Lynn Bushell has drawn on her own career as a painter and art historian to explore the relationship between the artist Pierre Bonnard and the rival women in his life. She has won prizes for her short stories and her articles have appeared in *Art Review*, the *Guardian* and the *Observer*. She is married to architect Jeremy Eldridge and divides her time between a house on the Suffolk borders and a working retreat on the Normandy coast.

Also by Lynn Bushell

Remember Me
Schopenhauer's Porcupines

Painted Ladies

LYNN BUSHELL

SANDSTONE PRESS

First published in Great Britain by
Sandstone Press Ltd
Dochcarty Road
Dingwall
Ross-shire
IV15 9UG
Scotland

www.sandstonepress.com

The publisher acknowledges subsidy from Creative Scotland
towards publication of this volume.

ISBN: 978-1-912240-48-7
ISBNe: 978-1-912240-49-4

Cover design by Rose Cooper
Typeset by Iolaire Typography, Newtonmore
Printed and bound by Totem, Poland

For
Pippa

PROLOGUE

Paris 1893

I sometimes wonder if our whole life isn't just a random accident. Ten seconds either way and we'd have missed each other. There I was, stuck in the middle of the rue du Bac, a costermonger's cart on one side and a carriage on the other, neither of the bastards willing to give way, steam coming from the horses' nostrils and sparks flying from the cobbles. And then there's the rain – the sort you only get in Paris. It's a mean rain, sleety, with a chill that gets you right through to the bone.

He's watching from the pavement opposite as if all this is a performance that I'm putting on to liven up the morning. He could be a toff or somebody who only has one coat and sleeps in it – it's hard to tell. He's dressed in black from head to foot. I can remember thinking, 'If I fall under the wheels of one of these carts, this is who'll be there to greet me on the other side. That, or he'll be the undertaker.'

There's a moment when the street and everybody on it seems to hold its breath. And then he steps into the road and takes my arm. Up close he's scruffy, but there's an expensive smell about him, as if he has washed first before putting on old clothes. He asks me where I'm going and I say, 'The dead house.' He's not sure he's heard me right. 'I work there,' I say. 'I sew flowers on the wreaths.'

'You don't regret it, Marthe?' he said later. 'Are you sure you wouldn't rather be back sewing flowers onto wreaths?'

'It's not the sort of job you miss,' I told him.

Paris 1917

She loves opening presents, getting her nail underneath the knot and easing it apart, unravelling it slowly, winding up the ribbon, finally ... Snip. Marguerite leans over her and cuts the string. It falls away. Now nothing separates her from the contents but the flimsy paper wrapped around the package, but she doesn't care what's in the box now.

'Happy birthday.'

Renée glances up and in the look that darts between them she feels Marguerite's desire and knows whatever she has bought her is a token of it. It's a signet ring. It isn't flashy – a plain setting with a blue stone in the centre – imitation sapphire. But it's not the sort of thing you'd pick up in the Marché aux Puces, which means that Marguerite has bought it from a jeweller's. There is a label on the box that says as much.

'It's lovely,' Renée says. 'It must have cost an awful lot.' The shrug that Marguerite gives isn't quite as careless as it might be. Renée hesitates. The ring is slotted with the jewel facing upwards on a satin-covered base that momentarily reminds her of the pillow underneath her father's head when he was lying in his coffin. She tries not to touch it when she takes the ring out. She rotates it underneath the lamp to catch the light, then slips it on the finger of her right hand. Marguerite gives her a quick glance.

'Don't you want to wear it on the other finger?'

Renée looks at her. 'The middle finger, do you mean?'

'I mean the finger on the other hand.'

'But that would look as if I was engaged,' says Renée.

'It would look as if you were committed. After all, you are committed, aren't you? We've been sharing this apartment for the past two years.'

'Yes, but I don't see why I have to wear it on that finger. Does it matter?'

'If it doesn't matter, why can't you just put it on the finger it was meant for?' Marguerite gets up and quietly clears the table.

Renée curls the twine around her index finger. There is not enough to be worth keeping but the ribbon circles it three times. She pulls it tight. Her finger reddens at the end and goes white at the base. She loosens it and blood flows back into the finger. Then she tightens it again. Her finger starts to throb. Her head begins to throb as well.

As they climb into bed that evening, Marguerite puts out her cheek and Renée plants the statutory kiss on it. They lie there rigidly, the space between them like a ditch they run the risk of falling into. They had hardly slept at all the night before. The sirens went off just before eleven. They'd unlatched the windows to avoid them blowing out and fifty minutes later they could hear air rushing back into the gas pipes; then the sirens suddenly went off again and people who had started coming from the cellars ran back down.

If there's an air raid in the middle of the night, they don't go down into the shelters. This is Marguerite's decision. When the shells start falling, she turns over on her back and lies there with her body open and her arms outstretched as if she has a rendezvous with death and is accepting every invitation that she gets in case she doesn't get another.

Renée rests her hand on Marguerite's arm. She turns over slowly. Renée feels her breath against her face. It's like the inside of a cupboard, dry and musty with a hint of lavender. She likes the fact that Marguerite's lips aren't wet like the swampy kisses she's received from men who've kissed her in the past.

'That's better,' Margo murmurs, pulling her into the narrow space between them. She wraps one arm round her shoulder. 'I'll look after you,' she whispers. 'You'll be safe with me.'

Once, they had turned the bed into a bier and Marguerite had laid her out. 'You're not to move,' she said. 'Pretend you're dead.'

When Renée's younger sister Emilie had died, she'd helped her mother dress the body. Emilie had had her cheeks and lips rouged. She looked healthier than she had ever looked in life. The faint smile on her face was almost smug.

'I'll have to wash your body and then dress you in a shift,' said Marguerite. 'No matter what I do, you're not to giggle. If you do, you'll spoil it.'

Renée lay completely still while Marguerite undid the buttons on her blouse and drew her arms out of the sleeves. She disengaged the buckle on her belt and eased the skirt over her hips. Her hands moved up from Renée's ankles and unlatched the garters on her stockings, rolling them back down towards her ankles and across the heel. She unlaced Renée's corset, opening it up, and Renée, who'd been trying not to giggle, parted her lips silently to draw breath. Marguerite leaned forward suddenly and kissed

her passionately on the lips. She looped her hands round
Renée's drawers and deftly drew them down over her thighs.
As Renée lay pretending she was dead, it struck her that
she'd never felt so much alive.

'If you were ever to tell anybody – ANYBODY – what we
did together, Renée, you would be shut out of Paradise for
ever. Do you understand?'

Although she rarely questioned anything that Margo
told her, Renée wondered how you could remain in Paradise no matter what you did, as long as no one knew about
it. She felt vaguely that if she were to confess her sins, she
wouldn't be forgiven. Marguerite was right, perhaps. It
wasn't what you did that counted, but how well you kept
the secret.

Bolivar got a direct hit in the night. The bomb fell on the
Metro. People who'd gone down there to escape the raid
were clambering over one another trying to get out again.
She's late for work, but Renée stops to buy a paper. On the
placard it says sixty-seven people died. She thinks about the
last one on the list and wonders if they're male or female, if
she'd ever passed them in the street, if they had ever come
into the store and bought some perfume.

On the Place Saint-Augustin, the barrage of the night
before has blown some of the shop signs off their hinges and
the metal brackets hang above the street like gibbets. Renée
sidesteps through the rubble, trying to avoid the clouds of
dust and grit that puff into the air each time she puts her
foot down.

She trips up as she's about to cross the Boulevard
Malesherbes. The strap has broken on her sandal; half of it
is still inside the clasp. She only bought the shoes last week.
She knew they wouldn't last but she loves anything that glit-

ters. She's spent nine francs buying shoes that would have cost her five last year and which are useless anyway.

When she looks up, the man is staring at her from the pavement opposite. This is the second time this week she's seen him. He's dressed like an office worker in a black suit with a bowler hat, but there's an unkempt look about him. He knows that she's seen him, but he doesn't move. She's only two streets from the store. She keeps her head down, curling her toes up inside the shoe to give her foot some grip. Once through the glass doors, she runs up the staircase to the top floor, lifting her nose to catch the first dense whiff of jasmine and cologne that floats up from the counters to the lantern roof and, finding no escape, floats down again to meet her. Gabi is already there and so is Mademoiselle Lefèvre.

'You're late, Renée.'

'Sorry, Mademoiselle Lefèvre. The roof collapsed over the Underground at Ménilmontant last night and I had to walk two stops.'

'A new consignment came this morning. You can stay behind tonight and help me to unpack it.'

'Miserable old trout,' Gabi whispers. 'After all, it's not as if we're being trampled underfoot by clients.'

Renée buttons up her uniform. She stops when she gets to the button at the neck, but then she does that up as well. She sees the man examining the rows of perfume bottles at the end of the display case. Gabi takes the roll of paper from the cash till and unwraps a new one. 'Isn't that the same man who was in here yesterday?'

'He followed me into the store this morning.' Renée sweeps her hair into the clasp behind her neck. She throws her head back and moves down the counter. 'Can I help you, sir? Perhaps you'd like to buy some perfume?' She's already noticed that the suit is shiny at the elbows and the white cuffs underneath are darned. He's not here to buy perfume.

He looks down the row of bottles and then glances back at her. 'I've no idea which one to pick,' he says. 'You choose.'

She could just take the most expensive one and say, 'That's it', but she goes through the rigmarole of taking out the stoppers, so that he can sniff them. He pretends he's taking all this seriously, but by this time it's a game that both of them are playing. Mademoiselle Lefèvre's looking at them, so they have to keep it up. He smiles. He looks much younger when he smiles. He points to the bottle she's picked up. She shakes her head. He moves his finger down the row and when he gets to freesia, she nods.

'That's settled then,' he says, and takes his wallet out. He does have money after all, then. While he's fumbling in his wallet, Renée takes a closer look at him. His hair is thick and still dark, but the beard has one or two grey streaks in it that have gone gingery around the mouth. He has nice eyes; eyes are important to her. It's the round-rimmed spectacles that give his face that owlish look.

She crooks her arm and holds the bottle in the palm. The gesture is flirtatious but he doesn't seem to notice. Mademoiselle Lefèvre, staring from the far end of the counter, knows exactly what is going on though.

'Shall I wrap it for you?'

'Yes, why don't you?'

Renée takes a sheet of the exclusive wrapping paper that they keep for regulars. She ties the ribbon round the box and draws the blade along it so it curls up prettily. 'There,' she says, handing it across the counter. 'I'm sure your wife will be pleased with that.'

He seems uncertain what to do with it now that he's bought it. 'Marthe doesn't wear scent. She says animals tell friends from foes by smelling them and that's the way we ought to do it.'

Renée thought the point of wearing perfume was to cover up your own scent. 'So why did you buy it?'

'It gave me an opportunity to speak to you.'

'And now you have?'

He weighs the parcel in his hands. 'Why don't you keep the perfume?'

'I'm afraid we don't do refunds.'

'Keep it for yourself, I meant. You chose it so it must be one you like.'

'I work here. I'm paid to like all of them.'

'Well,' he shrugs. 'Do you like this one or not?'

'I like it.'

'Take it then. Please.'

'Don't think I come with the perfume,' she says, but she takes it nonetheless. It isn't often that she gets to wear a scent that costs more than her wages for the week. Is he about to ask her out? She'd have to say no. She can't go out with a man who can't be bothered even to pretend he isn't married. Anyway, he's too old. 'Was that all?' She gives a brisk smile.

'Do you work here every day?'

'Except for Wednesday afternoons.'

'Would you be free to take on something else on Wednesday afternoons?'

'What did you have in mind?'

He rummages inside his pockets and takes out a notebook. There's a card inside. 'I wondered if you'd sit for me.'

'Sit?'

'Well, not sit exactly. Sometimes you'd be standing.' He flicks through the notebook. 'That's the kind of thing I do.' He hands it to her. There's a drawing of a woman standing, one foot in the bathtub and the other on the mat, without a stitch on.

'You want me to take my clothes off? Sorry.' She moves down the counter. There's another customer and Mademoiselle Lefèvre is beginning to make noises in her throat. She likes the girls to be polite to customers, but she's decided this one is a waste of air and so has Renée.

She's eighteen, although I don't discover that till later. It's the same age Pierre thought I was when we first met. Quarter of a century we've been together and he still thinks that I'm six years younger than I am. Too late to own up now. Most women only lie about their age when they're ashamed of it. I always felt ashamed of mine – too young to matter or too old. As for Pierre, he settled on an age for me and I was trapped in it for ever. Have you seen those pictures of me in the bath? How old would you say I was there? It doesn't matter what the date is; there I am, my hair still amber and my body like an hourglass, none of those ghastly blotches on my skin that later kept me in the bath all day. It was the perfect opportunity for him. I think he liked rooms that were small because they made him feel he wasn't meant to be there.

He was a voyeur; no doubt about it. I've known plenty in my time. There are the creepy ones who look at you as they would if they came across an animal run over in the road. If they discovered it was still alive, if they could see its heart was beating, they'd move on; real life is a distraction. Then there are the others – and he's one of them – who don't know what they're looking for until they find it. When they do, they never let it go.

I used to think I'd know the kind of woman he would be attracted by. I thought it would be somebody like me – dark, melancholy, antisocial. Was I always like that, or is that what happens when you've spent the best years of your life with somebody who sees you as a splash of orange in the background of a still life? At least up till now I haven't had to share the space with anybody else.

It's Marguerite's insistence that they have no secrets from each other that makes Renée want to keep things from her. 'We must tell each other everything,' says Marguerite, but Renée is already thinking, 'What if I don't tell her everything?' or, 'What if what I tell her isn't true?'

She always knew when she'd attracted somebody's attention. Normally it was her hair they noticed first. It was so pale that people often thought she'd bleached it. It was not just men – she often noticed women sneaking glances at her, too.

The stare she got from Marguerite when they got on the same bus in the mornings wasn't like the stares she got from women normally, the sort of stare that wanted what she'd got. This was a stare that wanted what she was. One morning when she had been hanging from the strap at one end of the tram and Marguerite was seated some way down the bus and facing her, she'd let herself swing slightly on the strap so that her eyes fell naturally on Marguerite's. She had expected Marguerite to meet the gaze or look away, but what she did was raise her eyes a fraction so that she seemed to be looking not at Renée but beyond her to a place of infinitely greater promise.

'Aren't you feeling chilly in that coat?' Those were the first words Marguerite had ever said to her.

'I grew up in a house in Bobigny that only had a fireplace in the kitchen. I don't feel the cold.'

'You travel in each day from Bobigny?'

'No. I've got lodgings in the 10th.'

'I work as a stenographer,' said Marguerite. 'I get off at the Mairie in Saint-Martin.' Had Renée been in any doubt, she now knew Marguerite was in a class above her. 'I allow myself an hour for the journey. You can never count on getting there in time.'

'I'm always late,' said Renée and then thought, why did I say that?

Marguerite gave her a condescending little smile. She sometimes read *Le Figaro* while she was on the bus. 'The war is going badly,' she said one day as she scanned the columns and then in a voice so low that she might have been talking to herself, she added, 'Do you ever wonder what it would be like to not exist?'

'Do you mean to be dead?' said Renée. She'd occasionally thought about it when there was an air raid and she hadn't managed to get down into the cellar. Once there had been a direct hit on the tenement next door and a woman she had often spoken to when they met in the market had been killed along with two of her small children. 'Yes,' she said. 'I think about it all the time.' That was the moment, she thinks now, when Marguerite's attention focused on her properly.

'The girl I share with will be moving out next month,' said Marguerite, one evening when they met up on the homeward journey. 'You could come and have a look at my apartment as you're here?'

Is she inviting me to share it with her? Renée wondered. So far, nothing they had said, apart from the discussion about being dead, had told them anything about each other. They got off together at the next stop, nonetheless, and walked the two blocks through the narrow streets to Belleville. It was not an area that had pretensions to gentility, especially since the outbreak of the war. The Zeppelins had targeted the 18th and the 20th arrondissements relentlessly. They walked through streets in which the only things left standing were the iron bases of the street lamps. Renée peered in through the shattered door of a *brocante*. Boys of six and seven scooted in and out among the debris carrying whatever loot they could lay hands on. In the rue de Borrego, the end wall of a tenement had been shorn off and in a first-floor bedroom Renée saw a black cat curled up on a brass bed with its sagging mattress still in place and, underneath, a chamber pot that had been shielded from the blast.

'That raid was mentioned in *Le Figaro*,' said Marguerite. 'The Zeppelins dropped nineteen bombs that night. They had a special funeral at Notre Dame La Croix for those who died.' She turned into an alleyway. The gunnels ran with water. Renée's shoes squelched as she followed her. They crossed a courtyard where smashed window boxes and the dead geraniums they had contained were piled haphazardly next to the rubbish bins.

'It's on the third floor,' Marguerite strode up the stairs ahead of her. Her footsteps echoed on the concrete tiles. The stairwell smelt of dust and cabbage. The two rooms inside the flat were similarly uninviting. There was very little furniture and nothing on the walls except a reproduction of the Pont Neuf and a print of Paris from Les Invalides. The only items that suggested comfort were a sofa with two cushions on it and a rag rug on the bedroom floor.

'It's very nice,' said Renée.

'What are you paying for the place you've got at present?'

Renée told her, and she did the calculations. 'All right, you can pay that here. It means I'm paying more but you can make it up in other ways.'

And that was how it happened. Three months later she was sharing Marguerite's apartment and discovering the ways in which she was expected to make up the shortfall in the rent. Although the flat had only one bed, Marguerite had not suggested that they get another. Renée wondered if the previous girl had taken her bed with her when she left. She had been used to sharing with her sisters, so it didn't feel unnatural to do that here. On Sundays, if they woke up early, she and Marguerite lay listening to the street sounds down below. 'I'm going to pretend that you're a little pat of butter,' Marguerite would whisper. 'I shall hold you so tight that you melt.' They giggled like two schoolgirls.

She occasionally fell asleep with Marguerite's hand on her stomach or her thigh and sometimes found her body answering the pressure of the fingers. She had grown accustomed in the past to pleasuring herself although she knew it was a sin. When Renée had to choose between a pleasure and adherence to a code of practice that forbade it, usually the pleasure won out.

One night after Marguerite had gone to sleep with her hand curled round Renée's thigh, the fingers quivering involuntarily, she had an urge to move her body just a fraction to engage with them. She lay there in an agony of longing until almost imperceptibly she felt the fingers relocating to the cleft between her legs that, in that instant, seemed to harbour every impulse and sensation she had ever felt.

As Renée's moans became more audible, there was no other sign from Marguerite that she had woken up except a whispered, 'There, there,' like an adult calming down a child it has provoked. As she lay, her hair plastered to her forehead, her heart banging so hard on her ribcage that she was afraid it might burst through, her gratitude was tempered by the knowledge that from now on Marguerite would have complete control over her life. Her small acts of rebellion were her only means of clinging to some last shred of autonomy. She sometimes felt that she was passing straight from childhood into middle age and that her one experience of what romantic love might be like was that night when Marguerite had first made love to her. But even then, it seemed like something she'd experienced, not something they'd experienced together.

'Is that where I'm meant to take my clothes off?' Renée pulls the curtain back. There is a ledge inside the cubicle and, hanging on a hook, a dressing gown. The room reminds her of the nests mice make, stuffed full of chewed-up rags and scraps of paper. There is nothing in it other than a chaise longue and a table with a palette and a jar of brushes – some round, some like chisels, some with handles so long that they look like brooms. The smell is cloying. Renée's brother, Tonio, has that scent on him when he comes back from the factory, but this smell is sweeter. It's the combination of the linseed with the vase of asters on the windowsill.

Next to a poster with a painting of a garden and 'Les Nabis' scrawled across the front in purple paint, a canvas has been tacked onto the wall. A light breeze catches underneath the fraying edges and the heavy linen lifts and sighs. She touches it. The paint is still wet and it comes off on her finger.

She looks back over her shoulder to see whether he has noticed. He picks out a paint rag from the pile next to the door and hands it to her. There's a blue smear on her finger after she has rubbed the paint off. She hands back the rag. He's not as friendly as he was when he was talking to her in the store. She wishes that she hadn't come. Her eyes move round the room like agitated butterflies, returning to the cubicle. The dressing gown is silk. It has a faint scent. Someone else has worn it.

'Who was here before me?'

'I've had several models. No one in particular.'

'What happened to them?'

'Some of them went on to sit for other painters. Some of them got married or found other jobs.'

'It isn't permanent then?'

'That depends.'

'There's no point in me giving up my Wednesdays if in three months' time you suddenly decide you've finished with me.' She sounds brittle. Who said anything about it being permanent? She came here thinking she would probably decide against it anyway. Now suddenly she's acting like she thought she'd get a pension when she leaves. She thinks she'll hit him if he smiles at her like that again. She keeps on saying things that make her sound naive or grasping. It's because he says so little that she's babbling.

There is something on the table that is helping to persuade her. It's a cake – a mille-feuille with cream oozing out the sides. The cream's not real, of course. The pastry won't be, either. Bread's been rationed for the past year. You can't even buy a brioche in the bakery. He sees her looking at it. On a Sunday, Mother usually does a suet pudding sweetened with molasses, but she can still feel the weight of that the next day. This looks so light it'll float into her mouth. She shrugs as if she doesn't care if there's a cake or not, but he knows that she does.

Outside it has begun to rain. The wind is blowing leaves onto the skylight. It feels warm inside. She notices the stove is lit. Unless she takes her coat off while she's in here, she'll feel chilly when she leaves. She slides it off her shoulders. 'What's the deal, then?' she says, airily.

I knew, of course. I knew the minute that it started. Women do. It's not as if she was the first. The others didn't matter.

There were some among our so-called friends who changed their mistresses more often than they changed their shirts. He wasn't like that. Sex for Pierre was never an obsession. It was something to be got out of the way so he could concentrate on work. I wasn't just the woman in his life. I was the muse. Without me, there would be no pictures. You can't wipe out quarter of a century.

I didn't care much for his painting to begin with, though I never said so. It was hardly my place to start criticising him before I'd even got my foot inside the door. I'd look at what he'd done and think, 'It's not bad and I like the colour, but he hasn't drawn the table properly. It looks as if it's been tipped up.' You'd see a plate that looked real, but there'd be an orange on it that was floating in the air. I thought, 'Well, after all, he hasn't been an artist very long. He'll probably get better.' I was wondering how I could fit into the space between the window and the door without the table cutting me in half.

'It's not important, Marthe,' Pierre said. Not to him, I dare say.

He was renting a small studio in rue de Douai with an alcove for a bedroom and a kitchen with a tin bath hanging on the wall. Not that I'd come from anything much better. I had seven brothers and my father was a navvy on the railways. I suppose my mother must have loved him, but in our class no one talked of love much. On a weekday he came home each evening, ate and went to bed. At weekends he got drunk and beat her. What's to love?

Pierre would have been riveted by Mother's bruises on a Sunday morning and the way they changed from blue to bluish-purple, then to yellow and eventually to black. It wouldn't have occurred to him to ask her where they came from, any more than it occurred to him to ask me where

I'd got a yellow headscarf or a vase. The only thing Pierre insisted on was that whatever came into our living space remained there.

If we'd had a child, that might have changed us. Children break things. They wear out the rugs. They eat the still lifes. Children were another subject that we didn't talk about. I lost one, three years after we moved in together, when my mother wrote to tell me that my father had been killed by falling masonry. I knew the baby was a girl. I called her Suzanne. On the day she died, a cat came scratching at the door. I should have turned her out, but I was needy, so I poured a saucerful of milk and let her drink.

If we had had a baby, I suppose he would have put that in the paintings, too: a white blob in what could have been a coffin or a crib. I sometimes wondered if the bathtub hadn't turned into a tomb, as well – a tin sarcophagus.

He's left three francs inside the cubicle. Is this so that he doesn't have to hand the money over to her? Renée hears him humming as he moves around the studio, the clink of glass, the glug of liquid being poured into a jar, the rustling of paper. She reminds herself she's not the first girl who has been here. She remembers that faint whiff of scent inside the cubicle the first time she pulled back the curtain. It's not there now. Either she's accustomed to it or already her scent has replaced it.

She can't stay in here for ever. She wraps the kimono round her, so that there's a double layer at the front, and clasps it to her stomach. Swishing back the curtain, she steps out onto the rug. There is a tin bath in the corner, underneath the skylight. When she came the first time, it was propped against the wall. He sees her looking at it. She's still clutching her kimono. 'What do you want me to do, then?'

'If you could take a position near the bath, as if you've just got out of it, perhaps, with one hand on the rim . . .'

She fumbles with the wrap. It's getting in the way but she can't bring herself to take it off yet. She goes over to the bath and bends down. 'Like that?'

'Yes, but I can't see your body while you've got the wrap on.'

It's all right for you, she thinks. She wonders how he'd feel if he was standing there with next to nothing on while someone stared at him. This isn't working out the way she had expected. She thought he'd be grateful that she'd bothered to turn up, concerned to put her at her ease. Instead, he grunts, makes huffing noises, mutters to himself as if she wasn't there and shunts her back and forwards like a piece of furniture. There is a moment when she thinks she'll straighten up, march back into the cubicle, get dressed again and leave.

'The wrap,' he prompts.

She hesitates. How does she get herself into these situations? Suddenly a beam of sunlight filters through the cracked glass of the skylight and illuminates her arm and the exposed part of her thigh. She sees the shadow cast across her foot by one side of the tin bath and the ripple of the light across the floorboards. She throws off the wrap. Her costume is her skin. She is no longer Renée Montchaty, a shop assistant on a perfume counter. She is Aphrodite, Liberty, the Sibyl.

'Yes,' he murmurs. 'Yes, that's very nice.'

Madame Hébert came by this morning. I would rather not have had a local woman in to do for us – I hate these Norman peasants with their mean eyes and their thin lips. 'No doubt you've been busy,' she says, knowing that my only task in life when Pierre is here is to have baths or sit around and wait for him to get the sketchbook out. The walls are choc-a-bloc with pictures and they all have me there, doing more or less what I am doing now – not much, in other words. She crops up in a couple of them too, though fortunately when she does she's on her feet and has at least got something in her hands. It wouldn't do for Pierre to imply that she's as lazy as his wife. They call me 'Madame' in the neighbourhood, but they know Pierre and I aren't married. That's the first thing they'll have sussed out.

When my mother was in service, she said that the women from the upper classes were all slatterns when it came to housework. That's why they got someone else to do it for them. I knew if I showed an interest, it would be a giveaway.

Pierre didn't see the dust as dust, in any case. Sometimes I'd sit there in the spot where he'd been sitting and I'd try to see what he saw. Once when he had left his glasses looped over a chair, I put them on. It made the particles of dust look bigger, but they were the sort of brownish-grey you see on uncooked chicken. Then the sun came out and all at once I saw what he saw – only for a second and never again – but I at least knew it was there. He wasn't seeing things. No, my Pierre was *seeing* things.

Madame Hébert and I sit down and have a chat before she starts to clean. She's always called me 'Marthe' whereas I've no option but to go on calling her 'Madame' because she hasn't told me what her Christian name is. It's deliberate. She knows we're equal and that means we can't be friends. Pierre must be the only person who accepts the lie. Perhaps there are so many lies between us that one more is neither here nor there. And he could hardly say at the beginning, 'Your name is de Méligny?' and give me one of those slow smiles of his and then add, 'I don't think so.' 'Marthe' is the compromise we both accept. At least I feel at home with it.

She's stopped undressing in the cubicle because the sight of her unravelling a stocking or unbuttoning her blouse will frequently turn out to be the pose he needs. Sometimes, when she is taking off her clothes in front of him, she knows he's watching her and that the look is not the same as when she's posing for him. She may not know what the difference is, but she knows that there is one.

When he's painting her, he seems so totally absorbed in what he's doing, it's as if she isn't there at all. Sometimes she speaks to him and there's no answer, or he looks up, startled, as if he's not certain where the voice is coming from. 'I'm sorry,' he says. 'Did you speak?'

She sometimes gets a glimpse of what he's working on, but usually when they stop he throws a sheet across the easel. Once, while he is busy at the sink, she lifts a corner of the sheet. She turns and sees him glance at her. 'Am I allowed to look?'

'I would prefer it if you didn't.'

'Why?'

'I don't want to be influenced by your reaction.'

She is flattered that he could be influenced by anything she said or did. 'I wouldn't tell you if I didn't like it.'

'That's not what I meant. I meant your attitude towards yourself might influence my attitude towards you.'

It's a bit too deep for her. 'But if I told you which bits didn't look like me, you'd know what needed changing.'

'Do you think you see yourself that clearly?'

'I know what I look like.'

'Yes, of course you do.' He smiles as if he knows some-thing she doesn't. 'You can see it when it's finished.'

He puts out two cups. He only has two. They're a cheap white china and they're both cracked. One leaks but so slowly that she doesn't think he's noticed. He sits opposite her on the chaise longue with his knees together and the cup and saucer balanced in his lap. He's not worn anything except the black suit all the time she's known him. Often he paints with his jacket on and there are blue stains down the front of it. It's odd that when he does spill paint it's always blue. He wears a white shirt buttoned at the neck. She's noticed that the cuffs and collars have been turned on all of them. She wonders whether Marthe does this out of habit since they can't be so poor that she does it from necessity.

'Why do you wear black all the time?'

He smooths the cloth on one leg with his hand. If she were looking at his hands in isolation they would conjure up a different sort of person altogether. He has dark hair on his forearms which she saw once when he rolled his sleeves up, but the hands are smooth except for a large vein running from his index finger to his wrist on both hands. 'I feel comfortable in black,' he says, at last. 'Why don't you eat your cake?'

He doesn't like it when the conversation turns to him. He'd rather that they didn't talk at all, but it's the only way for her to find out anything about him. When he asks her questions, she suspects that it's because he feels he ought to rather than because he's curious about her.

'What would you be doing on a Wednesday afternoon if you weren't here?'

'I'd take the tram to Bobigny to see my mother, or I might go to the cinema with my friend Gabi.'

'What films do you like?'

'Romances. Films with Rudolf Valentino in the tent.'

He's looking at her, vaguely. 'You know, where he plays the sheikh.'

'Ah.'

'I saw *Murders in the Rue Morgue* recently.'

'That one I do know. Have you read the book?'

'Why would I read the book if I can see it in the cinema?'

He nods. He casts about for something else to say. Her wrap has fallen open at the neck. She sees him glancing at her breast. At the beginning she had felt a vague sense of rejection when he made no effort to seduce her. She'd been told that she was beautiful, and beauty meant that men reacted to her in a certain way. She might not want them, but she wanted them to want her. When he showed no sign of wanting her, she wondered if he had detected something with that piercing gaze of his that left him ill at ease or maybe even that repelled him.

'I hope coming here won't have deprived your family of an opportunity to see you.'

'I can always go on Sunday. What about you? Do you see your family?'

'No.'

'Never?'

'We lost touch when I abandoned law to study art. I do see one of them – my sister Andrée. We were very close as children. Andrée always took my side.' He smiles. 'She has a daughter – that's my niece, of course. Her name is Renée, too.'

'The same as me.'

'Yes.'

'Nice.' As Renée bites into her cake, cream oozes out of both sides of her mouth. A blob of cream has fallen onto her left breast. He watches as it slides towards her nipple. When it gets there, it will have to do a detour round the areola or divide up into separate tributaries. She pauses, her mouth full of cake. He sees her looking at him.

'You've dropped cream onto your breast,' he says. She wipes it off.

When she is getting dressed one afternoon, she bends down with her back to him so that the gash between her legs is clearly visible. She glances back over her shoulder to see whether he's affected and is gratified when she sees that he is. He looks away, but it's too late.

Pierre knows Madame Hébert's been, the minute he walks back into the house. He's told her she is not to pick things up. She can dust round them, but they must remain exactly where they are. He says there's always something not quite in the right place after she has gone. She nudges things out of perversity.

'I have a new girl coming to the studio,' he says, as I am bringing in the cassoulet. He tucks the serviette into his shirt front. 'She works on the perfume counter at that big store in the centre – Printemps.'

I begin to spoon the cassoulet into the bowls. He helps himself to bread.

'We went there once to buy a birthday present for you. You remember?'

I nod. I remember everything. I'm thinking it's a long way from the studio.

'I went there looking for tobacco,' he says. 'Schiffs were out of it.' He waits for me to ask about the girl.

'And did you find some?'

'Fortunately, yes.'

I break the bread roll in the gravy, watching as the doughy lumps fluff up and take on colour from whatever's nearest to them. Poucette jumps onto the table and I move the water jug. The cat sniffs the tureen, its delicate antennae picking up the signals.

'Her name's Renée.' He's about to spoon the cassoulet into his mouth. He pauses as if it's an afterthought.

'The same name as your niece.' A pity, I think. It'll make her harder to forget.

'Girls like her are notoriously unreliable, of course.' He laughs and then I hear that little click inside his throat that comes whenever he's said something he's regretted. I don't draw attention to it. I don't want to spoil his dinner. Telling me he has a model is supposed to reassure me that he hasn't anything to hide, but that is not the way it works. Now both of us are wondering what he has to hide.

'How long have you and Marthe been together?' She is looking at a postcard reproduction pinned above the sink, a sculpture of a young man with his arms above his head. Beneath it, on the same pin, is a picture of another youth but this one's naked with his genitals on full view. Renée feels shy looking at it but since it's been pinned where anyone can see it, she supposes it's all right for her to look.

'I've been with Marthe almost all my life.'

'Do you still paint her?'

'Yes, of course I do.'

'That can't be very interesting after all these years.'

'It's different every time.' He takes a grimy teaspoon from the bench and uses it to stir his coffee. Renée makes a show of looking at the naked youth as if she's adding to her fund of knowledge.

'Are these statues made of stone in real life?'

'Marble. One is Michelangelo's *Rebellious Slave*. The other one's *The Dying Slave*. They're in the Louvre.' He says 'Michelangelo' as if she should have heard of him.

'He's famous, is he?'

'Michelangelo? He's quite well known, yes.'

'Are there any cards like this of your work?'

'You could probably find one or two on sale in the tabac or in the bouquinistes. The still lifes, mainly.'

'There'll be none of me, then?'

'As I say, it's mainly the still lifes.'

'Have you got any I can see?'

He takes a pile of cards out of the drawer under the workbench. Renée recognises corners of the studio – the tin bath hanging on the wall, the vase of asters on the windowsill.

'It feels odd, being here and looking at a picture of it.'

'That's because time normally moves on but when you paint it, it stands still.'

She comes to one that isn't of the studio. It's of a sunsoaked parlour with a woman sitting at a table in the foreground and a riot of laburnum and lobelia behind her. 'Is that Marthe?'

Pierre nods. Renée notices the pudding-basin haircut and the way the woman seems to lose herself among the objects in the room. There is a white cat on the table, licking milk out of a saucer from the cup the woman's drinking from.

'She must be quite old now.' It wasn't what she'd meant to say. He's giving her that look, as if he's miles away.

'A muse is different from a model. Age is not important.'

'What's the difference?' 'Muse' is not a word she's come across before.

'An artist might have several models, but he only has one muse.'

She feels obscurely that she's being shown her place. She might not understand what he is saying but she knows that it's important, that it's possibly the most important thing she'll ever know about him. She knows, too, that from now on her mission will be to become the muse in Pierre's life. She understands as well that it is not a question simply of seducing him.

'The Marthe'd Muse' is what they used to call me. It was Pierre's friend Édouard who came up with that. It was a play on words, Pierre said, although there was nothing playful in the way it came about. Pierre had put three paintings of me lying in the bath into the Salon exhibition. He was starting to be quite well known for them by that time and we'd rented an apartment separate from the studio. There was an easel and a fold-up table with his paints on in the bathroom. It had been a vicious winter. I was used to cold, but that year was the first one of the century and there seemed to be nowhere you could go to get away from it.

He liked to put the easel at an angle to the bath, so he was looking down at me. The dog would often crawl in underneath the bath and sit between the iron legs where she would be warm. I always made sure that the water started off hot, but once I'd been in there for an hour I could feel the pins and needles starting in my legs. The pain moves round your body looking for a place to settle and once it has set up camp it starts to claim the territory around it. You're a city under siege. The only way to bear it is to take your mind off somewhere else, the way the saints did on the rack. The pain is still there, but it's separate.

That day Pierre had started painting in the morning and it wasn't till the light began to fade that he took out his pocket watch. I'd been there in the water seven hours. In the painting you can see the goosebumps on my legs. I think he was as shocked as I was when he realised how long it had been. He spoke to me and when he didn't get an answer he knelt down beside the bath and plunged his hands into the water, trying to rub feeling back into my arms and legs. He lifted me out of the bath and carried me into the bedroom, piling blankets, coats and cushions, anything he could lay hands on, over me.

'I don't feel anything,' I told him. 'It's all right,' But then, as I began to thaw, that's when the torture started. It was like a thousand tiny, biting insects running up and down my legs – a scorching, scarifying pain. I wanted to peel off my skin so that the insects trapped there could escape. I howled. The sound was so unearthly that I thought it must have come from somewhere else.

Pierre was rocking, with his fists bunched up against his temples. 'Tell me what to do.' he begged.

I must have fainted. When I came around, the insects underneath my skin had gone, but I was shivering – my teeth, my legs, my insides, everything was shuddering. The bed was groaning underneath me.

Pierre took off his clothes. He climbed in next to me and rolled himself on top of me, his beard against my cheek, his breast against mine, his arms matching my arms and his legs on my legs. We lay like that till the morning. When I woke up, I was warm again, but Pierre was as cold as ice.

She is afraid that in the end she'll give herself away. Each time she leaves the flat she has to change the ring onto the middle finger of the other hand and then restore it to the left hand when she comes back in the evening. She is coming from the studio one afternoon when she hears voices arguing outside. She waits. The area is not as rough as Belleville, but it's better not to get involved in anything.

The argument goes on and Renée sees she has no choice but to walk past the pair. The man is leaning with his elbow on the wall next to the woman's cheek and has his back to

Renée. He is wearing a white linen suit. The girl is pale with short blonde hair, cut raggedly, and has her thin coat clutched around her. She assumes this is a client and a prostitute.

'Don't you come that with me, you little minx,' the man says. 'You get paid the same rate as the others and that's all you're getting.'

As they pass each other, Renée glances at her and the girl returns the stare. She's trying to look brazen, but she just looks frightened. Renée walks on. There's a lot of violence in the class she comes from, but it doesn't often happen in the street where everyone can see.

She hears a slap and then a cry. She forces herself not to look back, but she feels a sharp rush of adrenalin. She waits until she's reached the corner and then glances back just as the man looks up. He's heard the sharp click of her heels against the cobbles. Even though he's in the middle of an argument, the look he throws at Renée is appraising. It's the look that men give women all the time in her world, and as Renée throws the glance back she is wondering why a man like that would need to pay for sex.

She takes a shortcut through the market, stopping at the flower stall to buy a bunch of marigolds. On Wednesday afternoons she tries to make sure that she's home ahead of Marguerite so that she doesn't have to answer questions as to where she's been, but when she lets herself in, Marguerite is home already.

She puts down the flowers. Margo eyes them. 'What are they for?'

'I thought they would cheer the place up. And the man gave me an extra bunch. I thought you'd like them.'

'Marigolds? I've always found them rather fussy – all those little frills. I can see why you'd like them.'

'I don't like them in particular. They were the nicest flowers on the stall, that's all.' She takes her coat off. Marguerite comes over to her. She bends forward as if to kiss Renée on the cheek, then takes her chin and turns it so she's looking straight into her eyes. 'I called in at the store this afternoon to pick you up. The supervisor said you weren't due in.'

The stillness in the space between them feels like concrete hardening around her. 'Wednesday is my afternoon off.'

'But you said you were doing extra shifts for your friend Gabi.'

Renée feels her colour rise. She's never been much good at lying, which is curious because she's had a lot of practice. 'She and Jules were going out to buy things for the wedding. In the end they didn't go.'

'So what did you do?' She feels Margo's fingers pressing on the flesh above her elbow. 'Well?'

'I took the tram to Bobigny, to see my mother. She's not well. The shelling's getting to her. She can't sleep.'

'You should have said. Why didn't you?'

'She told me not to fuss. She's tired, that's all. It's hard for her to have to look after the girls at their age.'

'Can't your brother help her?'

'Tonio won't help her with the chores. He says it's women's work.'

While Marguerite has little time for men, she draws the line at criticising Tonio. 'You've had this oily smell about you lately.'

'Oily?'

'As if you've been going round a hardware store.'

'The bus back from the suburbs often has the workers from the factory on it.'

Marguerite grunts. Next time Renée leaves the studio, she

puts a small dab of the perfume Pierre gave her on her neck and wrists. But she knows time is running out.

'Who did that to you?'

She has tried to cover up the bruises with a mix of chalk and resin, but he notices immediately when she takes off the kimono. He comes over to her, taking her arm by the wrist and turning it towards the light. He rubs his thumb against the bruise. The chalk comes off on it.

'It was a game.' She colours underneath the look he's giving her. She's told him she shares an apartment in the 18th and she sometimes mentions Marguerite, but Wednesday afternoons are an escape from all that and she wants to keep the two apart. The bruises on her arm say things about her that she'd rather not have said. The light is shining from above and there's a sheen on them, like peaches when they start to rot.

'You know that games like this become more violent as time goes on.' He goes on staring at the bruises for a moment and then turns and goes back to the workbench. He picks up his brushes and begins to paint. For once she's grateful that she doesn't need to talk to him.

'That ring you wear sometimes,' he says, when neither of them has said anything for several minutes. 'Who gave that to you?'

'It was a birthday present from the girl I share with.'

'It's a friendship ring, then? If I'd known it was your birthday, I'd have taken you to lunch.'

'It was the day before I met you, so you couldn't have.'

He makes a mark and stands back from the easel to examine the effect. 'Does Marguerite know that you pose for me?'

'I haven't told her yet.'

'You think she'd mind?'

'She'd stop me coming to you.'

'Why would she do that?'

'She's jealous', Renée is about to say, but this is not a conversation that she wants to have with Pierre.

'Those bruises on your arms. Are those the way she stops you doing things?'

'Not always.' He does not pursue it. Last week, Renée came in with a split lip. She'd expected him to comment then, but he had not said anything. However, when she saw one of his sketches lying on the workbench afterwards, she picked it up and saw he'd drawn the split lip. Renée felt she might as well have been a milk jug with a crack in it; if it was there, he painted it.

He's looking at the ring. 'Blue. That's your favourite colour.' Renée sniffs. 'You don't seem very pleased with it. Would you prefer her to have bought you something else?'

'I wish she hadn't bought me anything.'

'Why's that?'

'She always ... wants something from me. She never gives me anything without me having to give something back.'

'And is the "something" something you don't want to give?'

She looks away. She doesn't want to tell him. She's afraid that telling him might make it worse, that once the thing is out there in the open it will have a separate existence and that once it does, she will be stuck with it for ever. 'I just wish she wasn't so possessive.'

'Ah.' He weighs the brushes in his hand, then lays them on the bench and comes across to her. He twists the ring between his fingers and then slips it off. 'It comes off easily enough.' She looks at him. She feels the muscles in her stomach clench. He slides it back onto her finger.

'Marguerite . . .'

'What?'

Renée shrugs. She's toying with the ring. She takes it off again and tries it on another finger. Then she tries it on the other hand. She holds the finger out. 'It's quite a nice ring.'

'Yes, it is.'

'I think I'll leave it on.'

He sighs. 'Good, that's decided then.'

They work on late into the afternoon and go down to the café when the session's over. La Rotonde is where the painters meet to talk and drink and it is always full of artists arguing and shouting. As they go in through the swing doors, Renée gets a whiff of freshly ground and roasted coffee beans, a scent you hardly ever come across outside the cafés any more. She's noticed that a lot of things that are in short supply – eggs, coffee, cigarettes – seem to be plentiful enough if you know where to go for them.

Pierre steers her deliberately to a corner of the room that's empty. Renée loves the noise and bustle of the café, but for Pierre it's a distraction. She doubts that he ever goes there when he's by himself.

'Why do the painters all live in this part of town?'

'It's cheap and painters like to live on top of one another. Some do, anyway.'

She picks up snatches of the conversation on the table next to theirs. 'What are they arguing about?'

He takes out his tobacco pouch. 'A Polish countess has been commandeering vans to transport soldiers to and from the front.'

'Is that a good thing?'

'If she wasn't Polish and a countess and if they were not the vans used by couturiers and if the chauffeurs weren't in uniforms that she'd designed herself, nobody would have given it a second thought.'

'I don't see ...'

'Nor do I,' says Pierre. 'They say she's doing it to advertise herself.'

'Who is she?'

'I believe her name is Misia Sert. Jean Cocteau is a friend of hers. The two of them were photographed together in *Le Figaro*.'

Occasionally, Margo brings home copies of *Le Figaro* or, if she finds one on the Metro, Renée picks it up, but normally she skips the news. She hasn't heard of either of them.

'So, are you on her side?' she says.

Pierre cups a hand over the pipe. 'I'm not on anybody's side. I just wish that the war was over.'

The noise ratchets up. One man lets out a swear word in a language Renée doesn't recognise although she gets the gist of it. The man is short and swarthy, and the energy is pumping out of him in waves. He throws his arms out to embrace the room but always ends up pointing back towards himself as if he's trying to corral a swarm of feathers that have just erupted from a bolster.

'That's Picasso.' Pierre looks away. 'He's recently been taken up by an American called Gertrude Stein. She picks up artists with a small amount of talent and recycles them as geniuses.'

Renée doesn't understand what half of them are saying but it sounds exciting, dangerous. She wishes she was sitting at their table.

'Is he someone I should know about?'

'I doubt you'll hear much of him in the future, but he's talked about a lot now.'

'Does he paint like you?'

Pierre turns so that he is not in anybody's line of sight. 'Picasso? No. He hates my work.'

'Do you hate his?'

'Let's just say that we differ in our attitude to art.'

'Why do you have to have an attitude? Why can't you just paint?'

'You don't have much choice about the way you paint, that's true.'

She lets the noise wash over her. She's not the only woman there, but none of them are making any contribution to the conversation. One man keeps on casting glances at her. Renée recognises him. This is the man she walked past in the street outside the studio. The same girl's sitting next to him. She's making small dips with a spoon into a water ice, then raising it with little darting movements to her lips.

'Who's that man in the white suit?'

Although Pierre has got his back to him, he knows who she's referring to. 'Roussel.'

'Why is he staring at us?'

'I imagine you're the one he's looking at.'

Since she's been coming to the studio, she has got used to being looked at in a certain way, but Roussel's look is like the ones you get from navvies when you pass them in the street.

'Try not to stare back quite so obviously,' Pierre says. 'I would rather that he didn't come across.' But it's too late. Roussel is on his feet already.

'Mind if I sit down?' He pulls a chair out without waiting for an answer. 'My name's Ker-Roussel. And you are . . . ?'

Renée glances at Pierre. He hasn't yet acknowledged Roussel. 'Renée Montchaty.' She notices how finely tailored Roussel's shirt is and how well it fits him. When he speaks to Pierre, he keeps his eyes on her. They are the coldest blue she's ever seen. 'We haven't seen you in here for a while, Pierre. You've turned into a hermit.'

'I've been working in the studio.'

'You must have come out of the studio at some point to have lit on this delightful creature.'

Pierre adjusts his spectacles. 'She came to me.'

Not quite true. Doesn't that make her sound rather forward, Renée thinks.

'You don't say? Well, I wish she'd come to me instead.' Roussel laughs. 'How is Marthe?' He is making sure she knows Pierre is spoken for.

'She's well. It's kind of you to ask.'

'You still spend time in Saint-Germain-en-Laye?'

'Of course. It's where I live.' He looks at Roussel. 'And your family? How's Isabelle? And what about the girls?'

'They're fine.'

'Annette must be . . . what, fifteen?'

'Fourteen,' Roussel says abruptly.

They are interrupted by the low wail of the siren and a groan goes up from the adjoining tables.

'Do you want to go down to the shelter?' Pierre says. No one else is moving.

Renée shakes her head. There's an explosion nearby. Glasses on the table rattle. In the first months of the war, Parisians came out onto the streets to watch the Taubes circling. People joked that you were more at risk from shells fired by your own side than you were from bombs dropped by the Germans. It's not like that now. The streets are clear within a minute of the sirens going off.

The girl on Roussel's table goes on spooning water ice into her mouth. Her face is pretty but her body has an undeveloped look about it. There's a small dog sitting at her feet. She pats it absently and dips her finger in the ice so that the dog can lick it. They wait till the noise of the bombardment has receded.

Roussel lights a cigarette. He looks at Renée as he throws the match away. 'What did you do before Pierre discovered you?'

She hesitates. She doesn't want to own up that she is a shop girl.

'She lived with her family in Bobigny.' Pierre gives a complicit smile. She's flattered suddenly to find herself the centre of attention, though she is embarrassed for the girl on Roussel's table who, now that the ice cream has all gone, is staring at them.

'Do you work for Pierre every day?'

'Not every day.'

'What days would you be free to work for someone else?'

Pierre is toying with a card of matches he has taken from the ashtray.

'I'm not free on any of the other days,' she says.

'You lead a busy life.'

'She has commitments,' Pierre says, quietly.

Roussel looks from Pierre to her and back again. 'I take it those commitments are exclusively to you.'

'Yes,' Pierre says evenly. 'They are.' There's silence round the table. Renée blushes. What Pierre is saying is that she's not just his model. She can't contradict him without giving Roussel the impression that she is available for anyone who cares to make an offer for her. She feels angry but she's not sure who she's angry with or why.

Roussel feels in his pocket. 'Take my card in case you change your mind. I'm always looking for a new girl.'

'Looking for a new girl' almost makes it sound as if he'd pick one off the street. Her eyes pass to the girl on Roussel's table.

'Caro works for several of us,' Roussel says. 'You earn more that way.'

Renée reaches for the card, then wonders if she should have left it on the table.

Pierre takes out a note and tucks it underneath the saucer. 'You'll forgive us if we leave you, Roussel; we still have some work to do.'

Roussel looks keenly at her. As he's gone on talking she's been looking at the sagging skin around his jaw, the drinker's raw cheeks. He is still a handsome man, but there is probably no more than three years difference between him and Pierre.

The girl on Roussel's table runs her finger round the inside of the ice cream bowl and puts it to her mouth.

'Is he someone you've known a long time?'

Pierre stops to button up his topcoat. It's cold outside on the pavement. 'We were students at the Beaux-Arts in the same year, although I was two years older; I'd already done my law degree.'

'The two of you were friends, then?'

'Not exactly. We were in the same place at the same time, that's all.'

It's begun to rain. She takes his arm; the pavement's narrow. 'Don't you like him?'

'I'm not keen on him.'

'You didn't have to make it look as if I were your mistress.'

'I said nothing of the kind,' he mutters. They walk on a few yards without speaking.

'That's what everybody thought.'

'If you knew Roussel better, you would know that it's the way he thinks.'

'So I'm no better than a street girl?'

'I believe I've always treated you with the respect that's due to you.'

Is this the problem? Renée wonders. 'Are you angry at me?'

He looks calmly at her. 'Why would I be angry?'

'You thought I was flirting with Roussel.'

'And were you?'

She stares back at him. 'Well, so what if I was? It's not as if you own me.'

'Quite.'

'I wasn't flirting with him anyway. I didn't even like him if you must know.'

'As you've been at pains to point out, Renée, I don't own you and of course you're free to work as Roussel's model if you want.'

'I don't...'

He puts a hand up. 'And you're equally free not to. When you came here it was understood that our relationship would be professional.'

'I still thought we were friends.'

'We are friends and because we're friends I would advise you to keep Roussel at a distance. Everything he does, he does for selfish reasons. I would hate to see your life spoilt. Can we move on?'

She walks sulkily beside him. She's not certain what she wants from him, but if she's going to continue to risk Marguerite discovering what she's been doing, she wants more than this. There was a moment in the café when she knew Pierre was jealous. Most men when they're jealous fight for what they want. He goes the other way. He's like a snail retreating back into its shell. Once there, it doesn't matter how long you stand over it, it won't come out again. She has an urge to shake him sometimes to wrest some kind – any kind – of a response from him.

They've reached the entrance to the studio, but Pierre keeps on walking. Renée runs to catch him up. 'Where are you going?'

'To the tram stop.'

'Don't you want to go on with the painting?'

'Not today. I don't feel in the mood.'

'Is that my fault?' She doesn't want the afternoon to end like this.

'Of course it's not. It's just that once I've stopped, it's harder to get started.'

'You told Roussel that's why we were leaving.'

'I preferred to spare his feelings. I could just have said I didn't care to spend another minute in his company.' He slides one hand under her elbow and propels her through the traffic to the stop. They wait in silence. When the tram comes, he stands back to let her on. She waits for him to kiss her, but he doesn't.

For months after that day, I dreamt I was floating in a lake just underneath the water with a film of thin ice over me. I couldn't breathe but in the dream I didn't need to; I was dead already. I think maybe for a short time, seconds possibly, I did die that day in the bath. My body never seemed to be entirely mine from then on. I would wake up in the mornings with odd welts and rashes on my arms and legs as if something had got in underneath my skin and couldn't find its way out.

Pierre was careful after that. Once we had got a proper bath, he made sure that the water never fell below a certain temperature and that I had breaks every hour. I was worried that he wouldn't want to paint me with the rashes on my skin but they were a reminder, I suppose, of that day when he nearly lost me. It became a bond between us.

There was no one else. He never introduced me to his family, even Andrée. When we first began to live together, I was glad I didn't have to meet them and then I began to wonder whether it was them or me he was ashamed of. Since I couldn't take him home to meet my family, I could hardly make a fuss about not meeting his.

He never knew about Suzanne. I wrote to her after she died. I tore the paper into little scraps and threw them from the window of the studio. They floated down into the street and gusted into doorways and shop windows, like confetti. Bits of them clung onto people's jackets and were carried home with them. It was my way of letting the world know she'd been here.

Pierre came up behind me and looked out over my shoulder. 'Look at all those bits of paper,' he said. 'I expect there's been a wedding in the church.'

'Yes,' I said, 'I expect there has.' Why couldn't I have said it was a requiem for our lost child? Perhaps because if he had known, he would have grieved. He would have looked to me for comfort and I couldn't give him any. I had none to spare.

There isn't anybody now, except Suzanne. She keeps me company. But I don't want to burden her with this. The dead have some rights. What's the point of being dead if you have to put up with everything you'd be expected to put up with if you were alive?

Last night when I looked in the mirror, I found two grey hairs both growing on the same side of my fringe. And now I see the rash beginning to appear again. It started in the little creases in my elbows and behind my ears – a faint bloom that gives colour to the grey skin round it. Now it's spread across my neck and upper arms. I shouldn't scratch it, but I do. The only thing that eases it is water.

∞

When she turns up at the studio the next week, Renée finds it locked. Pierre would normally be there before eight-thirty. His routine is stricter than an office worker's. She does not want to run into any of the other painters in the block, so she goes down and walks the streets for half an hour before coming back. The door is still locked.

She is angry that she's wasted not only the fare to get there but an afternoon when she might have been doing something else. That Pierre should finish with her like this goes against what Marguerite has told her about men and how they normally conduct themselves. When Marguerite was in her early twenties she had an affair with somebody she knew at work. 'That bastard had the best years of my life,' she used to say, 'and I got damn all in return. Let me be an example to you, Renée. Men are only interested in one thing.' But in that case, why would they give up before they've got it? Pierre's kept Marthe on for quarter of a century. But then, as he was only too quick to remind her, Marthe is his muse.

That they should quarrel over someone like Roussel seems unbelievable. She tells herself she wasn't flirting with him, but she can remember that sharp slither of excitement when she knew that finally she had got somebody's attention, and not just Roussel's.

'You're miles away. What is it?'

Renée looks down at the magazine, but Margo goes on staring at her and the colour starts to rise in Renée's cheeks.

'You've been behaving oddly all week. Is there something that you haven't told me?'

'No.'

'You haven't been laid off from work?'

She realises it's the perfume counter Marguerite's refer-ring to. 'Of course not. Why would I be laid off?'

'I thought something must have happened at the store.'
She waits while Renée goes through the pretence of thinking.

'Did you go and see your mother this week?'

Renée shakes her head.

'It must be three weeks since you paid your family a visit.'

'I don't think it's that long.'

'How long is it, then?'

'I'm not sure.'

'Won't she think it strange, her being ill and you not bothering to visit her?'

'It isn't that I can't be bothered.'

'We could go down this weekend together, if you like.'

The pause that follows is a fraction too long. 'Not this Saturday. The store is going on the outing to the Bercy funfair.'

Margo looks at her. 'You never said.'

'I thought I had. It's always the first Saturday in April.'

'Just because it's always then, it doesn't mean it always will be. There's no reason why I would remember, anyway.' She taps her pen against the form she's filling in. 'You're going, then?'

'It's only once a year. You don't mind, do you?'

'Not at all. The weekends are the only time we have together, but of course if you would rather see your friends ...'

'It's not ...'

'I've said go.' Marguerite writes for a moment and then puts the top back on her pen. 'I'd thought of doing some-thing else in any case, this weekend. There's a concert at the Châtelet. The head clerk at the Mairie invited me. It's Saint-Saëns.' She smiles cynically. 'Too serious for your taste.'

Renée doesn't answer. Margo does occasionally go to concerts on her own, but this time Renée knows she's doing it to get her own back.

'That's good,' she says. 'I'm glad you'll be doing something.'

It's not often she gets letters. When she moved into the flat with Marguerite, her mother used to write to her. She'd put the letter in the post on Tuesday so that it arrived on Wednesday. Renée sometimes wished it could be less of a routine. She often left the letter lying on the mat, or opened it at breakfast but then didn't bother reading it until the next day. There was never much inside that could be called news: stuff about the girls, what Alys had brought home from school, the nice girl Tonio was seeing. 'Nice girls' were what Maman talked about, as if by dint of constant repetition something of the niceness might rub off on Renée.

'Look what's come.'

'What is it?' Marguerite is sitting at the table toying with a croissant.

'It's a letter.'

'I can see that.' Marguerite dips one end of the croissant in her coffee. Renée weighs the letter in her hand. It's not official but her name is printed in block capitals, the way a child writes when it hasn't learnt to join the letters up. Some instinct tells her not to open it. She wishes that she hadn't been so quick to boast to Marguerite that somebody had written to her. Who would write a letter to her, after all? Apart from Pierre, the only people she knows are the people Marguerite knows too. She slides a knife under the flap. There is a single sheet of paper in the envelope. The message on it has been printed. '*FILLE SALOPE*'.

'Let's have a look, then.' Marguerite is holding out her hand.

'It's nothing.' Renée quickly slips the sheet of paper back inside the envelope, but Marguerite still has her hand out.

'Nothing?' She laughs nastily. 'I paid the rent to Monsieur Huppert last week, so it can't be that, but looking at your face it might be.'

Renée pushes back her chair. 'I need to go. I'm going to be late for work.' She thrusts the envelope into her bag and turns away, but Margo grabs her arm. She reaches for the bag and delves inside it.

'So it's comes to this.' She scans the letter and then lets it drop. She flicks it with her finger like a piece of dirt.

'I'm sorry.'

'Sorry? It's a bit late to be sorry. Who's it from?'

'I don't know.'

'Are you telling me there are so many people who know what you are, that anybody could have sent it?'

'I can't think of anyone who'd send it.'

Margo picks the letter up again. 'I knew that you'd been up to something. You do realise it's a warning? This is just the start. It won't end here.' She lets the implication dangle in the air between them.

'Should I take it to the police?'

'Oh yes, why not. Let's put a notice in the paper, just in case there's anybody left who doesn't know.'

'There isn't anything to know. It's not fair. Why is everyone so horrible?'

'You're telling me that you have no idea why anyone would say that you're a *fille salope*?'

'I'm not a *fille salope*!'

'Well, don't say that I didn't warn you.' Marguerite gets

up. 'When you've decided what it is the writer is referring to, perhaps you'd let me know.'

She leaves the letter lying on the table as she goes out. Renée puts it back into her bag. If she had really spent her afternoons at tea-dances or music halls – those places where girls were traditionally picked up, she would have confessed by now. What Renée hasn't yet considered is the possibility that Margo might already know her secret and is simply waiting for her to confirm it.

For the next five days, she takes the letter with her everywhere. Now she's told Margo she is going on the trip to Bercy, she will have to leave the flat, but she can't face the outing. She's not even able to confide in Gabi. Gabi is the only one who knows enough about her to have written it. They had been thrown together simply by the fact of working on the perfume counter. All the girls had backgrounds that were similar; it wasn't automatically a bond.

That Saturday, once she and Margo have had breakfast, Renée walks down to the river, buys herself a magazine and sits there on a bench until it's time to go back to the flat. On Sunday evening, Margo goes off to her concert. When she gets home, she finds Renée playing patience.

'Did you have a nice time at the concert?'

'It was most uplifting.' Marguerite smiles briefly.

'And the friend who went with you, did he enjoy it?'

'We agreed that the viola player wasn't quite up to the standard of the rest, but all in all it was a wonderful performance.'

'That's nice.' Renée takes the ten of Spades and lays it on the Jack. She's not sure how long she can carry on like this. She knows that in the end, however well she keeps up a pretence of ignorance, she will confess. And from that moment there will be no corner of her life that Marguerite does not have access to. She wonders what her punishment will be. Once, Marguerite had shut her in the wardrobe and gone off to work after an argument. She'd stayed there all day. By the time she was released, she'd passed out. When she came to, Marguerite was shaking her. 'I'm sorry,' she was sobbing. 'O God, Renée, I'm so sorry.'

Renée kept her eyes closed, partly out of curiosity to find out just how 'sorry' Marguerite was, partly because at that moment she would have been perfectly content to stay deliciously suspended between life and death for ever. As a child, she'd liked to hide in cupboards in the darkness. Putting out her hands, she felt the boundaries of the space that she was in. She felt safe. Outside, life went on as usual. She heard her mother shouting in the kitchen, Alys crying, Antoine yelling at them all to shut up. None of it impinged on her. The harder it became to breathe in there, the more she liked it. She felt dizzy with the lack of oxygen, intoxicated by the notion that unless she made an effort to get out, she could stop breathing altogether.

'Renée, say that you forgive me.'

'I forgive you,' Renée murmured. She had even hoped the punishment might be repeated. She would have preferred it to a slap or the discovery that Marguerite had sliced through all the clothes inside her wardrobe after she'd decided Renée had been flirting with the boy who punched their tickets on the tram. She was afraid that Marguerite would hurt her, but that she might kill her didn't bother her at all.

There is a raid that night. They hear the distant pop of gunfire and when Renée looks out from the window of the flat she sees smoke trowelling across the sky, illuminated by a holocaust of crimson flame as bombs fall to the north. An hour later it is their turn. Echoes of the detonating shells shunt down between the houses and they hear the crackle of the fires like dry crusts crumbled in a fist.

The next day she goes down to the patisserie as usual and finds it is no longer there. While her side of the road does not seem to have suffered any damage, on the other side a block of six or seven houses has imploded. In the smoking ruins, women wearing coal sacks on their shoulders to protect them from the dust and rain pick through the wreckage of what was a kitchen or a living room for anything that they can salvage.

Two young men with scarves over their mouths are lifting something from the debris. It's a meat safe, once an object to be prized, although of less use now that there is no meat to be had and nothing bought that isn't eaten straightaway. Between them they manoeuvre it onto the pavement, walking crab-like with the safe between them. They look slyly at her. Renée knows she should report them, but she won't.

She turns the corner onto rue des Cascades and sees what remains of the Patisserie Renard. She'd often wondered what lay on the far side of the swing door separating the Renards' apartment from the shop. A basket with the burnt remains of last night's bread lies just inside the door. All Renée glimpses of their living quarters is a heap of rubble and a square of velvet tacked onto the far wall. Underneath it, with its seat collapsed and both arms touching, is the carver in which Monsieur Renard sat to take his meals. A part of the dividing door stands upright in the ruins, still defiantly protecting land that is already lost. Glass crunches underneath her feet. One cabinet remains. The rest have shattered in the blast.

She picks a length of ribbon from the rubble and discovers it still knotted in a bow around one of the cardboard boxes used in the patisserie. The box is scorched a light brown and the ribbon's curling at the edges, but the seal is still intact. She eases up the flap. It's full of freshly baked chouettes, the pastry delicately caramelised in the heat. She slides her hand into the box. The crystals cling onto her fingertips. She puts them in her mouth. She can't smell burning, she no longer feels the grit that seems to permanently linger underneath her eyelids and in all the secret places of her body, she's unconscious of the mist that hangs above the streets as if embarrassed by the carnage and determined to conceal as much of it as possible. She is aware of nothing other than the agonising sweetness on her tongue.

She stands there in the rubble, stuffing one after another of the pastries in her mouth. The keen edge of her hunger lessens, and the scent of caramel reminds her all at once of something else. One morning she had passed the bombed-out barns behind the butcher's shop and smelt the carcasses of pigs mixed with the pungent odour of their swill – a mix of turnip, urine and whatever the *charcutier* had not been able to incorporate into his patés. Renée bends with one hand braced against her knee, the other holding back her scarf, and vomits everything she's eaten back into the dust.

After a week that seems to have gone on for ever, Wednesday comes around again. At midday, Renée leaves the store and takes a shortcut through the gardens of the Luxembourg to Montparnasse. The street door to the studios is open and she climbs the dingy staircase, littered as it always is with screwed-up newspapers and bits of rubbish. It feels unfamiliar, like a house you've lived in for a long time but no longer have a stake in. She stands at the door and listens. If the door is locked, there will be no point in her coming back again. But if Pierre is there, she's worried it might look as if she's desperate to be taken back.

She is still dithering outside the door when there's a movement on the floor above. The man who rents the top-floor studio comes out onto the landing and she hears him coming down the stairs. He glances at her. Renée's fingers are still curled around the doorknob. As he passes her she gives the knob a slight tug, as if to make sure she's locked it after her, and then she tucks her bag under her arm and follows him downstairs. He holds the street door open for her.

Renée wonders which direction she should go in, to avoid him, and turns right. He turns right too, but then somebody calls him from across the street. She can't go back immediately or she runs the risk of bumping into him again, but she can't bear to leave like this. The thought of going back to the apartment where she will be spending hours on her own again appals her. When there's nobody to talk to, it's like looking in a mirror; she sees nothing but her own reflection.

She goes past the café. There are fewer people in there now. The luncheon crowd are back at work and, while it's light, the painters will be in their studios. She sees that Caro is there by herself. It would be an extravagance she can't afford, to buy herself a pastry, but if she sits down with Caro she won't need to. She goes in. The dog is curled at Caro's feet. It wags its tail as she approaches.

'Mind if I sit down?' She curls her fingers round the chair back. Caro shrugs. 'It's freezing out there.' Renée keeps the two flaps of her coat wrapped round her. Caro finishes the boule she's eating, scooping off the cashews for the dog. He jumps onto her lap. Like Caro, he weighs almost nothing. He has small, bright eyes and three teeth missing from the right side of his jaw. The dog is basically a terrier but there is nothing pedigree about him. He and Caro are well matched in that respect. She strokes the dog's head absently.

'What do you call him?'

'Sweetie.' Caro shifts his weight onto her other leg. 'He turned up at the studio one day after a raid.' She stares into the empty glass dish and then runs her finger round the rim again in case she's missed some. There is a disturbing vacancy about her.

'Why do you eat ice cream all the time?'

'It hurts my throat to swallow. And my teeth are wobbly.' She is scratching at her lower arm and as her sleeve rides up around the elbow, Renée sees that there are scratches there.

'You've cut yourself,' she says. The cuts are each about eight centimetres long. 'It must have hurt.'

'It did,' says Caro. She draws up the sleeve. 'I did it with a razor blade.'

'You did it to yourself? Why?'

'I feel better afterwards.' The look that Caro gives her is defiant. This is something she has done before, thinks Renée, and now she can see the faint incisions further up the arm. She's curious. Whatever pain she's suffered in the past has been in consequence of other people. It had not occurred to her that pain was something you could use.

'You're always in the café, aren't you?'

'I live in the studio.' She pulls the empty bowl towards her so that Sweetie's near enough to lick it out. The waiter looks in her direction and then turns away.

'Do other girls live in the studios?'

'Some do.'

She wonders if the way that Caro lives means she's a '*fille salope*' too. If she saw the letter, would she even understand why Renée was upset?

There is a sudden blast of cold air as the door swings back. A couple come into the café, followed by two men. The couple peel off to a table in the corner and the two men come towards the table occupied by her and Caro. One of them is Roussel. Caro pulls her sleeve down. Renée doesn't want to be seen talking to Roussel, but he ignores her anyway. The men sit down and go on arguing. Roussel takes out his wallet and they order beers. He waits until they have their drinks and then he nods at her. 'It's Renée, isn't it?' He doesn't introduce her to his friend. 'You want a drink?'

'No thank you.'

Roussel turns away. She listens to their conversation. Whereas she and Gabi talked about the films they'd seen, the men who'd flirted with them and their hopes for a domestic future, these men talk of politics, the war, the latest exhibitions. Unlike Pierre who never raised his voice, it seems that every conversation with Roussel inevitably turns into an argument. Her nostrils catch the scent of something dense and yeasty.

His companion glances sideways at her. Renée sits back in her chair. She crosses one leg on the other and her skirt rides up an inch. Although she isn't in his line of vision, Roussel senses something going on behind him. He turns.

'Isn't this the day you model for Pierre?'

'He's not arrived yet.'

Roussel calls out for another beer and this time he includes a water ice for Caro. He takes out a note and looks at Renée. 'Let me treat you to a coffee or an iced tea while you're waiting.'

'No thanks.' Renée slides the bag across her shoulders. 'I expect he'll have arrived by now. I'd better go. He likes to start on time.'

Roussel looks at the clock but doesn't comment. He returns the wallet to his pocket. 'Last time you were here you didn't finish telling us what you did on the other days?' She hesitates. Roussel looks round at Caro and his friend and then leans back and stares up at the ceiling. 'Let me guess. You work behind the perfume counter in a big store in the centre.'

Colour rushes to her cheeks. She glances at the other man who's staring at her with an interested expression. Caro's barely looked at either of them since they came in. 'What makes you think that?'

'Each time you've been in here you've had a different scent on you. It's not cheap so I'm guessing that it's something you're exposed to every day.' He tilts his head towards his friend.

'You think you're clever, I suppose?'

'There's no need to get uppity about it. Caro here has never bothered to pretend she's anything except a little tart.' He glances sideways. Caro goes on staring vacantly ahead of her. 'At least she's honest,' he adds, carelessly.

'So what does that make you?' says Renée.

'If you were to ask my wife, she'd tell you I'm a navvy with pretensions just like yours. I don't deny it. Oh, for Christ's sake! Here, nobody gives a toss what class you come from. Stay and have a drink.'

'I've told you, I don't want one.'

'Has Pierre told you to stay away from me?'

'He didn't need to.'

Roussel snorts. 'We're old friends, Pierre and me. We go back years.'

'He doesn't seem to like you much now.'

'Ah.' He reaches for the ashtray. 'Shall I tell you what that's all about? He thinks I stole a girl from him in Rome. It happened years ago. If I had known he was so gone on her, I would have stepped aside. Pierre's not much good when it comes to courting.' He looks over at his friend again. The man laughs but she senses his discomfort. 'Women like men who know what they're doing.'

'Do they?' Renée scrapes her chair back.

'Don't you want to hear what happened?'

She does want to hear what happened, but she knows that anything she gets from Roussel will come at a price.

'I'm really not that dangerous, you know.' He turns to his companion. 'Stefan here will vouch for me.'

'I don't care if you are or not. I've better things to do than sit here listening to you gossiping.'

'The interesting part about it is that every model Pierre's had since then is the image of her.'

Renée hesitates. The tantalising snippet hovers in the air between them like a juicy apple with a vein of poison running through the core.

'That's not including Marthe, naturally.' He pauses. 'But then Marthe isn't just a model.' He regards her steadily above his glasses.

Renée turns and walks out of the café. Roussel calls out after her. 'That's always been the problem with Pierre. He's stuck. He can't move on. His pictures haven't changed in thirty years – the same old tablecloths, the same old tin bath on the same old rug. That vase of asters has been on the windowsill since 1890.'

As she steps outside onto the pavement, Renée hears their laughter.

She has barely gone ten yards before the sirens go off. People rush for the arcades. She stops and gazes up and down the street. Those buildings in the city centre that have cellars large enough to take in extra people have a stroke of white paint on the door, but there are none that she can see. A shell explodes nearby. A woman carrying a child bumps into her and Renée is shoved back against the wall. There is a sudden deafening explosion. For a second it's as if the space around her has been torn in half. Then shards of stone come pattering across the cobbles. Someone grabs her arm.

'Pierre!'

'For God's sake, Renée, why are you still on the street? You heard the sirens go off, didn't you?' He ushers her along the pavement to the shelter of a doorway. The shop signs are rattling on their hinges like a tinny orchestra. She squats down and Pierre leans over her, his head against the door so that she's wedged into a triangle. There is a sharp crack as another shell lands and the sickening rumble of collapsing buildings half a mile away.

'I came up to the studio. You weren't there.'

'I've been there since eight o'clock this morning. I was on my way down to the shelter when I saw you.' There's another thump and then a screech. A dog runs past them, its eyes white with terror, skittering from one side of the pavement to the other, like a clockwork toy. 'The door was open. You could just have walked in.'

Squatting with her neck in its uncomfortable position and her face pressed up against his jacket, Renée's glad he can't see her expression. 'You weren't there last week.'

'The terminus in Saint-Germain got a direct hit. There weren't any trams at all for several days. I couldn't let you know. I'm sorry.'

Renée tilts her face. His head is black against the sky. 'I didn't think the Germans bothered dropping bombs on Saint-Germain.'

'That one was probably a stray. I dare say it was meant for Belleville.' They wait for the all-clear. Renée gets up stiffly and her knees crack. 'Are you all right?' Renée nods. She dusts her coat down. When she looks up, Pierre is staring hard at her. 'I was afraid that when I wasn't there last week you might not come again.'

'I wasn't sure you'd want me to. I thought ...'

'What?'

'I thought maybe you were telling me you didn't need me any longer.'

He frowns. 'I would hardly do it that way.' They start walking down the street towards the studio. Pierre has looped his arm through hers. 'Where were you coming from?'

'The café.'

They climb up the stairs in single file. Pierre takes out his key. 'Was anybody there?'

'I spoke to Caro. Roussel came in later.'

'Ah, yes.' He stands back to let her in first. 'I'm surprised he ever gets a picture finished; he spends so much time there. Did he speak to you?'

'He offered me a drink. I said no.'

Pierre takes off his topcoat. 'That was sensible.'

'I didn't want to stay.'

'I'm simply saying that you did the right thing.' He takes out his pocket watch and flips the lid back irritably. 'There'll be no more visits to the café, I'm afraid. I need to catch up on the work I've missed.'

'I don't mind.' Renée slips her things off. If she never sees Roussel again, it will be too soon. She takes up the pose. It takes her seconds, normally, to distribute the weight so that she doesn't feel the pain, but she can't get into the right mode. Her left leg still aches from squatting in the doorway and there is a dragging in her stomach which reminds her that her period is due. After the tensions of the past week, she feels agitated. This is where she's longed to be, but she can't settle. She's not in the mood for standing still.

'Does Caro live in Roussel's studio?'

'I've no idea.'

'She's always in the café, isn't she? As if she's nowhere else to go.' He doesn't answer. 'Did you know that Caro cuts herself? She's got marks up her arm. She does it with a razor blade.'

'I think that Caro is a lost cause,' Pierre says, mildly. 'She strikes me as someone who is crying out to be destroyed and if she doesn't find someone to do it for her, she will do it to herself.'

'You don't think Roussel is to blame, then?'

'Roussel should have left her where he found her – on the street. At least there she had friends. You'd do well to keep clear of both of them.' He goes on making alterations to the picture, but it isn't going well. She knows because he keeps on reaching for the rag and using it to wipe off what he's done. Eventually he gets up and goes over to the bench where he has left the keys. He takes one off the ring and puts it down beside her wrap. 'You ought to take this. If you have a key and I'm not here, you can at least be comfortable while you're waiting. Wouldn't that be more convenient?'

She stares. The way he says it makes it sound as if the key is of no real significance, but Renée knows it is. He'd talked about 'convenience' before, once, when she had been getting dressed after a session which had twice been interrupted by the sirens.

'You know you could stay here sometimes if you don't like going back to your apartment in the dark. There's always the chaise longue,' he'd said then.

Renée had been drawing up her stocking, one leg stretched, the toes extended, gently easing the silk up over her calves. She'd gone on pulling up the stocking as if she was only half-attending to the conversation.

'Well?'

'I wouldn't do it for convenience,' she'd said, a hint of

sharpness in her voice. She smoothed the stocking up over her thigh and reached under her shift for the suspender belt.

'What would you do it for?'

She looped the stocking-top over the buckles and pulled down her shift.

'I wouldn't do it for convenience,' she'd said again.

'Convenience' on this occasion meant that he could guarantee her being there on Wednesday afternoons. It meant he wanted to continue painting her. The studio is like the inner sanctum of a temple; no one enters without invitation. He is trusting her and in return she feels she has to trust him. In the break, she takes the letter from the pocket of her coat and shows it to him.

He is silent for a moment. 'Do you have the envelope?' She hands it over. Pierre squints at the postmark. 'It was put into the box at Belleville.'

'Yes.'

'Do you know anyone apart from you who lives there?' Renée shakes her head. 'Who do you know who might have sent it?'

'No one, really.'

He regards her patiently. 'Could it be Marguerite?'

She's toying glumly with the sleeve of her kimono. 'I suppose so.'

'Why would Marguerite say you're a slut?'

'I take my clothes off, don't I?'

'You're a model. That's what models do.'

'Try telling that to Marguerite.'

He folds the letter up and lays it on the worktop. 'I think you should tear this up. Why carry it around with you? Ignore it. Throw the thing away.'

'It's different for you.'

'Of course, if you would feel more comfortable not

coming here again, then I shall understand. I wouldn't want to make your life more difficult.'

'This is the only time I feel alive.'

He looks at her a moment and then takes his glasses off. He smooths his thumb across the rim. 'I didn't realise it meant such a lot to you.'

'It does. I couldn't bear it if I had to give up coming here.'

There is a pause and then he pulls a chair up and sits down in front of her. He takes her hands. 'You realise, Renée, that there's very little I can offer you, apart from what you have already.'

'I'm not asking you for anything.'

'But I still feel responsible. You shouldn't have this happen to you.'

Renée sniffs. 'It's just a letter.'

'No, it isn't. What it says is slanderous. It's completely unacceptable. Whoever wrote it hasn't got the least idea what working for an artist means.'

'What does it mean?'

'You're part of a tradition that goes back two thousand years. Those pictures on the pinboard over there would not exist if someone like you hadn't modelled for them. You're a vital part of the artistic process.'

'Like a muse, you mean?' She didn't mean to sound sly.

It's as if the safety curtain has come down belatedly between the actors and the common people in the stalls. 'If you prefer to call it that.' He's giving her the sort of look you might give someone who'd come begging at the door.

'I don't mind what they say as long as you still want to go on painting me.'

'I've said I do.'

But later, when the session ends and she is getting dressed, she finds her money – which he usually leaves discreetly in an envelope inside the cubicle – is not there. Renée hovers by the door. 'I'll see you next week.'

He looks up and smiles, then pats his pocket and takes out his wallet. 'Wait. You mustn't go without your money.' He counts out the notes onto the workbench. Gathering them up into a pile, he hands them over to her.

'Must you go?'

He half-turns in the door. I hear that little click of irritation in his throat.

'You're being foolish, Marthe. It's not like you. What's the matter?'

'I don't see why you would want to travel into Paris every day when all the Germans use it for is target practice. You could work here.'

'When the terminus was bombed I had no choice, but now I need to get back to the studio. I've work to finish.'

'Can't you bring it back?'

'I'd have to wait for it to dry and since it's going straight into an exhibition there's no point in bringing it here just to take it back again.'

When Madame Hébert came on Tuesday, she said there's a rumour that if the Americans do come into the war it could be over in a month, but that the Germans plan to raze the city to the ground first. I know I'm not going to persuade him, but I go on chivvying him anyway. 'They say the shells from this new gun rise thirty-five kilometres into the air before they come to earth. Suppose a bomb drops on the studio?'

'I'd count myself exceedingly unfortunate.'

'I'd say that you were asking for it.'

'Don't let's quarrel, Marthe. I can't spend the whole war hiding out in Saint-Germain. Don't worry, I'll be careful.'

Tell that to the Germans, I think. Maybe if he asks them nicely they'll drop bombs on someone else.

That night, I see the jagged lights of the artillery and hear the cracks as bombs explode and debris flies into the air. The city has been targeted for five nights in a row. It goes on hour after hour, till I wonder whether by the morning anything will be left standing. I imagine factories manufacturing the bombs as quickly as they are released into the air.

Pierre is terrified of being suffocated. The idea of being underneath the rubble haunts him. He'd be whimpering with terror, calling for me. He once said he couldn't come to terms with the idea of death. Not even the idea of it. So how does he think he would cope with the reality? Of course he wouldn't have to, I think. 'I'm the one who'd have to cope with the reality.'

As Renée comes out of the Underground on rue de Ménil-montant, she sidesteps the soldier squatting at the entrance. It's beginning to get dark and he'll have finished for the day. The first time Renée saw him, she thought he was standing guard outside the Metro. He stood to attention with his head back and his chin stuck out. She was preparing to slow down and give her hair a little toss as she went past. It wasn't until she'd drawn level with him that she realised one side of his face was missing. Where there should have been an eye, there was an empty socket and the flesh and bone on either side of it was raw and scarified. He held his tin cup like a rifle butt in front of him, with both hands curled around it.

Paris swarmed with beggars. Many were the same age as the boys she'd been at school with. Usually she gave them something. This one wasn't more than eighteen. Even with his terrible disfigurement, the left side of his face suggested he had been a handsome boy. His mouth had not been damaged and the lips were full and soft. As she was fumbling in her purse she'd felt a hot flush creep up from her neck. She heard the shiny jingle of the centimes as they dropped into the tin cup.

He had looked at her expressionlessly. 'Merci.'

'De rien.' She felt the hunger kept in check behind the tin cup, which was now his only weapon. She wished she had not put lipstick on that morning.

Since he didn't ask for money, people didn't always notice he was begging. They assumed, as she had, that he was on duty to protect them. She'd have liked to ask him how much he could count on being given on a good day, where he went at night, if he had anybody to look after him. But still, she was relieved when every time she dropped the centimes in the cup, she got the same reaction.

'Merci.'

'De rien.'

It's after seven when she comes out of the Metro. He is squatting on the pavement with the cup between his knees and counting out the coins into the palm of one hand, holding them up to his good eye to examine the inscription before slipping them into his pocket.

He looks up and Renée gives a brisk smile. It's a smile that has already moved on somewhere else. She's never had a conversation with him. That would have meant looking at his face and Renée wouldn't have known what to focus on. If she looked straight into the good eye, wouldn't that suggest she was disgusted by his wounds, but if she let her gaze move to the right side, wouldn't that imply a morbid curiosity? The two of them were trapped inside the ghettoes of her beauty and his ugliness.

She walks on past him, conscious that his head is turned in her direction. She turns onto Rue de Belleville. They've had raids on two nights in succession and the soft light is shot through with ash. It leaves a grey smear on her jacket when she tries to brush it off. She passes underneath the archway at the entrance to the alleyway that comes out onto rue des Peupliers. She might have gone the long way round and not turned off the main road. Renée knows already that he is behind her. She can hear the soft thud of his heels against the cobbles. As he gains on her, she hears his breathing. Like the rest of him, it is contained, the kind of breathing that men practised in the trenches before going into battle.

Renée steels herself. She's waiting for the breaths to change. This was the moment when they went over the top. A lot of men were sick; some wet themselves or worse and some said afterwards that they felt nothing, just relief that there was no more waiting. She knows there's no point in running. If she does, her panic will excite him. She is only yards from the apartment, but she knows that she won't make it to the entrance. She hears what sounds almost like a sob and then she sees the hand as it comes round the front of her. He's clawing at her breast, but he is hardly touching her. There's something reverential, almost tender, in the gesture.

Renée lashes blindly at his face. They tussle for a moment and she sees the tramlines that her nails have left across his cheek. Blood is already seeping from the cuts. He looks surprised, as if he'd suddenly been wrenched out of a dream. He takes a step back and stands looking at her. Then he turns and runs back down the street.

She leans against the wall. Her legs feel weak. Her breath is coming in short, wispy little squeaks. She rubs her thumb against her fingertips. There is a rime of dirt and skin under her nails. She feels sick. If he'd only spoken and not simply panted after her like that.

She wishes she had quietly let him grope her in the street. For once, behaving like a slut might have redeemed her. 'If you want to, you can feel my breasts,' she might have said. 'They're nothing special. It's what Marguerite does every night; she never bothers asking. If I can put up with her, why should you be denied?'

It's not as if she'd have to look at him. She could have closed her eyes. It would have been her sacrifice, an act of charity.

The first time there is hardly any blood at all. She has to press the skin on both sides of the cut. It hurts more than she had expected. It had started hurting her before the blade had even touched the skin. She doesn't want to cut twice in the same place, so she goes a little higher up her arm, but there she finds the flesh more sensitive. She clamps her teeth together while she makes a second cut. This one is marginally deeper, but still she is disappointed. She is conscious of the pain as something shrill but at the same time small and insignificant. The way that Caro had described it somehow made it grander. She puts down the knife and lays her forearm on the table. Caro had made four cuts on her arm. I couldn't even manage two, thinks Renée. She's not sure why it should feel so much like failure.

Where she's laid the knife, a smear of blood has come off on the tablecloth. She spits into her handkerchief and tries to rub it off. It turns from bright red to a soft pink, but it is still visible and Renée knows that Margo, who is blind to her environment as long as it remains the same, will notice it at once. She bunches up the handkerchief and leans her forehead on the table. Why does she make such a mess of everything she does?

∽

When Renée finds the cat, she thinks at first it's still alive. When she was in her other flat, they often got strays coming to the door and Renée always gave them something, but it's rare, now that she's living on the top floor, to find animals in the apartment. This one is an alley cat with black streaks, scrawny, as are all the residents of Paris these days. It's out on the landing, curled up but with all four legs in running motion.

It's when Renée sees its mouth that she knows this cat isn't going anywhere. Its lips are drawn back on its teeth, its mouth half open. It's not only dead but it's been dead for some time. Renée prods it gently, but there isn't any doubt about it. Did it crawl up to the top floor before dying, or did someone leave it there? She needs to make sure that there isn't any message underneath it. But perhaps this is the message. Renée looks at it. She's sorry that the cat's been made to suffer. She hopes it was dead to start with and not killed just so that somebody could leave it on her landing.

She will have to take it downstairs to the dustbins in the yard. In half an hour Margo will be home. She goes into the flat and fetches half a dozen copies of *Le Figaro* piled up behind the kitchen door for throwing out. She wraps the cat in newssheet, cradling its head while she attempts to loop the paper round it. The scent coming from its mouth suggests it has already started rotting on the inside. Renée turns her head away.

'How long has it been going on?' No use now trying to pretend that everything is as it should be. She'd run into Margo on the stairs as she was carrying the cat down to the yard. The first thing Margo looked at was the bundle in her arms. 'What's that?'

'It's only rubbish,' Renée was about to say, but she would

have felt outraged on the cat's behalf if she had said that. 'It's a dead cat.'

'What's it doing outside our apartment?'

'I don't know. Perhaps it crawled up there to die.'

'Don't be ridiculous. Cats crawl off into corners or behind the furniture to die.' She folded back the paper from its head. 'It's been dead ages.'

'Maybe it was poisoned.'

'Maybe it was left there purposely by somebody who knew you'd find it.'

Renée suddenly felt weary. Marguerite's determined silence had begun to wear her down, but not as much as this continual insinuation that she'd somehow brought things on herself. 'I don't know who would do that.'

'Don't you?' Marguerite's eyes narrowed. 'Think about it.'

'I have thought about it.'

'I suppose you think about it every Wednesday afternoon while you're pretending to be helping your friend Gabi with her wedding preparations, or behaving like a normal daughter, visiting your mother.'

'If you must know, I've been working somewhere else on Wednesday afternoons.' It's out before she can do anything about it. 'I was having trouble finding my half of the rent and there aren't many jobs that you can do one afternoon a week.'

'And what is it, precisely, that you do?'

'I help an artist in his studio.'

'What help would you be to an artist?'

When she tells her, Renée has the feeling Marguerite already knows exactly what she does. She just wants Renée to condemn herself by saying it out loud.

'How old is he?'

'I don't know. In his forties, I suppose.'

The look that Marguerite is giving her is pitiless. She brushes past her and goes on up to the next floor. Renée goes down to the yard and lays the cat as delicately as she can among the other detritus. She says a prayer for it before she puts the lid down. If the rubbish isn't covered up, the foxes get at it.

In the apartment, Marguerite is sitting at the table with a pile of papers. Once they've eaten, she spreads out the documents again and reaches for her glasses.

'Don't you want to talk about it?'

'What's the point? You did it without asking me. Why would you bother taking my advice now?'

'You'd have disapproved. That's why I didn't mention it.'

'Of course I disapprove. If Mademoiselle Lefèvre knew how you were spending your half-days off from the perfume counter, you would lose your job. Then what?'

The dirty plates from dinner are still on the table. One of Margo's papers lies next to the blob of gravy Renee had spilt to disguise the bloodstain on the cloth. She wonders whether she should move the plates into the sink and wipe the table down, but she's afraid that Marguerite will think she isn't listening to her if she does.

'It isn't me you've let down, Renée. It's yourself. Well, and your family, of course. I can imagine how your brother would react.'

'You won't say anything to them?' says Renée, tightly.

Margo fixes her. 'You know what really hurts me, Renée? No, let's say what really disappoints me, is the fact that you deceived me. I thought our relationship was based on trust.'

'I would have told you in the end.'

'It's just as well, because as far as I'm concerned this is the end.'

There is a pause while Renée takes in what she's just said. 'You don't mean it . . .'

'There's no point in our continuing to live together. It would be dishonest.'

'No!' Why does the thought of Marguerite abandoning her terrify her so? For two years, Marguerite's dictated every move she makes. Becoming Pierre's model is her one act of rebellion. At the start it carried no more weight than treating herself to a matinee or buying chocolates and then eating all of them at once.

'Don't go.'

'It's you who would be leaving, Renée.' Marguerite gives her a faint smile

'But I haven't . . .'

'Haven't anywhere to go? Perhaps you should have thought of that.'

'I didn't think . . .'

'Precisely.' Marguerite sighs. 'That's the problem, isn't it?'

If Renée cries in front of her, she knows that this will signal some new phase in their relationship, a phase in which whatever slender ground she held, has now been occupied.

'I'm sorry if you think I let you down.'

'I've told you, Renée, it's yourself you're letting down. You either give up working for this man or you start looking for a new apartment.'

'Why? It's not as if . . .' She bites her lip.

'It's not as if what? Dead cats, letters telling you that you're a trollop? What more does it take?'

'It's not as if what I've been doing is a sin or something.'

Marguerite gives her a long look. 'You're a wretched little liar, Renée, and if you're not careful soon you'll be a wretched little whore.'

'I haven't ...'

She puts up her hand. 'Don't tell me. I don't want to hear about it. I'm just telling you the way these things go. You might think it's all right, but in six months' time when this man's had enough of you, you'll end up opening your legs for one of those mille-feuilles you've always been so keen on.'

'That's a dreadful thing to say.'

'Believe me, I know how the world works, Renée. You have no idea.'

It's over. In the minutes afterwards, there is a lull – the sort that follows an explosion; then an echo. She's not sure if it's the echo of the silence or the echo of the noise preceding it. She hears a rumble in the distance that could be the sound of thunder. It expands into a roar; then suddenly the noise is all around her. It's the guns, she thinks. They haven't stopped. They promised, and they haven't stopped. But as it grows, the rumble gradually transforms itself into the sound of voices cheering. People pour onto the streets. They're waving flags and banners; soldiers throw their caps into the air; she sees a small boy shinny up a lamp post and pin streamers to the metal hood over the light. As he is sliding down again, his breeches snag against the rough edge of the metal stanchions and he lets go, hanging in the air a moment while the crowd gasps. Renée thrusts her way towards the edge. The shouting blends into what sounds to her ears like a keening dirge – the kind that cows make when their calves are taken from them. She keeps walking, but she feels hands pawing at her. Strangers throw their arms around her. They want her to join them; it's a party nobody must be left out of. Renée isn't certain what she feels. Then suddenly she knows. She feels old.

∞

He would like to close the windows, but without the draught of air the studio would be oppressive. They must be the only people left in Paris who aren't on the streets. The Stars and Stripes are pinned onto the front of every shop in every quarter, hanging out of windows and taped to the front of cabs and trolleybuses. Music is erupting from a hundred different sources – violins, accordions, street vendors selling paper flags and ticker tape and, somewhere in the distance, the battalions marching from the Rond Point to la Concorde.

Renée gives a quick glance at the window. 'They've begun the march past. Shall we go and look?'

'I doubt we'd get within a mile of it.'

'We'd hear it, though.'

'But we can do that just as well from here.' He takes the sketchbook from the worktop and begins to draw. They work for quarter of an hour and then Pierre puts down the crayon.

Renée shifts her weight onto the other leg. 'Why have you stopped?'

'You're tense. Why don't you take a break?'

She straightens up and presses one hand to her back. She has been waiting for the break to tell him that she isn't coming to the studio again. That it should be today of all days, when the whole of Paris is out celebrating. Pierre will think she isn't capable of making up her own mind, or that she is letting Margo bully her. He'll tell her to stand up to her and Renée knows she can't. She wanders over to the window and looks out over the street.

'You'd better put your wrap on.'

'Nobody can see me up here.' They can hear the sound of the parade now. The whole building starts to tremble.

'Let's hope the enthusiasm isn't premature. What better

triumph for the Germans than a raid on Independence Day.'

'We've managed to survive raids up till now.' And so what if we didn't? she thinks. Everything she looks at, everything she touches in the studio, she tells herself she's touching for the last time. She will leave here when the session's over and she won't be coming back. The studio has been as much her home as the apartment in the rue des Peupliers. The room is littered with her personal possessions. She will leave them, she decides. She doesn't want him to forget her. He will find another girl to pose for him, a girl who when she goes into the cubicle to take her clothes off for the first time will detect the faint scent of the previous incumbent.

When she goes back to the flat this evening, Marguerite will be there waiting for her. They'll sit down to dinner. Marguerite will be solicitous; she won't want to be seen to crow. I ought to hate her, Renée thinks, but she is fearful of the future Marguerite's predicted for her. Life is merciless to girls who break the rules.

An engine roars and splutters overhead and there's a sudden eerie silence as the crowd looks up into the sky to see if the bombardment has begun. But it turns out to be a Liberty Machine. The engine stutters and then fires as if at any moment it might cut out altogether. As the pilot swoops and dives over the crowd, it breaks into spontaneous applause and there are shouts of 'Plus! Plus!' Renée stares up at the sky.

'For God's sake, Renée. Come away and put on a kimono. Someone's bound to see you.' She comes back into the room and starts to pull her clothes on. 'Are you getting dressed?'

'I'm going down.'

He reaches for his jacket. 'You can't go down by yourself. All right; we'll both go.'

Once they're on the pavement they're immediately

swallowed up into the crowd. There's no choice but to let themselves be swept along in the direction of the Champs Elysées. They can hear the tramp of marching feet. A *mutilé de guerre*, without legs, is careering round the square on wooden slats with wheels attached. He has a tray of paper flags. The boy is barely twenty. He's lost everything but he's still cheering. 'I'm not finished yet,' he says. 'They haven't seen the last of me.'

The band is followed by the march past. First in line are the Marines, still in their uniforms with battle stains and tin hats. Women rush out of the crowd, bombarding them with flowers. Some are tucking notes with their addresses in the pockets of the soldiers' uniforms. It isn't just the city that's been liberated.

Renée catches sight of Roussel in his white suit. He is standing back, a cigarette in one hand, casually looking on as if what's happening in front of him has no connection with him. From the way he's leaning back against the wall, she sees that he's already drunk. A woman steps out of the crowd towards him. She stands with her face up close to his and says something. He looks away. She puts her mouth up to his ear and Roussel snorts. He looks over her shoulder to where Renée's standing. She's not certain if he's seen her.

On an impulse, Renée breaks away and hurls herself into the line. She flings her arms around the neck of a Marine and kisses him. The soldier laughs and whispers something. They walk on a few yards with their heads together.

Pierre looks on, stonily. She makes her way back through the crowd and stands beside him. 'What's the matter?' she curls one hand round his arm and nuzzles up against him. When she looks back, she sees Roussel's disappeared. The woman has, too.

'Quieten down. You're acting like a schoolgirl.'

'It's a celebration. Can't we just be happy for an hour or two?' The look he gives her isn't one she's seen before. 'What are you thinking?'

Pierre looks away. 'You should be celebrating with your own friends – people of your own age.'

Renée isn't sure she has friends of her own age any more. 'I'd rather be with you.'

'Why?'

'I don't know. I just would.'

His mouth twitches. 'What a funny little creature you are.'

'What about you? Would you rather have been back in Saint-Germain with Marthe?'

'Marthe won't be celebrating. She was never for the war. She thinks it's an abomination.'

'Do you think all this is wrong, then?'

'No, of course it isn't. People have a right to celebrate. They've had enough of suffering. It's harder for my generation. It's not only that you've seen it all before; you know that you'll be seeing it again.'

'There couldn't be another war.'

'Let's hope not.'

'If it had gone on another year, my brother would have joined up.'

'That sounds like another reason to be grateful that it ended when it did.'

'Why not enjoy it, then?'

'When you're as old as I am, you'll discover nothing makes much difference to the way you live. Provided I could still get hold of paint and canvas, I would have survived whichever side had won.'

'But still you're pleased it's our side, aren't you?'

'I doubt either of us would be standing here now, had it gone the other way, so yes, I'm pleased it's our side.'

By the time the soldiers have passed out of earshot, it's late afternoon. The crowd breaks into factions and goes off in search of further entertainment. Every street is littered with small paper flags. Now the excitement's over, Renée's mood begins to darken. She's already later than she said she'd be and she has not said anything to Pierre.

'You're very quiet,' Pierre says.

'So are you?'

'Did you enjoy it?'

'It was wonderful. I'm glad we came.'

'Yes, so am I.' He tucks her arm through his. She leans her head against his shoulder.

'Let me take you out to dinner. Why not round the day off pleasantly?' Her face lights up and then the light goes out of it again. 'We could start with champagne at Maxim's. How does that sound?'

'That sounds lovely.' She's about to say she has to go, that Marguerite is waiting for her.

'There's no need to agonise.' He laughs. 'The choice is between dinner and an early night, that's all.'

No, Renée thinks, that isn't all.

She's never been inside a restaurant as grand as this. It's like a palace. Ornate mirrors with frames in the shape of trailing vines reflect her image everywhere she looks. The tables are divided by screens filled with stained-glass images of poppies, irises and dragonflies. The dark red ceiling and the red banquettes add to the hothouse atmosphere. The waiter leads them to a table at the back. He pulls a chair out for her. Renée sits. She looks around her.

Pierre shakes out his napkin and she does the same. 'This room is famous. It's been decorated in a style called Art

Nouveau. In 1899 it was the setting for an opera called *The Merry Widow*.'

'It was set in this room?'

'In this very room. For pudding you can have a *Crêpe Veuve Joyeuse* if you want.'

She takes the printed card the waiter hands her, casting her eyes down the list of dishes. Most of them she's never heard of.

'Would you rather have meat or a fish dish?'

'You choose.'

'Well, then, let's have both.'

'All on the same plate?'

He hands back the menu. 'One after the other might be nicer.'

Renée sees the waiter smirk. He brings a bucket to the table with a bottle of champagne. He grins at Renée as he eases out the cork and it explodes into the air and shoots into her lap. She gives a little shriek. He makes a big show of apologising, reaching for the cork and tossing it into the air before he pockets it. He pours a little of the champagne into Pierre's glass and he tastes it. Renée wonders why the waiter doesn't serve her first. She waits. Pierre nods and the waiter comes to her side of the table.

Pierre is watching her the way you'd watch a child to see how it responded to a new experience and maybe to decide how safe it would be to repeat it. He leans over, tapping Renée's glass with his. She takes a sip. The bubbles stay a moment on her tongue and start to fizzle in her nostrils.

'Do you like it?'

'It feels odd.' She takes another sip and splutters.

Pierre hands her a serviette. 'Small sips are better.'

She's about to take another sip, but then she puts the glass down.

The first course arrives – whole scallops in a seashell with a white sauce over them. She scoops the sauce onto her tongue and lets it rest there for a moment. 'It's delicious. Can I keep the shell?'

'I think they might regard it rather as they would if you asked whether you could take a plate away with you.'

'But aren't these like the shells you find on beaches?'

'Yes. I'll get one for you if you like, but possibly not this one.'

Is she being ticked off? With Pierre it's sometimes hard to know.

'You often come here, do you?'

'Hardly ever.'

She looks round the tables. There are several women with men decades older than themselves. She wonders whether Maxim's is another of the *maisons closes* that have sprung up in Paris since the war began. They often have a restaurant up front to make it look respectable. She feels as if she's walking on a tightrope. Underneath her if she slips – and now she knows she will – there is a bubbling cauldron waiting to consume her. It's not just a question of her going back to Marguerite; it's what she might or might not do instead that matters and what that will mean from then on.

'Now you're looking sad again.'

'I'm not. It's only that when something nice is happening I keep thinking that tomorrow it'll all be over.'

'Isn't that a reason to enjoy it while you can? What is it you're afraid of?'

'I don't know – the usual things, old age, death, being poor, not having anybody except Marguerite.' And maybe now not even having her, thinks Renée.

'That's an awful lot to be afraid of. But you wouldn't

want to stay with Marguerite for ever. You'll move on at some point. You'll get married and have children.'

'I suppose so.'

'Well then,' he smiles. 'Marguerite is just a staging post.'

'Why didn't you have children, you and Marthe?'

'I'm afraid that painters make neglectful parents.'

'Marthe didn't want them, either?'

'I think Marthe might once have discovered she was pregnant, but she never mentioned it. I thought that if she didn't want to talk about it, that was up to her.' He clears his throat.

'What happened to the child?'

'It went away.'

'You mean it died?'

He looks round for the waiter. 'It was over twenty years ago.'

'You never talked about it?'

'As I said . . .' He raps his fingers on the tabletop and casts about him. 'What will Marguerite have done today?'

'She had to stay on at the Mairie. They had documents to work through for the Armistice.'

'She won't be working now, though?'

'No. She'll be at home.'

'Will she be worried that you're not back?'

She'll know who I'm with, thinks Renée. From the way he says it she knows that it isn't something he's concerned about. Already she can sense a certain rivalry between them, although Pierre is not aware that Marguerite now knows about him.

'What did you do with that letter you received?'

'I did what you said.'

'Good. If you can show you're unaffected by these things, they usually stop.'

She nods. She hasn't told Pierre about the cat. He fills her glass again. With each sip, Marguerite seems to recede a little further. There's a pattern of acanthus leaves with berries on the wall behind Pierre's head and suddenly his face looks like a gargoyle in among the foliage. She throws back her head and laughs. There's so much noise inside the restaurant that no one notices.

'It seems the champagne's having the desired effect at last.'

'Is it the champagne? So it isn't real, this feeling?'

'If you're feeling it, it's real.'

'I mean, it won't last.'

'I think we've agreed that nothing lasts.'

There is an altercation at the door as three Marines are turned away. The diners look round, momentarily diverted by the prospect of an incident. The Maître d' is called and remonstrates with them. They don't speak French and although Renée knows Pierre speaks English he makes no attempt to intercede. The boys are clumsy; they're already half drunk and now that they've been released onto the streets, they don't know what to do – the city is replete with opportunities beyond their reach. They offer up a token protest and then meekly take their leave. One of them catches Renée's eye. He's barely older than her brother, but the look he gives her is both covert and respectful. He takes in the room as they withdraw and gapes.

The Maître d' turns to the diners and holds up his hands. A titter goes around the tables. Pierre sees her face.

'Why weren't they let in?'

'They're not wearing suits.'

'But they've just won the war for us.'

Pierre's eyes flicker to the other tables. 'It's a rule they have sometimes in restaurants.'

'It's not right. I feel sorry for them.'

'They'll find somewhere else to eat. Don't worry.'

She toys with her serviette. 'Why can't they be allowed to celebrate?'

'Nobody wants to stop them celebrating, but I'm not sure Maxim's is the kind of place where they would want to celebrate. They're soldiers; they'll be looking to get drunk and they can't do that here. They'd only end up being thrown out later on.'

'The French are such snobs.'

'Yes, they are.' He mouths the words. 'Especially the Parisians.'

The second course arrives in front of them. 'What's this?'

'It's escalope de porc.' He cuts a piece and puts it in his mouth. 'It's excellent. Do try a bit.'

She carves a slice of meat and spears it with her fork. Outside, the city is erupting into life again after the temporary hiatus of the afternoon. The Maître d' looks anxiously towards the window.

'Just as well we chose a table near the back.' Pierre smiles. 'Any plate-glass windows not already shattered by the blasts are likely to be targeted this evening.'

'I hope they come back and burn the place down.'

'You don't mean that.'

Renée looks at him. His face looks raw and viscous in the red light. She takes in the other diners in the room. There's not a single face here that she can relate to.

'What's the matter, Renée?'

'I must go.'

He looks over his glasses at her. 'Very well, but surely we can stay until the meal is over. You don't want to miss out the dessert.'

'I promised Marguerite I would be back at six o'clock.'

'That's totally unreasonable. What is this hold that Marguerite has over you?'

'It's not that.' Renée screws the serviette up in her hand. 'I don't belong here.'

'Dear girl, it's a restaurant, that's all. There isn't any need to feel intimidated.'

'You don't understand.'

'I think I do. You don't like how they treated the Marines. Well, nor do I. I hate society. It's why I don't go out in it unless I have to. I just thought you might enjoy the spectacle. I wanted to do something special for you, something that you would remember.'

'Yes, I know. It's lovely, but ...'

'I think you ought to wait for the dessert. I promise you it's worth it.' He leans over and unclasps her fingers from the serviette. 'I'd like it if you stayed. Please do.'

He knows, and so does she, that it will be too late once they have finished eating for her to go back to Marguerite. The longer that she sits here, the less choice she has.

They have to walk back from the restaurant. The Metro has stopped running and there are no cabs. To walk the streets without the wail of sirens and the constant crack of shells exploding is a new experience. The street lamps, turned off in the last months of the war to make it harder for the enemy to see what they were bombing, flood the boulevards with light. The party that will go on for the next ten years has started.

It's past midnight when they cross the Boulevard du Montparnasse. They climb the staircase arm in arm. Pierre takes off his overcoat and lights a candle. She is out of her clothes in a fraction of the time it takes him to undo the buttons on his shirt and take his tie off. He is fumbling with his shirt cuff. As he tries to disengage the button on it, it pings off onto the floor. He curses. Renée has the feeling he is no more used to this than she is.

'Do you always take this long to get undressed?'

'I'd get there quicker if you didn't watch me.'

'You watch me.'

'You have the option of undressing in the cubicle if you don't want me to.'

'Why would I bother when you've seen me naked every Wednesday afternoon for eighteen months or more?'

'You know that watching someone get undressed is reckoned to be more erotic than the sight of them with nothing on?'

'Is that right? Not when someone's making such a mess of it. Would you like me to help you?'

'Not at all. I hope I can still manage to undress myself.' But it is soon apparent that he can't. He stands there with his shirt half off, his hands hung limply at his sides. She gets up and uncurls the shirt across his shoulders, down his arms. She takes the buckle of his trousers and unloops it. He sinks down onto the chaise longue. Renée kneels in front of him to take his socks off. He rests one hand on her head and waits for her to look up.

She has often wondered what his body looks like underneath his clothes. Whereas she can't go past a mirror or a window without studying her own reflection, Pierre seems unaware that he has even got a body, other than the parts of it he needs – hands, eyes, brain.

There's a thatch of dark hair in the middle of his chest that tapers down towards his navel and continues in a thinner line towards his groin where suddenly it sprouts into a forest. She's seen few men naked but once some girl in the factory where she worked before the perfume counter had brought in a cache of photographs of men, their penises erect, their arms crossed, staring baldly at the camera, daring anybody looking back to be impressed. His penis looks like an exotic breed of caterpillar nestling in the undergrowth.

She wants to take it in her hand and whisper to it that it needn't be afraid, but as she reaches out to touch the outer skin, it comes alive. There is a pulsing down the length of it, the tip protrudes out of its cloak of skin and thrusts itself towards her. She is fascinated and appalled. It seems to have a personality distinct from Pierre's and when she glances up at him, she sees the horror on his face. 'It's all right,' she says, 'I don't mind.' She wants to go back to observing it, discovering its habits, how best to approach it. But a second later Pierre's hands close around her shoulders and he thrusts her sideways onto the chaise longue. She feels his penis jabbing at her, blindly, still acclimatising to the monstrous transformation it has undergone.

Eventually, he puts his hand down, grasping it along its length and easing it inside her. She'd expected to feel pain. The girls at work had said the first time would be painful. She had thought there would be blood, but there was no blood either and she wondered if the games that she and Marguerite had played had somehow taken her virginity without her noticing.

His body clenches and convulses and then Renée feels the weight of him on top of her. He groans. His face is buried in the cushion next to hers. She wonders what will happen next. She feels him shrink inside her and loops both arms round his back. She wants to keep him there. She is afraid that once he has withdrawn she will feel lonely.

For a while, his breathing slows down and she wonders whether he's asleep. She lies there without moving, listening to the distant sound of revellers still on the streets in a remote part of the city. Moonlight filtering through the skylight throws a ghostly white veil over the familiar objects in the studio – the vase of dead chrysanthemums left on the windowsill till Pierre has finished painting them, the easel and the worktop with its brushes and its jars of oil and turpentine. When she recalls that night, the bitter odour of chrysanthemums, the smell of linseed and the sweat from both their bodies is what she'll remember.

When she wakes up, she's not certain where she is. Pierre is lying next to her. He has his eyes closed, but she knows he's not asleep. He turns his head. 'You slept a long time.'

'I was tired.'

'We had a full day yesterday.'

'I shan't forget it ever.'

'Nor shall I.'

She wonders whether he'll invite her to stay in the studio. She'll have to go back to the flat at some point; all her things are there. But she can't bear the thought of going back yet. They lie quietly listening to the city waking up below them. 'Will you work this morning?'

'No.' He bumps the cushion up behind his head. 'I need to go home. Marthe will be anxious.' Marthe. She'd forgotten her. She turns so that her chin is buried in his neck. 'I know we have to talk about this, Renée, and we will, but Marthe will be wondering what's become of me.' He puts an arm around her. 'What will you do?'

'I don't know?' She hardly dares to think of the reception she will get from Marguerite when she returns.

'Would you like me to come with you to Belleville?'

Renée sighs. 'I don't think that would help.'

He draws her in towards him. 'You can't let a woman like that run your life. You would have had to distance yourself from her in the end.' He strokes her hair back from her forehead. 'You don't have to go back there at all, you know. You could stay in the studio.'

Although it's what she hoped he'd say, there is a hesitation in the way he says it. She could tell him that she may not have the choice of going back to the apartment any more, but she does not want him to feel obliged to take her in.

His thumb continues moving back and forth under her hairline. 'Do you wish it hadn't happened?'

Renée gives a slight start, as if she'd forgotten he was there. She blinks. 'Of course not. No.'

'It's only that you seem preoccupied.'

'I feel a bit odd.'

'Odd in what way?' His hand moves down to her forehead. 'Aren't you well? Your forehead's damp.'

She throws the cover back, distractedly. 'Hot,' she says. 'I feel hot.' She stares about her and then clutches at him.

'Darling, what's the matter?'

'Promise me you won't forget me, Pierre.' She's scrabbling at his chest. She has a sense that everything around her is about to fall away.

'Forget you. What a thing to say.' He strokes her cheek. 'How could I possibly forget you?'

'Will you keep the paintings that you've done of me?'

'Of course I will.'

'You won't let anyone destroy them?'

'No, I won't.'

'You promise?'

Pierre takes both her hands in his. He bunches them against his lips and kisses them. 'I promise.'

Margo flings a case at her. 'So you've come back at last! You've got a nerve. You little whore.' The buckle on the suitcase catches Renée's ankle and she flinches. She begins to speak, but Margo puts a hand up. 'I don't want to know. Just pack your things and go!'

She watches her as Renée goes into the bedroom and begins to pull out drawers and throw clothes in the suitcase. There is still a pile of items on the carpet. 'Can I come back for these later?'

'No, I want you out of this apartment.' Renée starts to cry. 'You'll have to hope he doesn't throw you over straight away. You could be wandering the streets with half a dozen bags under your arms. I wouldn't put them down if I were you. Thieves had a field day yesterday.'

'Please could I have a glass of water?'

'Get it. Don't think you'll be getting any help from me.'

She limps into the kitchen. Marguerite comes after her. She leans against the doorpost. 'Don't imagine that he'll leave his wife now. At least we know what you are. There isn't any need to be polite about it. You can always go home to your mother, I suppose, though she won't be so keen to have you once she knows what's happened.'

Renée leans her forehead on the wall above the sink. The sound of Marguerite's voice is like linen tearing right next to her ear.

'Cat got your tongue? And you can take that ring off. I don't want you wearing it on any finger, let alone the third one.'

Renée glances at her wearily. 'You gave it to me.'

'You were someone else, then. Do you think I would have given it to you if I'd known how promiscuous you were?'

'I don't know what that means.'

'It's what you call a woman who's prepared to sleep with anybody.'

'That's not me.'

'It clearly is. You'll find it's easy now you've started. Soon it'll be anyone who offers you a meal. That's how it is. You've lost the only thing you had to offer.'

Renée bends to clip the fasteners on the case. It's heavy. She has no idea how she will get it down the stairs and out onto the pavement.

'You can leave the rest out on the landing.'

If she does, the tenants on the floor above will think it's rubbish. Nothing will be there when she returns. 'Perhaps you'd like to keep a few things to remember me.'

'I don't want to remember you. I'll have forgotten you before you've turned the corner.'

'That's not true,' says Renée. 'If you didn't care, you wouldn't be like this.'

'I'm angry that I've wasted so much time on you. I'm angry that you've turned out to be such a ... such a ...'

'What?'

'Such a nonentity. Oh ... get out.'

Renée grips the handle of the suitcase and attempts to drag it the few yards towards the door. It comes to rest against the rug. She tries to hoist it up over the edge and then gives up. Collapsing on her knees, she pounds her fists against her sides and wails. She feels her shoulders being shaken.

'Stop it, Renée!' Marguerite's face peers into her own but Renée is immune to anything that Marguerite can do to her now.

'Calm yourself! We'll have the people downstairs beating on the door. 'Stop crying, Renée.'

Renée wraps both arms around herself. She's rocking back and forwards and begins to retch. 'I feel so ill,' she gasps. She puts a hand out to support herself and ends up clawing at the carpet. 'I can't breathe. There's something happening in my chest.' She's listing sideways and then suddenly she's on the floor, her knees bent underneath her.

Marguerite leans over, shaking Renée's shoulder, but less violently this time. She draws Renée's hair back from her face and looks at her intently. Renée hears the note of triumph in her voice. 'What has that bastard done to you?'

The newspapers are full of it. The whole of Paris was out on the streets. I spent the day re-potting the geraniums.

'You saw the march past after all, then?' There is something in the air so rank that I can almost touch it. He's brought back a copy of *Le Figaro*. The Champs Elysées is awash with faces. There are thousands of them. I can hear the noise, just looking at the photograph. 'I thought you hated crowds.'

'I do, but this was different.' He sits down and then gets up again. 'You sensed that history was being made. It was exciting. I wish you had been there, Marthe.'

'Eleven million dead boys and it's called a victory celebration. Tell that to the mothers. Pity their sons couldn't have been there to celebrate.'

He makes a little hissing sound. I've spoilt it for him. 'There's not much that we can do for them and people have a right to celebrate the victory; they've waited long enough for it.'

There's plenty that we don't agree on, Pierre and me, but I thought we were of one mind about the war. I hand him back the paper. 'I doubt Monsieur Clermont will be celebrating; he lost two boys. Or the Canvilles. Their son's missing.' He takes off his glasses and pinches the bridge above his nose. 'You must be tired,' I say. 'Out all night on the streets.' I'm waiting for him to say what has happened, even though I know.

He starts to pace the room. He jerks his head from side to side to ease his neck. The energy is pulsing out of him. He's giving me the fidgets. 'Oh for goodness sake sit down,' I feel like saying. He keeps sniffing, as if he has caught a cold.

He doesn't say much over breakfast, although once or twice I have the feeling he's about to. Afterwards I take the string bag from behind the door. 'I have to go down to the market. I need brisket for the casserole.'

He sniffs. 'We could afford a better cut of meat, you know. It's not as if we're that poor . . .' He stops.

Oh my, I think. He knows better than to interfere in household matters. 'Brisket's good enough,' I say. 'Unless you want me to get something different.'

He looks sheepish. 'Brisket will do very well,' he says. 'I'm not ungrateful, Marthe. I just wish that sometimes you could be a little more adventurous.'

Adventurous? It wouldn't do for both of us to go down that road. What if he came home one day and found I'd bought a pair of stays – the sort with ribbons that you tie in bows to make yourself look like a Christmas present? There would be no point in me at all if I were just like her, but older.

'Now the war is over, it'll be much easier to travel, for example.'

'Into Paris, you mean?'

'I was thinking of abroad.'

'Abroad?' I don't have much time for 'abroad.' Why bother going somewhere else to do what you'd be doing here? It's not as if Pierre would draw the landscape. He would sit inside and sketch the kitchen table and the vase of flowers on the windowsill, the way he does now.

'Wouldn't you be interested to see Morocco or Tunisia? You've barely left this house in ten years. There's a whole world out there waiting for you.'

I don't think it's me the world is waiting for, somehow. 'I'll see if there's a tarte aux pommes at the patisserie.'

'Good. Splendid.' He starts whistling.

'Shall I buy food for tomorrow, too?'

He stops his pacing and stares out over the garden. He won't look at me. 'No, I'll be going back into the studio tomorrow. I have work to finish off.'

'No partying tomorrow, then?' He gives me one of those quick looks of his. 'There won't be anything else left to celebrate.'

'The peace is something we'll be celebrating for a long time, hopefully.'

'Unless some silly bugger shoots another archduke.'

'There aren't many archdukes left,' says Pierre. He sinks into a chair. The energy seems all at once to have leaked out of him, like air escaping out of a balloon. 'I do feel quite tired, actually. I think I'll have a bath. I feel as if I've got the city underneath my nails.'

That's not the only thing, I'm on the point of saying, but I've learnt to curb my tongue. He doesn't like baths, normally. He doesn't share my love of water. When we lived in rue de Douai, I would offer to heat up the water on the stove and scrub his back for him, but no, he didn't like the feel of it all round him. This time, I don't offer. My adventure will be buying brisket from the butcher and a bit of offal for the dog. 'You won't mind filling up the bath yourself?'

'Of course not. Thank you, Marthe.' He comes up behind me, putting both hands on my shoulders. 'I don't mean to criticise, you know that.'

So why do you? I think. But I know it isn't me he's criticising; it's himself. I take the string bag and the purse of money and leave, closing the door quietly after me.

∽

When Renée comes around, she's wearing a thin linen nightdress and there is a jug next to the bed with water and a flannel in a bowl. The fever is so all-enveloping that it's as if she's wrapped up in a blanket.

'Take these.' Marguerite holds out two tablets broken into four. 'I got them from the pharmacy. They'll help to bring your temperature down.' She holds the glass to Renée's lips while Renée tries to swallow them. 'You've been a naughty girl. You disobeyed me and you're being punished for it. You got back to the apartment just in time. Imagine if you'd been out on the street. I could be looking for you in the morgue now.'

Renée feels the dry hand on her forehead and sinks back onto the pillow. Marguerite returns the glass of water to the bedside table and tucks Renée's hands under the sheet. 'Sleep.'

Later, she feels Marguerite slip into bed beside her. She rests one hand on her shoulder. 'Renée.' She lies with her mouth to Renée's ear. 'You're very ill, pet, but I'm taking care of you. From now on it will just be you and me. I love you.'

Renée feels a wave of gratitude sweep over her. 'I love you too.'

The next day Pierre puts on a clean shirt. Yesterday he told me it was time he got some new ones – I don't need to go on darning cuffs and collars. He stands at the mirror while he loops the scarf around his neck. It used to be the outside world he looked at; he preferred to be invisible himself. Now suddenly he spends his whole time looking at his own reflection. It must be hard work at his age, to have so much to live up to. I see that he's trimmed his beard as well. I usually do that for him. Pierre has never visited a barber.

I'm the one who cuts his hair and clips his nails. I even took a tooth out for him once.

I tell myself he's following the 'normal' path for men of his age – feeling insecure about themselves and looking for a woman who will make them feel young, or at least a woman who will take their minds off being old. I've seen enough of it to know the way these things go: the excitement, then the blind infatuation, months when you can think of nothing else. And then a gradual return to normal. All I have to do is wait. But that's not easy.

He goes back into the studio the next day and the next and each time I think maybe this will be the last time. Maybe this time he will go and not come back. But every evening he sits opposite me at the table, toying with his food. I ask him how his work is going. Nothing usually gets in the way of that. But he's distracted, locked inside his head. The silence used to be companionable. Now it's filled with questions that I dare not ask and secrets he won't share with me.

I see him staring at the water jug and whereas in the past I'd know he was imagining what it would look like in a painting, now he's simply staring at it, like a drowning man stuck in the middle of the ocean with a lifeboat fifty metres off. He isn't urging me to have adventures any more. The one he's having doesn't seem to be affording him much satisfaction.

'Eat something,' I say. I stand behind him, resting one hand on his shoulder. I can't bear to see him brought so low. I ask him, 'What's the matter?' He is looking at his hands as if he isn't sure they're his. I look at them and feel afraid. I'm not sure they're his, either.

In the afternoons, he goes for long walks down the footpath by the riverbank. It's not the sort of walk you take because it's pleasant being out there in the fresh air. He walks up and down as if he's punishing himself – a mile in one direction, two miles in the other, one-two, one-two, back and forth until he's worn himself out. And he still can't sleep. At night he lies there with his eyes wide open, staring at the ceiling till I wonder if he's still alive.

I whisper to him, 'Are you ill?'

'No,' he says. 'Not ill.'

'Can I get you anything?'

He seems to be considering. 'No,' he says, finally, 'I don't think that you can.'

'Are you the painter?' Marguerite peers through the gap. She hasn't taken off the chain. 'I thought we'd seen the last of you.'

Inside the room where she lies wrapped up on the sofa, Renée picks up snatches of the conversation. Marguerite removes the chain and steps outside onto the landing so that now she has to strain to overhear them.

'What's the matter with her?' Pierre says.

'She's gone down with influenza. She's been very ill. She could have died.'

'Why didn't someone tell me?'

'Why would anybody bother telling you?'

'There must be something I can do.'

'There isn't. What's so hard to understand? She doesn't want to see you.'

'Margo.' Renée calls out feebly from inside the flat.

'I'm coming,' she shouts back over her shoulder and then hisses 'Go away.'

'I'll leave after I've spoken to her.' Pierre pushes past her. He comes over to the sofa and kneels down beside it.

Renée indicates the bowl tucked underneath the sofa with a wrung-out cloth in it. 'You'd better not come too near. I might be contagious.'

'Half of Paris is contagious. I shall either get it or I won't.' He takes her hand. She looks at Marguerite who turns round pointedly and goes into the kitchen.

'How did you find where I lived?'

'I went into the store and spoke to Mademoiselle Lefèvre. I was desperate to know what had happened to you. She refused to give me your address, but your friend Gabi let me have it.'

Renée sees him taking in the room. The fire is lit but hardly any heat is coming from it.

'You have seen a doctor, haven't you?' She shakes her head. 'For heaven's sake, you must. I'll pay.'

'It's past the worst. My skin turned blue at one point.'

'I was frantic when you didn't come back to the studio the next day.'

'It was difficult. I didn't mean to . . .' Renée sinks back.

'I can't leave you here in this place, Renée. Let me bring the car next weekend and I'll drive you out to Bobigny so that your mother can look after you. It's Christmas soon. You'd rather be there, surely?'

Renée's eyes flit past him. 'Marguerite would never let me go.'

'I'll speak to her.'

'No!' Renée clutches at him.

'Dearest, you can't let her bully you like this.' He kisses her. 'I'll come for you on Saturday.'

He goes into the kitchen. Renée gazes after him. He takes a wad of notes out of his wallet. 'I want you to call a doctor in,' she hears him say.

'There's nothing they can do,' says Marguerite. 'The germ is in the air. It came across with the Americans.' She looks at Pierre. Behind him, she sees Renée watching them. 'We don't need any help from you,' she says, but her eyes linger on the roll of notes he's holding out to her.

'I've said I'll take her to her mother's next weekend. I'll bring the car on Saturday.'

The notes are now in Marguerite's hands. It's too late for her to give them back. She thrusts them at him, but he wards her off. 'I'll come in time to get her there for lunch.'

'Don't. She's all right here. I'll look after her.'

'You can't object to Renée visiting her mother, surely.'

'She can come here if she wants to see her.'

'But that's not the point,' says Pierre. 'Renée needs to get out of the city. Here, she could pick up another virus and she would be too weak to recover. You don't want to be responsible for killing her.' He turns to leave.

'She doesn't want you,' Marguerite calls after him. 'She won't come.'

Pierre's voice drifts up through the stairwell. 'Saturday,' he calls.

He's calmer. Something's been decided. It seems what was bothering him isn't bothering him any longer. Something else is bothering him now.

It's been a week since he last went into the studio. Perhaps this is his way of reassuring me that he can live without her. But it doesn't reassure me. For Pierre it's not what happens in his life that matters; it's what happens in the paintings. What's been said there can't be unsaid.

This is different from the other times. Then it was more a case of getting rid of something so that he was not distracted by it. Afterwards he could go back to work. He might have favoured laziness in women, but he didn't like it in himself. He often said that he felt lonelier than ever after making love and working was the only way that he could deal with it.

This morning, I went through the pockets of his overcoat.

I don't know what I thought I'd find. There was his pocket diary, which he uses as a sketchbook, several scraps of paper, sticks of graphite and a bill from Maxim's for as much as I'd spend in the market in a year.

Tucked underneath the rubber band that stops the loose sheets in the notebook falling out, I find a pencil sketch. It's just a few lines and so faint it's like a whisper, but I know at once that this is her. It's not the sort of face you would expect to see on working-class girls here in Paris. They peak, if they're going to, around sixteen. The bloom goes off them pretty quickly after that. She looks Italian, though he hasn't shaded in her hair, so I suppose it could be blonde. Her face reminds me of a figure in Giotto's *Lamentation*. My word, doesn't that make me sound grand? I've never been to Italy, but Pierre showed me a picture of the *Lamentation*. It's the nose; that's what reminded me. It's long and fine and with her head in that position she looks proud.

He's hatched the shadow underneath her chin so delicately, I can feel the outline of the jaw. I'd like to ram my fist against it, but instead I press my thumb down on the cheek and when I take my hand away the imprint of my thumb is there. I don't want Pierre to know that I've been going through his things, so with my fingernail I try to scratch the smudge off. But instead I find I've scored a ridge across her cheek. She doesn't look as wholesome now.

He says he plans to take the Dietrich into Paris. Since the war began, the car has hardly been out of the garage. 'I'll be bringing back some canvasses,' he says. As long as he's not bringing her back with him, I think.

I must run a bath. The rash is getting worse. It's spread all down my back and formed a crust between my thighs that scuffs and crumbles when I walk. I feel as if a chrysalis is forming round me and that inside I am turning into something else. The creature that I used to be is not there any more.

'She isn't coming.' Marguerite goes out onto the landing.

'Let me past.'

'The doctor says she isn't well enough to travel.'

'That's not true. You can't keep Renée here against her will.'

'It's not against her will. It's what she wants.'

'You mean it's what you want.'

'Why can't you go away?' There is an edge to Marguerite's voice. Renée hasn't dared to pack a suitcase. Margo is determined that if she is going to her mother, it will not be Pierre who takes her there.

'But Pierre has a car.'

'In two or three days you'll be well enough to take the trolleybus. If you still want to see your mother, we can go together. All that man is interested in is taking you away from me. He'll drive a wedge between us and then he'll abandon you, you'll see.'

When Saturday arrives, she's told to stay in bed and Margo brings her hot milk and a madeleine. 'If he turns up, I'll deal with it,' she says. 'You stay here.'

Renée tiptoes over to the door so she can hear what's going on out on the landing. Pierre is standing two steps from the top, so Marguerite has the advantage over him in height. He's clutching at the rail. He needs to get himself onto the landing so that they are on a level. Marguerite leans forward suddenly and Renée is afraid she is about to push him down the stairs.

Pierre grabs Marguerite's arm with his free hand and she pulls herself back, hauling him unwillingly onto the landing after her. They're face to face now. He lets go of her and turns towards the door.

'No, you're not taking her!' shrieks Marguerite. She locks her hand around his arm.

'For God's sake!' Pierre turns back. He puts his face up close to Marguerite's. 'I'm taking Renée to her mother. She's expecting her and one way or another I intend to get her there. I'm asking you to stand back.'

Renée wonders whether this show of bravado is for her sake. Marguerite stares at him for a moment and then slams the heel of one hand into Pierre's shoulder, shoving him away from her towards the edge. There is a scuffle. Pierre grabs the bannister and swings his body in an arc. His left hand lands on Marguerite's chin. Her head jerks back and there is a sickening crack as it makes contact with the wall behind. She looks at him with mild surprise and then she crumples.

Pierre stands looking down at her. He slides a foot out, tentatively nudging her. Her eyelids flutter. 'What?' She looks about her. Her gaze settles on the foot wedged underneath her calf. Her own legs are stuck out in front of her and she regards them, curiously.

Renée has crept over to the door. Pierre turns. Marguerite's abrupt collapse seems to have robbed him of initiative. He frowns. 'We need to get you out of here.'

'We can't just leave her.' Renée stares at Marguerite. The scene reminds her of a boxing match she went to, once, where one of the contestants suddenly fell down. The other went on punching at the air until they realised that the first man wasn't getting up again and then they stood there stupidly, not knowing if the referee should start the count, since theoretically the first man hadn't been knocked out.

'She's dazed, that's all. It's better that we go now.' He

bends down to look at Marguerite and straightens up again. He wipes his palms against his jacket. They both know what Marguerite will be like if she comes around.

'I'll carry you downstairs.' He sweeps her up into his arms. As they descend the staircase she looks back over his shoulder. Marguerite remains hunched up against the wall.

Once they are in the car and out of danger, Renée starts to shiver. She's brought nothing with her in the way of luggage but she can't go back now. Pierre has wrapped a blanket round her, but it's not that sort of cold. This is the first time since she moved into the flat with Marguerite that someone's wanted her enough to fight for her. There is a scent the body gives off when it's driven by adrenalin and she can smell it on them both.

Pierre looks sideways at her. He puts one hand on her knee. 'I'm sorry, darling. That must have been ghastly for you.'

Renée turns to look at him. 'You hit her. You hit Marguerite.'

'I pushed her. I had no choice.' Pierre takes her hand. 'Perhaps I should have stayed to make sure she was all right, but I felt I ought to get you out of there.'

She rests her head against his shoulder. 'You did that for me,' she murmurs.

'It was good of you to bring her, Monsieur.' Renée's mother hovers in the doorway. She looks tired, thinks Renée, but she's brought her best dress out for the occasion. 'I've been wondering how we could get her here. It isn't far from Paris, but I'm sure the air is better.'

'I could easily have organised a car for her,' says Tonio, resentfully. He reaches out to Renée and she lets him carry her inside. His arms are straining underneath the weight of her, but he's determined not to let it show. 'I'll take her upstairs, shall I, Maman?'

'No, dear, let her sit downstairs. She'll want to be with us.'

He lays her on the sofa with a rug across her knees. The younger girls are staring at Pierre. He waits for her to introduce them.

'This is Claire and Alys.' Claire is standing with her finger in her mouth. She draws back shyly into the protection of her mother's skirts. 'Claire's six and Alys will be eight in two weeks' time,' says Renée. 'Pierre's an artist.'

'What's an artist?' Alys, who is standing next to Pierre, is staring up into his face.

'It's somebody who paints things,' Pierre says.

'Pictures?'

'Yes.'

'I did a picture. Do you want to see it?'

'I would love to.'

She goes over to a drawer and comes back with a scribble on a sheet of paper. 'It's an angel.'

'I can see that. Very good.' There is a snort from Tonio.

'You're not like we expected,' Alys tells him, when her mother has gone off into the kitchen to bring on the lunch.

'You are quite old though,' Claire adds, peering at him sideways as if wanting to peek round behind the beard.

The conversation round the dinner table is relaxed and noisy, although Tonio says little. Renée's mother tries to compensate.

'You make a living from your painting, do you, Monsieur?'

'These days I sell most of what I do.'

'And Renée's in the pictures?'

'Some of them.'

'Imagine!' She's not certain whether to be pleased or not, but Tonio has made his mind up.

'She already had a job; what's wrong with working on the perfume counter?'

'Mademoiselle Lefèvre had to bring in someone else when I was ill. You're not allowed more than a fortnight off. I'd had enough of working there, in any case.'

The conversation's starting to acquire an edge. Pierre stays for an hour after lunch and Alys sits for him so he can do a portrait of her.

'Alys, it's just like you!' Claire says. She looks up at him as if he's managed to produce a rabbit from a hat.

'I'll leave the drawing with you; in return for Alys's.'

'Look, Maman,' Claire says, even more enthusiastic now that they have rights of ownership. When Pierre leaves, Renée sees him following her mother out into the scullery. He presses half a dozen notes into her hand.

Her mother's flustered. Her hand wanders to her neck. 'I couldn't, Monsieur. No, I mean it.'

'It's expensive caring for an invalid,' Pierre insists.

'It's far too much.'

'It's been a while since Renée had an appetite, but on a good day she can eat her own weight in mille-feuilles.'

'She always did like cakes.' Her mother slips the notes into her apron pocket. 'Thank you, Monsieur. You've been very good to her.'

'Please call me Pierre. You have a charming family, Madame Montchaty. I hope I'll meet them all again. Perhaps when Renée's ready to come back to Paris, I can pick her up.'

'That's kind. I don't suppose she'll want to stay with us for long.' She herds the girls into the kitchen, leaving Pierre to say goodbye to Renée. He squats down beside her on the sofa.

'I'm afraid your brother doesn't like me.'

'Tonio thinks he's responsible for us. He thinks you want to take advantage of me.'

'What do you think?'

'I know you would never hurt me.'

Pierre hesitates. 'You can't go back to that apartment, Renée.'

'It's a shame you had to see it. I was hoping that you wouldn't.'

'It's not the apartment I object to so much; it's the way that Marguerite behaves towards you.'

Renée turns her face into his shoulder. 'She kept telling me I'd brought it on myself. The way I'd carried on over the past year meant my body couldn't fight off germs.'

'For God's sake, Renée, that's ridiculous.'

'It's what she said.'

'And you believed her?'

'You don't understand the way it is with us. When I began to work for you, it was the first time I'd done something without asking her first. She had been about to throw me out once she knew you and I ... well, that it wasn't just a job. She would have, if she hadn't seen how bad I was. The thing is, she does care about me and I care about her too, but it's as if she wants to eat me up and when she finds she can't, she spits me out. As long as I was ill, she had me to herself. I think she wanted it to last as long as possible.'

'I'd be afraid for you if you went back there, Renée. She's obsessed. The woman is unhinged.'

'But all my things are there. I'd have to go back sometime.'

'We'll go back together, then, to fetch your things.'

There is a question mark in her expression.

'You can move into the studio. It's not ideal, but it at least gets you away from Marguerite. I want you with me, Renée.'

∞

When they go back three weeks later so that she can pick up her belongings, Pierre insists they ring the bell first. There's a long pause. 'Do you think she could be out?' The thought occurs to both of them that maybe Pierre hurt Marguerite more than he thought.

'She's always there on Sunday afternoons,' says Renée.

When he rings again, he keeps his finger on the bell.

There is a muffled answer. 'Yes? Who is it?'

Renée puts her mouth up to the voice-tube. 'It's me, Marguerite. Can I come up?'

There is another long pause. Renée gives up waiting for an answer. She takes out her key. Pierre follows her into the hall. She puts a hand up. 'I'll go by myself. If you're there, it'll only make her angrier.'

'But darling, I can't possibly allow you to go up there by yourself. Suppose she's violent towards you?'

'You're the one she blames for taking me away'. It's not the threat of violence that's preoccupying Renée. What she needs from Marguerite is a defining gesture, something that gives meaning to the time they've spent together. 'I can't simply vanish from her life. I have to see her one more time.'

'I'll wait down in the hall, then. But you have to promise me you'll call out if you need me.'

As she climbs the stairs to the apartment, Renée is remembering a film she saw once, where a woman just like her had visited her lover in a hotel room to break off their affair. As she was going down the staircase, he had leant over the bannister and shot her. She had spiralled down into the stairwell and the film had slowed down so that you could see her body turning in the air and floating like a leaf towards the ground. Her lover had called down to her in anguish, 'Darling girl, forgive me!' But the look on her face when she landed, with her eyes wide open, was of blissful triumph.

There had been a violin sonata playing in the background and a crash of cymbals as she reached the ground.

The flat door's closed when Renée gets there. As she lets herself in, there's a faint sound coming from the kitchen. Marguerite is ironing. As she presses the iron down onto the linen, there's a light thud and the wooden struts under the board give little mousy squeaks. She looks up, fixes Renée for a moment, and then goes on ironing.

'I've come back to say goodbye,' says Renée. Marguerite holds up a pillowcase and folds it into quarters, brushes off a speck of fluff and runs the iron across it one more time before she lays it on the pile. 'I'm moving out.'

'I heard you.' Marguerite picks up another pillowcase and once again goes through the ritual of folding it in half, then into quarters. Renée watches her. 'You have somewhere to move to, I presume?'

'I shall be living in the studio.'

'You'd sacrifice your independence for a man like that?'

'It's not as if I have much independence living here with you.'

'That's what relationships are meant to be about. Have you considered what you'll do when he gets tired of you? I'd give it six months at the most before he's off back to his wife.' She turns the iron and spits on it.

'He never left her.'

'You're more stupid than I thought, then.'

Renée clasps her hands behind her back. 'I wouldn't be like this if it was you who'd found someone. I would be happy for you.'

'What's the point of me pretending to be happy for you, when I know you're going to be miserable? I know what men are like.'

'I didn't want to have to choose between you.'

'No of course you didn't. Much more satisfying to have both of us lined up and panting after you.'

'That's not the way it was,' says Renée.

Marguerite gives her a long look and then tosses back her head. 'You haven't got a thought for anybody else.'

'It couldn't last for ever – you and me, though, could it? It was only until one or other of us found someone.'

'That's all it was, eh? What a shame you didn't say so at the time. I saved your life. You would be dead now if it hadn't been for me.'

'I know that and I'm grateful. I'm not saying that it didn't matter, only that . . .' she bites her tongue.

'What?'

'That we couldn't ever have been more than friends, so why can't we be friends now?'

'We were never just friends.' Margo fixes her. '"Just friends" don't do what we did. You think all that will just go away now you've met someone else? It won't, because it's in you, Renée, and you can't escape that any more than you can suddenly decide you're not a Catholic any more.'

'I am a Catholic. I believe in God.'

'You do? Why don't you ask Him what he thinks about it?' Marguerite says, smugly.

Renée puts her suitcase down and looks back up the stairs. The door to the apartment stays shut.

'Was she very angry?'

'No, she wasn't.'

Pierre takes the suitcase. Renée follows him onto the pavement and he offers her an arm to get into the car. He stows the suitcase in the back and climbs in next to her. 'What happened?'

'Nothing, really.' She feels vaguely cheated. There had

been no pleas for her to stay, no declarations that she'd loved her. All that Marguerite had said was, 'If you go, you go for ever. Don't think you can change your mind.'

Pierre is looking at her. 'You're not sorry that you've left her, are you?'

Renée turns and gazes at him. 'No, it isn't that. I thought she loved me, that's all.'

Once they're safely locked inside the studio, they fall into each other's arms. They spend the rest of that day and the next one feverishly making love, with intervals of torpor in between in which they sleep and wake up groping blindly for each other. After three days, Pierre puts Renée's canvas on the easel. They work through the morning, make love through the afternoon and finally collapse in an exhausted heap from which they wake and work again into the evening. If she goes down to the market to buy food, she sees him watching from the window till she disappears and when she reappears, he's still there waiting for her to come back along the street. If she had any doubts about his love for her, she has no doubt about it now.

He takes his leave of her on Friday, promising to be back in the studio first thing on Monday morning. Renée listens to his footsteps on the stairs. She hears the street door clang and waits until he steps onto the pavement. That's my lover, she thinks, watching the dark figure walk away from her into the twilight. We shall be together always.

The sun sinks below the level of the rooftops opposite. When she looks round the room, she feels as if she's gone into a time warp. Nothing looks familiar any more. There is an untouched look about the chaise longue with the rumpled drapes that testify to a brief, frenzied interlude while Pierre was getting ready to depart, the worktop with its crusted palette and the brushes left to soak in half an inch of turpentine.

She gets up, making her way round the room and touching all the objects in it, repossessing them. She puts a pot of water on the stove to boil and settles down to plan her evening. There is nothing Pierre has said she shouldn't look at, so she goes round opening drawers, examining the contents. She's afraid that if she doesn't occupy herself, her thoughts will keep on creeping back to Marguerite.

She finds a cardboard box stowed underneath the worktop with a camera and a cache of photographs. There's one of Pierre standing with a group of friends outside the Beaux-Arts. Several feature women and one woman in particular – a small, slight figure dressed unfashionably who never looks directly at the camera. Is this Marthe? She goes through the pile, occasionally holding one or other photograph up to the light until she comes to one she recognises. Roussel's arms are draped round Pierre's shoulders in the photograph. There's no doubt which of them was better looking. Roussel is exuding confidence and charm. Beside him, Pierre looks reticent, uncomfortably aware that he is being scrutinised. He might have used the camera but he didn't like the camera being used on him.

There is a separate folder of girls posing in the nude. Pierre had told her that he'd bought the camera in 1906, so these women would be middle aged now. She tries not to wonder whether Pierre slept with any of them. There was nothing after 1910. His interest in the invention had evaporated overnight. She puts the box away. It makes her sad to think of all those lives that have passed on and, in some cases, passed away entirely.

Finally, she's ready to explore the drawer under the table. She has left this till the last but now she eases it out, guiltily, so that it won't squeak, and inside she finds a folded square of silk. She knows what this is, but she's never seen one close up. Working-class boys and the *poilus* on leave from the trenches used pigs' bladders or, occasionally, squares of cotton. There are rumours that the flares sent up in no-man's land had small silk parachutes attached to them to slow down their descent and soldiers on both sides would risk their lives to go out and retrieve them for their girlfriends. Two could be sewn up to make a pair of knickers. Four would make a good-sized blouse.

She's never come across one used in this capacity. She strokes it reverently. It's not something Pierre has used with her and Renée wonders what this recklessness, if that is what it is, suggests. Perhaps now that they're lovers he's decided to leave Marthe after all. She feels a rush of giddiness, a fluttering inside her which perhaps might be the start of new life. He would have no choice but to leave Marthe then.

She stops herself. This isn't something Pierre would do. He can't bear hurting people. Though he did hurt Marguerite, she thinks with satisfaction. He hurt Marguerite for her sake, so perhaps he would hurt Marthe, too. She should feel sorry for her, but she doesn't. There's no room for Marthe in their lives now.

It's got dark while she's been sitting there. She eases back the drawer and crosses to the window. In the street below, the lamps are lit. She hears a woman laughing. A cart rumbles down the street over the cobbles. At the bar across the road two men are sitting at an outside table, arguing. Pierre will be in Saint-Germain by now. Perhaps he's sitting down to supper at this very moment, telling Marthe . . . what?

She shakes her head. Each time she thinks about it, she gets to the point where Pierre is ready to tell Marthe everything and then it's as if her imagination shuts down.

She looks round the studio for something she can occupy herself with.

Then she sees it, wedged into the gap between the rug and one leg of the chaise longue. It's the button Pierre lost from his cuff on their first night together. Renée picks it up and turns it over in her hand. It's white with two holes – one of those soft linen buttons that are difficult to fasten. Renée fingers it. It's as if she is holding him there in the palm of one hand. She feels certain now that everything will be all right. The button links her to him. There is half an inch of thread still in the holes and Renée teases it between her thumb and index finger. She looks round for somewhere she can put the button where it will be safe, and tucks it underneath the bowl of apples on the windowsill.

Tomorrow, she decides, she'll look for Caro in the café. It's through Caro that Roussel will find out that Pierre is now officially her lover.

I lie in the bath, my head against the rim. My knees bob up above the water – rocky outcrops in a green sea uninhabited except by guillemots, a surface to cling onto in a high wind. My toes rise out of the sea like calloused reptiles and sink down into the depths again. I pat the water absently and send waves eddying towards them. I can lie like this for hours, patting at the water like a mother calming down a restless child. I am the lighthouse keeper and the ocean is my kingdom.

Downstairs I hear Pierre's key in the lock. The front door opens and then closes. He calls, 'Marthe?' I don't answer. He'll be hanging up his coat and taking off the bowler hat. He only wears it going to and from the tram stop. He pretends he does it out of deference to me, so that the neighbours will mistake him for an office worker or a clerk.

But after all this time they've probably decided he is neither.

He is coming up the stairs now. He knows that, if I am not downstairs, I will be in the bath. I used to have my baths each morning after he had left, but I have two or three a day now. He taps on the door and comes in without waiting for an answer. He looks down at me. He's painted me so often like this that he would have been disturbed to find me sitting up or with my knees bent, scrubbing at my back or rubbing soap into my arms. I am the 'done-to' not the 'do-er'.

There's a jar of ointment on the rim next to the tap. He kneels down, rolling up his sleeves, and scoops a little of it out onto his fingers. I hold up my arm obligingly and he begins to rub the ointment on my skin in circles till his fingers run dry. When they catch against a shred of loose skin, I start and he hesitates. I keep my eyes closed. He is working his way up towards the elbow.

'Do you think the rash is getting worse? Should we call Doctor Dolbecq in to have a look at you? Perhaps he can suggest a different ointment.'

'This one's good enough.'

He takes my arm and turns it gently. There are weals along the inside that have bled. He puts his lips against the hard skin. 'I'm so sorry.' What is he apologising for? Look at him, kneeling on the bathroom floor as if he's genuflecting at the altar. This is where he worshipped me.

'Poor little bird,' he murmurs. 'My poor little bird.'

That night we lie like two spoons, Pierre with his arms around me. When he touches me, I feel the hard skin on his knuckles and I'm grateful for the roughness of it. My skin must feel like this too. A quarter of a century of lying in the bath as it gets colder, of my hands plunged into boiling water in the sink or washtub.

Pierre sees through his fingers, so I know that when he

touches me he sees the texture and the colour of my skin and tucks it in the secret places of his mind for later. When he paints me now, he's drawing on what he remembers. I know this is not a new beginning. I can recognise an ending when it comes.

Roussel keeps an account at La Rotonde and Caro sometimes has her breakfast there while she is waiting for him. Renée thinks the brown shape by her legs is Sweetie; then she sees it's Caro's satchel scrunched up on the floor beside her.

'Isn't Sweetie with you?'

'He escaped the evening of the victory celebrations. Ricki put up posters with his picture on, but no one's seen him.'

'Caro, I'm so sorry. You must miss him dreadfully.'

She shrugs. 'He wasn't really mine.' She looks at Renée. 'You've not been in here for ages, either.'

'I went down with 'flu. I nearly died.'

'Poor you.' She dabs a handkerchief against her nose.

'I've left the place in Belleville I was in. I shall be living in the studio from now on. We'll see more of one another.'

Caro nods.

'Why isn't anybody here?'

'The painters are all working.'

'Why aren't you with Roussel in the studio, then?'

'I'm still waiting for him to arrive. He goes to church on Sundays.'

'Church!'

'He's Catholic,' says Caro.

Pierre is an agnostic. Renée had assumed that went for all the painters in their circle. 'I'm a Catholic, too,' she says.

'Yeah?' Caro looks at her with mild enquiry. 'Don't you go to church, then?'

Renée looks away. 'Not lately.'

'Nothing to confess, eh?' Caro grins.

'Too much,' says Renée. 'Where to start?'

She hasn't been to church since she moved in with Marguerite. Before that, she had hardly sinned at all, it seemed to Renée. Afterwards, she was too busy sinning to have time to think about it. Churches in the centre had been closed down in the last months of the war after a shell went through the roof of Saint Gervais, an old church in the Marais, and killed eighty-eight. It was incomprehensible to Renée that God would allow a shell to fall on people who were at that very moment praying to be kept safe. Some of the department stores, including hers, allowed those worshippers with nowhere else to congregate to use their basements. Renée heard them singing sometimes as she left the store, but she had never felt inclined to join them and she didn't now.

'Are you and Pierre . . . ?' Renée nods. 'Where is he now?'

'He's gone back to his house in Saint-Germain-en-Laye. He's got a wife there.'

'Does she know about it?'

'Not yet.'

'Can't you go home too? You've got a family, haven't you?'

'My flatmate will have told them that I'm living with a married man.'

'Right.' Caro nods.

'I wondered if you'd like to walk down to the river later.' Caro's looking at her, blankly. Walking isn't something she does very often. 'Or you could come over to the studio.'

'Sounds fun,' says Caro, vaguely.

When Pierre comes in on Monday morning, Renée's still asleep. With no one there to wake her up, she can sleep twelve or thirteen hours at a stretch. Her body is completely hidden underneath the blanket. When her face emerges, it is pale and bleary-eyed. She yawns and stretches out her arms.

He's bought a brioche. For the first time since the war began, these are back on the shelves. She hauls herself into a sitting-up position, balancing the slice of brioche on her knees. She scoops the flakes of bread into her mouth and mops the crumbs onto her fingers.

'How is Marthe?' She knows better than to ask directly what's been happening in Saint-Germain. She'd been aware of a reserve in him when he arrived, as if he was embarrassed by the memory of their last encounter.

He is perched beside her on the chaise longue, brushing stray crumbs absently onto the floor. She scrunches up the paper bag and sinks back on the cushions. Pierre rests one arm on her knees. 'She isn't well. She knows that something's going on. Her body senses it and that's how it responds. I couldn't make it worse for her.' He's telling her he's not said anything to Marthe. Renée feels a rush of disappointment. She begins to plait the loose threads on the silk kimono she is wearing. For a moment neither of them speaks.

'And how was your weekend?' he says. 'How did you occupy yourself?'

'I went down to the café.' She was going to pretend she'd spent the weekend in the studio, but she wants Pierre to know that there are other options open to her. He does not respond. 'I thought it would be nice to talk to Caro. It's a long time since I've seen her.'

Pierre lays a hand on Renée's calf. Because she's nearly naked and he isn't, there is something in the gesture that's uncomfortably proprietorial. He senses it as well and takes his hand away, then seems uncertain what to do with it.

'Her dog went missing on the evening of the victory celebrations.'

'Yes, I'd heard. Is she upset?' He rests the hand beside her foot, but Renée notices the fingers are still quivering.

'Not really. Not as much as I'd have been.'

He loops his fingers round her ankle.

'Did you know that Roussel was a Catholic?' She is watching him for a reaction. Roussel is the stick she beats Pierre with when she has no other weapon.

'No, I didn't.' His hand moves down to her instep. 'Caro's not a Catholic, presumably.'

'I don't think Caro's anything.'

He cups her toes into the palm of one hand. Renée wriggles them. 'That tickles.' Her toes feel like small birds fluttering inside his palm. He's looking strangely at her. Suddenly he puts his face down to her feet and takes the big toe in his mouth. She feels the bristles of his beard against her foot. His tongue dips down into the crevices between her toes, exploring parts of her that nobody has accessed since her mother bathed her as a child. The tongue flicks back and forth as if it has an independent life. Each time it dips into the gulley, Renée feels the flesh between her thighs contract and melt. The churning in her stomach is so powerful she's frightened she might come before he's even got undressed. She wrenches at his collar. He is struggling to get his trousers off. He thrusts himself against her and she curls her legs around his back. She's whimpering and calling out to him. Once he has spent himself inside her, they lie drifting in and out of sleep until the bells ring out for midday.

That night he stays with her in the studio and in the morning they start early and work through until the afternoon. The next day is the same. She brings in food and cooks it on the stove. She often has to clean paint off the knives when Pierre has used them to prise open tins or scoop whatever pigment is left over back into the tin it came from. He looks on, amused, as she puts one pan then another on the hotplate, alternating them until whatever they contain is heated through. He turns her face towards him as she stands there with a saucepan in each hand and kisses her. 'My darling girl,' he whispers.

Sometimes when they've finished eating and she's cleared away, he reads to her. She isn't used to reading by herself; it seems to take a lot of effort. Even when the story draws her in, she can't help riffling through the pages to find out how many more there are to get through. But when Pierre reads, she sees the characters in front of her. He reads to her from Dickens and she gasps with horror at the passage in which Bill Sykes murders Nancy.

'Did he really kill her?' She has read of such things in past copies of the penny dreadfuls that she picks up in the market.

'In the story, yes.'

'She won't come back to life, then, even at the end?'

He smiles. 'It's not a fairy story, Renée. People don't come back to life.'

'But stories aren't true.'

'No they aren't. But they reflect life. That's why they affect us in the way they do.'

'You don't think that could really happen?' Renée knows it can. It happens several times a year in Belleville.

'It's not so much the event itself; it's the emotions that lead up to it – love, passion, anger, jealousy. Those things exist in all of us and Dickens shows us what the consequences are when we don't keep a rein on them.'

She's sitting at his feet and gazing up at him, her arms wrapped round his legs. Her chin is resting on his knees. 'I wish you hadn't read that bit,' she says, but next time when he settles down to read to her, that is the passage Renée asks for.

'Are you sure? You seemed upset the last time.'

'Yes, but now I know what happens, it's all right.' What Renée's interested in is not so much the suffering of Nancy as the rage of Bill Sykes. That is what she wants to understand.

'Is this the button off my shirt cuff?' Pierre turns it over in his palm.

'I found it underneath the chaise longue.'

'Clever girl.' He goes to put it in his pocket.

'Are you taking it away?' says Renée.

'Marthe will have noticed there's a button missing from the shirt.'

'Why don't you let me sew it on for you?'

'I wouldn't want to put you to the trouble.' He goes back to tapping down the paint lids with the little hammer he keeps underneath the workbench.

'It's no trouble,' Renée says. She tries to keep her voice flat.

'I think Marthe would prefer to sew it on,' Pierre says, quietly.

Renée goes on pulling on her clothes. Who cares which of them sews the button on? she thinks. What else has Marthe got to do all day? She pulls her stockings up and fastens the suspenders.

Pierre looks sideways at her. 'What's the matter?'

'Nothing.'

He puts down the hammer so that he can press the lids down with his thumb to make sure they are airtight. 'If you want to sew the button on . . .'

'I don't. Of course I don't. Who cares about a rotten button?'

'Quite.' He smiles. 'It's not the button; it's the principle. I understand that.'

'I wish I did.'

'There are certain things that Marthe's always done, you see, and if I take those things away from her ...'

'You don't have to explain.'

'And there are other things that you do.'

'What?' She looks at him. 'What things do I do?'

'When I'm with you, I feel more alive. You've opened up a world I had forgotten. Does it matter which of you sews buttons on my shirts or trims my beard?'

Her eyes pass to the beard. 'Does Marthe trim your beard for you?'

'Yes. And my toenails. Maybe that's a job you'd like.'

'No, thank you.'

'Well, then.' He lines up the paint tins ready for the next day.

Renée throws her wrap across the screen. 'Does Marthe have a button box?'

'Yes, I believe she does.'

'My mother has one. We were always begging her to let us play with it. We liked to sort them into piles, pretending they were people – big, fat men and skinny women, grandmothers and babies. Tonio pretended they were soldiers.'

'It's true, buttons seem to have a personality.'

'Yours don't. They're all the same size and they're white or black. Those are the ones that Tonio sent out to battle. They were always getting killed. He said it didn't matter; there were always more.'

'Your brother would have made a first-rate general.'

It's been three days now since she set foot outside the studio except to buy food from the market. Pierre is lying on the chaise longue with one arm draped round her neck. She's sitting with her back against it. Pierre is humming something out of an Italian opera where the heroine is dying of consumption, although Pierre said Violetta died because she'd sinned. It made her think of Marguerite.

'Can we go out tomorrow?'

He stops humming. 'To the café, do you mean?'

'I thought we might go to the Tuileries? I want to see the rose garden.'

He shakes his head. 'The rose garden was shelled during the last bombardment. It's a crater.'

'But that's what I want to see.'

'You want to see a vast hole with a few sad roses clinging to the edge of it?' He laughs, but it's a nervous laugh. If they go out, they run the risk of meeting someone Pierre knows and that will inevitably lead to gossip. Anyone who didn't know already that he had a mistress would know now.

'I saw a photograph in *L'Illustration*. Someone had left a copy on the Metro. It's become a sort of shrine, they say. The roses have already started rooting in the soil again.'

'If you would like to go, we will.' The sigh he gives is almost imperceptible but still she hears it.

'We don't have to. We can stay here.'

'No, you're right. You can't spend all your time cooped up in here. We'll start off at the Tuileries and afterwards I'll take you to the Louvre.'

'Really? That place where they have all those enormous pictures?'

'Would you like that?'

She is flattered that he is prepared to take the risk for her. She spends more time than usual on her appearance, pinning up her hair and putting on a dress that Pierre has bought her. There's a little parasol that goes with it, which she's been longing to show off. The day is sunny and although Pierre is wearing his habitual black overcoat, she doesn't even bother with a shawl. She revels in the glances thrown at her by passers-by. She wishes Gabi or one of the other girls from work would suddenly appear and see her like this, walking down the pathway with a gentleman. But it's a Thursday afternoon. The girls are all at work. The only people out this afternoon are those who have no work or have no need to work. Pierre keeps his hand looped round her arm.

The hoardings put up in the last months of the war to try and offer some protection to the city's monuments are being taken down, but scaffolding still masks the entrance to the Louvre. Renée delicately picks her way among the planks of wood and sandbags.

They stroll down to the Renaissance galleries. She isn't interested in the paintings; it's the outing she's enjoying and the prospect of the tea to follow, but she makes an effort to appear engaged.

'Will your work be here one day?'

'I doubt I shall ever be that famous.'

'Aren't you famous now?'

'You'd never heard of me when I approached you that day on the perfume counter.'

'Till I met you I had never heard of Michelangelo. I only know of him because you've got his picture on the wall.'

'That isn't Michelangelo. It's by him.'

'I'm just saying that before we met I'd never heard of either of you.' She looks up. 'Why are you laughing?'

'I'm not laughing. To be classed alongside Michelangelo is very flattering.'

'You're making fun of me.'

He looks at her a moment. 'I would never dream of making fun of you.'

They pause before Mantegna's *Saint Sebastian*, his body pierced with arrows and his flesh grey. Renée makes a face. 'Why couldn't he have painted something nice?'

'He wanted what he painted to be meaningful.'

'You're saying if it's nice, it can't be meaningful?'

'It doesn't need to be nice in order to be meaningful, is what I'm saying.'

She walks on. The *Saint Sebastian* is not a painting you would want to spend much time in front of, meaningful or not. 'Those bunches of chrysanthemums you did a picture of last week; could they be meaningful?'

'They could and naturally I hope they are. I hope that everything I paint has meaning.' He knows what she wants to ask. 'It isn't only the chrysanthemums you're interested in. You're wondering whether Renée Montchaty is "meaningful".' He smiles. 'I wouldn't have asked you to sit for me unless I thought there was at least a chance that what resulted would be meaningful.'

'And if it turned out that it wasn't?' She's remembering the conversation they had after they had spent that first night in the studio.

He is remembering as well, perhaps. 'I'd put the painting to one side and come back to it later.'

'And if it was still not meaningful?'

'Then I suppose I might consider painting over it.'

'But you'd have nothing to remember me by!'

Pierre looks round. A couple walking through the gallery glance curiously their way. Pierre takes her arm, but Renée stands her ground. 'There would be nothing left of me without the pictures.'

'Hush, dear. You're forgetting that before you came to me there were no pictures of you.'

'But it's different now there are.'

'Well, what would you remember *me* by?'

'I don't know.'

'You would remember me the same way that I hope I would remember you. Up here.' He taps his forehead. 'You would go on influencing future paintings.'

'Even if I wasn't there?'

'You would be there. Perhaps as ... well, a still life or the pattern on a tablecloth.'

'That's silly. It's like saying someone you pass in the street could end up as a shrub.'

'That isn't what I'm saying. What I mean is that if there's a meaningful connection between people in the first place, it will influence whatever happens afterwards.'

She tosses back her head. It doesn't sound like much to her.

She's thankful when they're outside on the path again, although she is aware of Pierre's eyes flitting nervously across the faces of the people passing by. He takes her elbow suddenly and turns her in towards the verge.

'What is it?'

'I've seen somebody I know.'

'Another artist?'

'Yes.'

An artist won't think anything of seeing them together, Renée thinks, but when she looks in the direction Pierre is indicating, what she sees is a stout, middle-aged man, dressed impeccably with a cravat and a Malacca cane, who's waddling as opposed to striding down the path ahead of them. 'It's Édouard,' Pierre says. 'Roussel's married to his sister.' Now she can't help staring. 'We'll stand here a moment till he's gone.' They turn towards the gardens. Édouard is now fifty yards away, but then he stops to take out a cigar and with his hands around the match he turns back to protect it from the breeze and sees them.

'Pierre!' He gives a bluff wave and comes back along the path towards them. Pierre lets go her arm, but it's too late now to pretend they aren't together. He comes up to them.

'Dear chap!' He shakes Pierre's hand. Renée's first impression is of someone with a very large head and a coarse beard. There is something gingery about his whole appearance. She had been concerned that anyone they met might snub her, but when Édouard reaches her, he bows. He takes her hand and lifts it to his mouth. His brown eyes twinkle. This is someone who likes women.

Once Pierre has introduced them, they do not immediately turn away from her and start another conversation. Édouard asks her courteously if she lives in Paris, which arrondissement, is this the first time she's been to the Louvre and what does she think of it? He leans towards her, nodding as if what she says is of supreme importance; he congratulates her on her dress, her hat, the colour of her hair. She feels herself bloom underneath his gaze and when she catches Pierre's eye she registers a touch of envy at the ease with which some men can make themselves agreeable. When they eventually walk on, Renée glances back over her shoulder.

'I like Édouard,' she says. Pierre has looped his hand around her arm again and Renée feels him nudging her along the path a little faster than before. He doesn't want to run the risk of meeting someone else. For Renée on the other hand, it's been the highlight of the afternoon.

'You'll never guess who I saw in the Louvre.' Pierre sits down and takes his pipe out. 'Édouard.' He begins to stuff the bowl with loose shreds of tobacco from the pouch. 'He asked to be remembered to you.'

Was he with her when they met? Is that the reason why he's telling me? It isn't likely Édouard would have given him away. The painters always stick together. I avoid them if I can. Oh, I know. They think Pierre ought to have married someone of his own class and kept me on as his model. As things stand, I'm neither one thing nor the other. They don't feel they owe me their respect.

I never felt like that with Édouard. He insists his mother is his only muse. I like that. She was nothing special, after all – a corset maker. I thought he had stayed a bachelor out of respect for her, but Pierre said Édouard only falls in love with married women. After that, I wasn't sure I ought to like him. Still, he was the only one of Pierre's friends who made an effort to be nice to me.

Pierre is not a cruel man. He tells me things he thinks I want to hear and leaves me to fill in the gaps. He asks me if I've had a nice day, did I go to market, what's the gossip in the village? Pierre's not interested in gossip. For a long time, we were all the village talked about, but they've moved on. Of course, it only takes the slightest breath of scandal for it to begin again.

It's only ten weeks till the opening of the Salon. There's a painting of me in the parlour here, which he still has to finish. It's a view onto the garden with the rhododendrons in the background and me leaning on the windowsill. I wear a loose red shift to match the colour of the walls and on the table in the foreground is a wicker basket full of apples. Every two weeks I replace the ones that have gone rotten, sifting through the apples on the market stall for others of the same size, the same shade of red and green. I even try to match the scent. The stallholder insists they're all the same, but I know what I'm looking for. Not that it's made a lot of difference to the painting. Every now and then Pierre brings down the canvas, makes a few more brushstrokes, adds a bit more colour to it. But his heart's not in it. I've been leaning on that bloody windowsill for seven months.

I'm standing at the looking glass over the mantelpiece. Pierre comes up behind me and we gaze at our reflections in the glass. 'What are you thinking?' Pierre says.

'I was thinking of that morning when we first met. You asked me where I was going, and I said the dead house.'

'That's an odd thing to remember.'

I look back at him a moment. 'Yes, it is.'

'Where did this come from?'

It's a china shepherdess. She has pink cheeks and yellow hair. There is a small lamb tangled in her skirts. 'I found it in the market. Don't you like it?'

Pierre puts it back onto the windowsill next to the china dogs and the glass figurine with a viola da gamba tucked under its arm. 'You're building up quite a collection.'

'There's this stall I go to in the Marché aux Puces. The man knows what I like. He keeps them for me.'

'So we can expect some more?' Pierre says, lightly. He goes over to the workbench.

'I thought you might want to paint them.'

He looks back at them a moment. 'Oh no, I don't think so.'

'You paint everything that's here.'

He starts to ladle paint onto the palette. 'I expect to someone looking at it with a strange eye this room would seem full of clutter, but the things in it are chosen very carefully. None of it is accidental.'

'These aren't accidental either,' Renée says. 'I chose them very carefully.'

He looks at her a moment and then smiles again and this

time without turning down the corners of his mouth. 'Yes, I can see you did,' he says. 'They're very nice.'

He bends down to retrieve the stocking she has dropped onto the floor. He stands a moment with it draped across his hand and gazes round him as if looking for a home for it. She takes it from him and returns it to the cubicle. She's suddenly aware how many of the items in the room are hers. He rarely adds to what is there already, whereas every time she comes back from the market Renée brings a token of her visit – magazines, another ornament to add to the collection, a silk scarf to swell the dozen she already has.

If it was Margo, she might not have noticed, but Pierre sees everything. He sometimes spends a quarter of an hour when he comes into the studio adjusting the position of the flowers so that the reflection is the same as it was yesterday. He likes the skylight to be open no more than an inch so that the light comes through it at the same intensity, the screen is always *contre-jour* so that it forms a backdrop to the picture.

She takes up the pose, but she can feel the tension in the air. 'You don't like what I've bought?'

'It's not to my taste, that's all.'

'What does that mean?'

'Caro loves her water ices; I prefer black coffee; you would rather have a café crème. We all have different tastes. In this case it's your eyes and not your taste buds that are making the decision.'

'Shall I keep them in the cubicle?'

'Of course not, Renée. At the moment this is your home. You have every right to have your own things round you.'

'But if you don't like them . . .'

'I'll get used to them.' He takes his brushes and begins to paint again, but they stop earlier than usual and for the first time Pierre leaves without making love to her. She looks on from the window as she always does, until he's out of sight. It isn't dark yet; she could go down to the street and find some entertainment there, but she's not in the mood.

She settles down to read a magazine. She is uncomfortably aware that there are situations where her beauty doesn't work for her, when it might even be a handicap. She's worried that her lack of education irritates him, and his moodiness is an attempt to hide his disappointment.

There are pigeons scratting on the skylight, sliding down the glass pane to the gutter and then climbing crab-wise up again like skiers on a steep slope. Pierre's studio is one floor from the top, but the façade is terraced with a slanting patch of roof above each storey. Renée watches as the pigeons strut and slide, occasionally taking off and fluttering together in the air before collapsing awkwardly again onto the sloping roof.

Somebody in the room above turns on a tap. She finds the sounds that percolate through from the other studios consoling. Having grown up in a family where there were other children, she is used to noise. It doesn't bother her whereas she knows that Pierre is irritated by it. Noise, crowds, smells – all those things Renée welcomes as distractions Pierre avoids whenever possible. She hears a cough and there's a tinny sound as something drops. It bounces, and the echo resonates.

There is a footfall on the stairs. A woman sometimes comes to see the painter in the flat below. Once Renée passed her on the stairs. The girl was pasty faced and sourlooking and did not respond when Renée smiled at her. The footsteps reach the landing underneath and start to climb the next flight. She looks up. The door clicks open. Pierre stands there. He keeps one hand on the door. The other hangs beside him.

Renée puts the magazine aside. 'Did you forget something?'

He doesn't answer her. Eventually she gets up. 'Better shut the door,' she says. She climbs out of her clothes. He doesn't bother getting out of his. He drops onto his knees and stretches out his hands. She stands in front of him and cups his cheeks in both hands, pressing his face hard against her stomach. She sinks back onto the chaise longue and he climbs between her legs. She feels the terse hair of his beard against her thighs and cries out as his lizard tongue darts in and out between her legs. The hard ridge of the chaise longue digs into her back. She arcs her spine. She's lying with one foot on either side of him, her knees bent, scrabbling with her toes to get some purchase on the rug. The carpet skids under her feet. She pushes herself forward rubbing herself frenziedly against his mouth until it feels as if she's drowning in him.

They sink down onto the rucked-up carpet afterwards. Pierre sits hunched up with his arms crossed on his knees, his head bent. She says nothing. She is conscious that what is a victory for her is a defeat for him. She doesn't want to think of it like that, but she has lived with Margo long enough to know that only one of them can occupy the throne at any one time. For the first time in her life she knows what power feels like.

Pierre pulls himself up. Renée sees him wrestling with the buttons on his trousers and she helps him. There are times when she feels almost motherly towards him; he seems so incapable. When he has finished he stands looking at her.

'Why did you come back?'

'I think you know that.'

'Do you wish you hadn't?'

'At the time it didn't feel as if I had a choice.'

'I didn't ask you to.'

'I know you didn't.' He is patting at his pockets as if he's been robbed.

She smooths her stocking up over her calf. The desperation of the previous half-hour has left both of them with jarred nerves. 'Would you rather I found somewhere else to live?'

'Why would you do that?'

'I don't know. It's only that you don't seem very happy with me being here.'

'It's not your being here that is the problem.'

'Well, what is it, then?'

'I hate deceiving Marthe.'

'Are you sure she doesn't know?'

He rubs the heel of one hand on his forehead. 'If she doesn't know, then I'm deceiving her and if she does know, she'll feel compromised.' He turns towards the door.

'Why don't you stop it, then?' She says it sulkily, but she can hear the note of panic in her voice.

He turns back. Renée bites her tongue. 'I didn't mean that.'

He comes back into the room and takes her in his arms. 'Please don't let's quarrel, Renée. There would be no point in any of it if I couldn't even make you happy.'

'You have made me happy,' Renée bunches up his shirt front in her fist. 'I'm happy,' she insists.

'That's good.' He gently takes her hand and pats it at her side.

His footsteps echo down the stairs and Renée hears the street door slam behind him. When she rushes to the window for a last glimpse of him disappearing down the street, he has already gone.

One weekend Renée crosses town with Caro to the Galeries Lafayette. Pierre has given her some francs so they can have tea in the café. Caro never seems to have the money to buy anything, in spite of Roussel's generosity. Although she doesn't class her as a friend exactly, Renée now spends most of her weekends with Caro and because she talks so little, Renée finds herself revealing aspects of her former life that she has not told anybody else. When she let slip that there had only been one bed in the apartment that she shared with Margo, Caro had asked baldly, 'Did you kiss her?'

Renée hesitated. 'More than that,' she said.

The look on Caro's face was mildly curious. 'I've never kissed a woman,' she said. 'What's it like?'

'It's all right,' Renée said. She hoped that Caro wouldn't ask her to go into detail.

'When my sister was at home, we shared a bed,' said Caro.

'So did we. I shared a bed with both my sisters.'

'Did you kiss them?'

'Not like that,' said Renée, shocked.

'Like what?' said Caro, fixing Renée with her pallid eyes in which the pupils were so small they barely registered at all. This is what gave her that remote expression, Renée thought. Whatever she told Caro would pass fleetingly into her consciousness and out again without inviting either praise or sanction.

'Like this.' She'd bent forward, and her lips brushed Caro's. Caro's lips drew back obligingly, and Renée moved her own across them. She experienced the damp interior of

Caro's mouth with its faint aura of vanilla. When she sat back, Caro was still gazing at her vacantly.

She nodded. 'Yes, I see.'

It wouldn't matter what I said to her, thought Renée. I could tell her anything. And, as the days passed, she confided more and more to Caro. It was an alternative to going to confession.

Caro offered little in return and Renée wondered whether there was anything to Caro other than a love of ice cream and her look of wide-eyed innocence, based not on ignorance but an acceptance of whatever human beings did to her or to themselves. Perhaps that was why Roussel kept her on and maybe that's why Renée needed her as well.

They wander past the counters on the ground floor and then take the staircase to the upper storeys. Renée wants to see the scarves and jewellery. They sift through clothes and lingerie and try out lipsticks on their wrists. An hour later they are sitting in the café. Caro scoops the white froth from her coffee cup into her mouth.

'What happens when you finish working for Roussel?' asks Renée.

Caro shrugs. 'I'll probably move on to someone else.'

And would you sleep with them? This is the question Renée wants to ask. She doesn't think that Caro would resent the question, but she feels shy about asking it. 'You wouldn't mind, then, if it wasn't Roussel you were with?'

'I'd miss the ice creams. Some of the painters in that set are really mean; the girls don't even get a cup of coffee.'

'Does he ever hit you?' She's remembering the argument that day outside the studio. Roussel behaved to Caro generally like an indulgent father, but his moods changed in an instant.

'Sometimes; if he's cross.'

'And you don't mind that?' She already sees that this is something Caro takes for granted and it's something Renée understands, this need for violence. It's what separates them from the other girls that painters bring into the café. No one speaks to Caro. It's as if they recognise her as a different species and are wary. There is something sphinx-like in her.

'Are you Roussel's muse?' says Renée. From the blank stare she receives, she gathers that if Caro is his muse, she's not aware of it.

'His what?'

'His muse. It's like a model but it's more than that.'

'How, more?'

'I don't know exactly.'

'Do you get paid more if you're a muse?' The look that Caro's giving her reminds her of a woman who'd once helped her mother carry Alys in her baby carriage up the steps into the Gare du Nord and then demanded money from her.

'I think you might have to be with someone for a long time.'

'It's a kind of pension, do you mean?'

'Perhaps.' She suddenly feels foolish. For the first time it would seem that she knows more than Caro but that neither of them knows enough.

Once she sees that the waiter isn't looking, Caro tips her satchel out onto the table. Inside is a brooch, a jar of cold cream and a scarf and more incongruously, since she has no money of her own, a leather wallet. Renée is appalled. 'You stole them,' she says. Caro smiles. She puts the jar of cold cream next to Renée.

'You can have that if you want. I wouldn't use it anyway.'

'Why did you steal it, then?' says Renée, mystified, but

Caro's blank expression tells her this is something else she's never thought about.

When Pierre complains a few days later that his pocket watch is missing, Renée helps him look for it, but she's remembering when she invited Caro to the studio one evening and they had dropped off to sleep. When Renée woke up she found Caro trying out the colours in a box of chalks, a sheet that she'd torn out of Pierre's sketchbook on her knees. Although she had the freedom of the studio when Pierre wasn't in it, Renée knew he didn't like his paints and sketchbooks to be touched and she made sure that anything she moved was put back where she'd found it. She can't mention it to Caro without seeming to accuse her. Caro has no scruples when it comes to theft and Renée worries that she might see no distinction between robbing friends and robbing strangers.

'Let's go back to yours,' says Caro, when they're walking back the following weekend from an excursion to the cinema.

'Not this time,' Renée says. 'Pierre would rather not have other people in the studio. He says we move things and then when he comes back on a Monday morning, he can't find them.'

'What things?'

'Just things.'

She decides to wait for Caro to produce the missing watch or evidence that she has pawned it. In the meantime, she hopes Caro might invite her back to Roussel's studio. She doesn't want to spend the evening on her own. But Caro just shrugs.

From then on, they meet outside the studio. She doesn't want to give up Caro altogether, but the missing pocket watch is dangling in the space between them like a ticking bomb.

'Who is she?' Renée slips her stockings off behind the screen. She'd been determined not to make a fuss. She didn't want him thinking she was jealous.

On the far side of the screen she hears the scratching of the knife as Pierre removes the dried paint from the palette. He'll be wondering what she was doing in that part of town, if she's been following him. She would not have minded so much, Renée thinks, if it had been a woman of her own class, someone less well dressed, less elegant, less . . . everything. She'd caught a glimpse of them outside a tearoom on the rue de Rennes. It had been Caro's turn to choose how they should spend that weekend and she'd opted for an ice cream at Le Vaudeville.

'I can't afford Le Vaudeville,' said Renée. 'Let's go somewhere cheaper.'

'It's my birthday,' Caro had insisted. 'Ricki's given me some money.' She had taken out a wad of notes that she had stuffed inside her satchel.

'Caro, if you'd said it was your birthday, I'd have bought you something!'

Caro shrugged. 'It doesn't matter. I can pay for both of us.'

They had been watching from the top deck of the tram when Renée had caught sight of Pierre stepping from a cab onto the pavement with a woman on his arm.

'You told me you were going back to Saint-Germain-en-Laye on Friday.'

'I spend every Friday night in Saint-Germain.'

'And then on Saturday you creep back into Paris.' She is anxious not to look as if she is accusing him, but that is what it sounds like. 'Couldn't you have told me you were meeting someone?'

'With respect, you very rarely tell me how you spend your weekends.' He is managing to make it look as if it's her who is at fault.

'I saw you kissing her,' she throws out.

Pierre rolls up his sleeves. 'I kissed her on the cheek.'

She knows she's being tiresome, but she's gone too far to let it go now. They are having their first argument. This is the moment when the battle lines are drawn. It's been polite till now. It still is, but it's like the crust you get on top of a crème brûlée. If you tap your spoon on it, it cracks. 'I don't care anyway,' she says. He doesn't answer. Renée feels a sudden rush of anger. If it had been Margo, they'd be twisting each other's arms by now.

He stands back from the easel. 'Can we start?'

She flings the wrap aside. The next time he comes to the studio, she won't be there. She'll come in later and refuse to tell him where she's been. Let him know what it's like. She's standing with the weight on one leg, bending forward with her hands above the knee. It's not a comfortable position to be in. Her neck is permanently cricked. 'Why don't you start?'

'I'm waiting for you to relax into the pose.'

'I am relaxed. I've been stood here for quarter of an hour and you haven't made a single mark.' There is a pause. He puts the brushes down. She feels the air between them tighten like elastic when it has been stretched too far. He comes across to her and cups his hand around her chin. She thinks he's making an adjustment to the angle of her head but then he turns her face towards him.

'She's my sister,' he says.

'This is Gallagher.' The name is English, but the emphasis is on the final syllable when Caro says it, so it sounds French. Renée puts her hand out. Gallagher just nods. She stands there waiting for them to invite her to sit down. 'You want something to drink?' says Caro.

'No thanks. We were going for a walk, remember?' She hopes Gallagher won't want to tag along. He sits back in the chair and loops his thumbs into the pockets of his waistcoat. He has mousy hair and pimply skin. She'd put him in his early twenties, although he could pass for seventeen without the weasel eyes, which look at Renée with a guarded curiosity.

'This afternoon, maybe,' says Caro. 'Gallagher and I have things to talk about.'

He curls his lip as if there is some secret that he's party to and Renée isn't. Renée doesn't like him. 'Right, I'll walk down to the river by myself, then,' she says.

Caro nods. 'I'll catch you up.' Throughout the conversation, Caro hasn't looked at either of them. Gallagher is smoking one of those short black cheroots that the Americans brought over with them and which cost a lot unless you're in the know. The suit, the angle of the hat, the waistcoat and the black cheroot all mark out Gallagher as a black-market racketeer. She wonders what else he is peddling.

So that Caro won't think she's dependent on her, Renée walks down to the river by herself. She buys a postcard of the Mont Saint-Michel and another of the Pont Neuf. She has nobody to write to, but she likes to pin the cards up in the studio.

She gets back to the café to find Caro on her own. 'He's gone, then?' she says. Caro looks at her as if she's not sure who she means. 'Your friend,' says Renée.

'Gallagher?' She dips her spoon into the sugar and licks off the crystals. 'He's a cousin.'

'With a name like Gallagher? He's English, Caro.'

'We just call him Gallagher. His real name's Charlie.'

Renée wonders whether Caro ever tells the truth. She is like Renée used to be, but Renée likes to think she doesn't tell lies any more.

The sketch has been ripped down the centre. The two halves are lying on the bench, the edges lined up as if they've been left to knit together of their own accord. On one side is a figure with two sticks for arms and two more for the legs. A cock's comb on the crudely drawn head with its yellow hair proclaims this as a princess and her dress is spattered with gold flakes that are continuing to moult. It doesn't look like one of Roussel's drawings.

'Lisel did it,' Caro says. 'She's Ricki's daughter.'

'What's the drawing doing here?'

'He brought it in to put it back together.' Caro says it carelessly, but Renée knows she should have left the two halves as they were. She tries to match them up again, but the alignment has been lost. 'Why did he tear it up?'

'He didn't. She did. He said he was trying to explain how you could make the eyes less starey.' Caro moves a plate with the remains of couscous on it to the sink but doesn't wash it up. It sits there with the dirty bottles and the empty plates. A poster tacked onto the wall next to the window replicates the one in Pierre's studio but here the purple lettering proclaiming that the artist is a Nabi has been bleached a pale grey by the sunlight. There's a pile of drawings stacked haphazardly at one end of the draining board and Renée notices the top one is already stained with splashes.

'It's a mess in here.'

'Yeah,' Caro yawns. She flicks a blob of rice into the sink. The air in Roussel's studio is different from the slightly sweet, decaying atmosphere of Pierre's atelier. It smells of sex and sweat and anger. It smells powerfully of Roussel. She turns back to the drawing.

'So how do you make the eyes less starey?'

Caro looks over her shoulder. 'That dot in the middle of the eye needs to be lower down. If you have white all round it, that's what makes it starey.'

Renée puts her thumb over the lower eyelid. 'How did you find that out?'

'Ricki told me. He talks all the time about his daughters – how intelligent they are, how beautiful.' She gives a mean laugh. 'When he tried to tell Lisel how she could make the drawing better, she just ripped it up. I don't know why he bothers with them. Isabelle won't give him any money and the girls both hate him.

Renée wonders what else Caro knows about Roussel's domestic life, what little there appears to be of it. 'You've met them, have you?'

'No, but I've seen pictures of them.'

'Does he paint her ... Isabelle, his wife?'

'He said he's never seen her naked.'

Renée's shocked. 'He told you that?'

'She came once to the studio before they married, and he had to put his jacket on the chaise longue so that she could sit down without dirtying her dress. He uses photographs and sketches if he wants to paint her.'

'Why do you suppose he married her?'

'For money, I suppose. She's rich.'

'But you just said she doesn't give him anything.'

'Who knows? He said she represented something finer than himself.' She gives a trilling little laugh.

This isn't something Caro would have made up. These are Roussel's words, not hers. She'd thought of Caro as a sponge absorbing anything that anybody said to her. Until now it had not occurred to her that someone else might squeeze the sponge and water would come pouring out of it.

'You don't tell Roussel any of the things we've talked about together, do you, Caro?'

Caro looks at her, her face which had been mischievous and full of mockery a second earlier, now blank. 'Of course not.'

With the Salon only weeks away, the café's empty in the daytime as the painters rush to get their pictures ready for the exhibition. Renée has been in the café on a couple of occasions when Roussel has stormed in and dragged Caro off, or shouted at her to put on her clothes and stop behaving like a slut. She sometimes goes down to the café in the middle of a session wearing nothing but a shift and sandals with a thong between the first and second toe to keep them on. The shift sags open at the neck to show the slight curve of her breasts and as her leg jogs up and down, the sandal swings loose at the heel.

She's sitting next to Roussel in the café late one afternoon, a hand clamped underneath her chin, a teaspoon dangling from the fingers of the other hand. There is a heated argument in progress between Roussel and Bénard about a painter Bénard likes but Roussel thinks is rubbish.

Suddenly the teaspoon drops from Caro's fingers, clattering onto the marble tabletop. The conversation stops abruptly. Roussel glances at the spoon, which is still juddering. He looks at Caro and she gives a shrill laugh.

'What's the matter with you?' he says, roughly. Caro pulls

her bottom lip in. Roussel turns away and then looks back over his shoulder as a thin wail rises from her throat. She holds her arms out to him like a baby crying for a cuddle.

'I don't feel well, Ricki.'

Renée looks on, horrified, as Caro slides out of her chair and climbs onto his lap. There is an awkward silence round the table. Caro loops her arm around his neck. She curls her knees up underneath her chin and sucks her thumb. There's something not quite right, thinks Renée, about Caro, who admittedly is no more than a child, behaving like one and with someone like Roussel, who isn't anybody's idea of a parent.

Bénard gives a short 'Tch'. Renée waits to see how Roussel will react. He seems impervious to the discomfort of the other men around the table. He shifts Caro into a more comfortable position and takes up the argument again. When Renée looks at Caro, she appears to be asleep.

The next time Renée goes into the café, Caro isn't there. She's not there on the Sunday, either. Renée waits for Roussel to come back from church.

'I haven't seen her,' he says. 'When I do, she'll have a lot to answer for. I paid her for the week on Wednesday and I haven't seen her since. She said she needed money for the clinic. Clinic!' He scoffs. 'Heroin's her medicine. I gave her just enough to get some. More fool me. And she's been going through my wallet. I suppose she thought I wouldn't notice, but a couple of weekends ago she helped herself to more than usual.'

'It was her birthday.' Renée falters. 'I thought you had given her the money ...' She tails off.

'Her birthday? Is that what she told you?' Roussel snorts. 'I hope you spent the money wisely.'

She's embarrassed, as if she's the one who's cheated him, but Roussel looks amused. 'She always managed to get what she wanted, didn't she?'

'What will you do about her?'

'If she isn't back by Wednesday, I'll ring up the hospitals and check the morgue.' He sees the look on Renée's face. 'It's not the first time she's gone off. She comes back when there's nowhere else to go and she's run out of money.'

But the days pass and there's still no sign of Caro. Renée is surprised how much she misses her. It's not unusual for models to take off, but it's not easy to imagine Caro finding someone as accommodating as Roussel to give her shelter and look after her. His popularity is largely based on his capacity for drinking and his readiness to buy rounds. He'd been at the centre of that little crowd, but now what troubles Roussel's friends is not the fact of Caro's disappearance, it's that she's the same age as their daughters and the same age as his own.

They start avoiding him and gossiping behind his back. He sweeps aside the rumours with his usual swagger. Word goes around that he is looking for another girl to poach from one or other of the painters. They close ranks against him. Renée waits to see if he'll ask her to pose. She's not forgotten his humiliation of her in the café that day and a part of her looks forward to the satisfaction of refusing.

Ten days after Caro's disappearance, Roussel gets a visit from the gendarmes. When he comes into the café afterwards, his face is ashen and his eyes are rheumy with exhaustion. He stands looking at the group around the table.

'All right, Roussel?' Bénard says.

One of the girls gets up. She goes across to him and loops

her arm round his. 'Why don't you come and sit down, Ricki?'

'I don't want to. I've got things to do.'

'What things are those?'

'None of your business,' he says, throwing off her arm. 'None of your fucking business.'

For a moment, he looks round as if he isn't certain what he's doing there and then he turns and walks out.

They see nothing of him in the next week. Groult, the painter in the studio below Roussel's in rue Delambre says he heard him arguing with Caro on the night before her disappearance. Others add their own accounts of Roussel's preference for young girls, his shortcomings as an artist and a man, his tendency to violence after he's been drinking.

Renée is surprised how little loyalty the painters seem to feel for one another. While they go on arguing and speculating about what's become of Caro, no one seems to care about Roussel's predicament.

When she goes to his studio, a part of her is still expecting to find Caro there. The door is open. Listening, she can hear a faint tap-tapping on the other side, suggesting somebody is there, but when she knocks, there is no answer. Still the tapping goes on. She peers round the door. Inside, it's empty, but a cord is dangling from the open skylight and the draft is rapping it against the wall. The room looks even more chaotic than it did when Caro lived in it. Her foot knocks up against an empty bottle. The same plates are piled up in the sink and there's a saucer full of cigarette butts on the carpet by the chaise longue. Roussel's clothes are strewn across it and the cushions have been bunched at one end with a rug spread out along its length, as if someone's been sleeping there.

The room reeks of neglect. The only item that suggests Roussel might have a life outside it is the drawing pinned above the sink that had lain in two halves on the bench the last time she was there. The torn halves have been taped together and Roussel has put a cardboard frame around it.

Renée sees that several of the tops are off the paint tubes and the dipper has been filled with oil. A dozen brushes are laid out across the worktop. He's been working on the painting Caro had been posing for before she left. When Renée puts her face up close to it she sees a smear of fresh paint on the surface.

She goes over to the cubicle. The curtain rings have come adrift at one end of the rod and, as she draws it back, she sees the marks of Caro's fingers in the grey stains on the curtain. Caro's wrap is on the hook. She bunches it against her face. There is a scent on it, but it is not the scent of Caro. She has taken her scent with her, if indeed she had one. Renée glances up and sees her own reflection in the grimy surface of the mirror hanging from the curtain rail. As she steps back, she stumbles over Caro's sandals.

She goes out onto the landing, leaving the door open as she found it. Outside on the pavement, she sees Roussel coming down the street towards her.

'Lost your way?' He's carrying a heavy-duty bag in one arm, with the other wrapped around it. Renée hears a clink of glass. There's three days growth of stubble on his chin and she can smell the whisky on his breath.

'I wondered whether you'd had any news of Caro?'

'Given all the trouble that girl's caused me, I'd have done myself a favour if I'd left her where I found her.' He is rummaging inside his pockets with his free hand for a cigarette. His hand shakes as he lights it.

'You look dreadful.'

'I've been living in the studio. My wife has kicked me out. Some kind friend has been spreading rumours that I pick my models off the streets and dump them back there when I've finished with them.'

'Do you?'

'I admit there have been times when I could cheerfully have murdered Caro, but I wouldn't have been mad enough to do it just before the autumn exhibition.'

'I once saw you slap her.'

'She would have despised me if I'd let her get away with it when she got greedy. Every now and then she'd try it on. It was as if she felt she had to keep her hand in. Me and Caro understood each other.'

'Pierre said . . .'

'What?' She shrugs. He throws his spent match in the gutter. 'I know what they're saying out there, but you can't corrupt someone unless they're innocent to start with. She'd had several lovers when she came to me. At least I paid her for the work she did, I kept her off the streets; she had enough to live on and as much ice cream as she could eat.' He rests his back against the wall as if he's having trouble staying upright. 'If you don't mind, I shall crawl back to my bogey-hole. I'm not fit company for anyone at present.'

'Is it Caro or your wife that's got you into this state?'

Ash is dangling from the cigarette in Roussel's mouth. He doesn't seem to notice.

'Isabelle is trying to deny me access to my daughters. I may be a bastard, but I'd never harm them.' The ash settles on his sleeve. The linen suit looks grey. 'You know the trouble with posh women? They insist on sitting down to dinner with a knife and fork, but they still chew your balls off when they've got them on a plate.'

'You can still work. She can't take that away from you.'

'You may have noticed that I haven't got a model.'

'Can't you get somebody else to pose for you?' Roussel gives her a long look. 'I can't do it. Pierre's got work to finish, too.'

'You wouldn't do in any case. You're not the same shape.'

Renée bridles. 'Fussy, aren't you?'

'I would need to start from scratch. You can't graft figures onto one another. If I had you for two afternoons I could white out the figure and paint over it.'

The idea that the ghost of Caro would be permanently underneath Roussel's depiction of her bothers Renée more than the idea of sitting for him.

'Pasting me on top of Caro; it's like rubbing someone out.'

'You must have been rubbed out a dozen times while you were sitting for Pierre.'

'But only so that he can paint another one of me on top. He's not replacing me.'

'I need a model. Caro isn't here. Unless I get it finished, I'll have wasted three months on that picture.'

'Show it as it is, then.'

Roussel gives a weary smile. 'For someone of your class, you're quite bright, Renée, but you don't know anything about art.'

'What's it got to do with art?'

'You think I'd be betraying Caro if I painted over her?'

'You would be killing her,' says Renée, simply.

'What's a Nabi?'

There's a pause before he answers. 'Where did you hear that word?'

Renée hesitates. She doesn't want to tell him she has

been in Roussel's studio. 'It's written on that poster by your workbench.'

Pierre glances at the poster. 'They were artists who met up as students in the 1880s. When they left the art school they continued working as a group.'

'Were you one?'

'Briefly.'

'What about Roussel?'

Pierre picks out a brush and tests it with his fingers. 'He was there at the beginning, yes.'

'Why did you call yourselves the Nabis?'

'We wore beards, a lot of us were Jews and we were very earnest.'

'Is that what the word means ... earnest?'

'It means somebody who speaks the word of God. I know, it sounds unbearably pretentious. I can only say that we were very young.'

'Is that the sort of thing they did?' She nods towards the poster.

'That's a painting by Serusier. It's fairly typical.'

'And Roussel painted like that, did he?'

Pierre looks at her. 'What is it that you want to ask me?'

Renée colours. 'Roussel's asked me if I'll sit for him, so he can finish off his painting for the Salon. He would only need two afternoons.'

There is a slight pause. 'Did you say you would?'

'I said no, but without a model he can't finish off his picture.'

'Any time you spend with him is taken off the time you have with me.' He has his back to her, but Renée knows by the determined setting of his shoulders that he's trying not to say what he would like to. 'You must please yourself, of course.'

'I just felt sorry for him.'

Pierre glances at her. 'Last week you were blaming him for Caro's disappearance.'

'I'm not sure it was his fault, exactly. He looked after her.' She wonders if she ought to mention Gallagher. 'You said yourself she was a lost cause.'

'At the point when she met Roussel, I suspect she was.' Pierre takes out his pocket watch and flips the lid back.

Renée stares. 'You found your watch.'

He looks up. 'Did I not say? It was in the studio at Saint-Germain. I found it when I went back that weekend.'

'I thought . . .' she stops. Her life feels skewed. She crosses over to the window.

Pierre is winding up the watch. 'I dare say I could spare you for an afternoon,' he offers grudgingly.

She gazes down into the street. She's thinking of the white space in the centre of the canvas with the hazy image of her predecessor underneath it and of Roussel blocking in the shape of her on top of it, obliterating anything that still remains of Caro. She sees Caro scooping cashews off her ice cream with a spoon and feeding them to Sweetie, Caro staring back at her defiantly when their eyes met that morning in the street outside the studio, and gazing proudly at the cuts along her arm. She sees her blank face after Sweetie disappeared. She hadn't understood why anyone would grieve for Sweetie and she wouldn't understand why anyone should grieve for her.

'Well?'

'Actually, I think I won't,' she says.

There is a pause before he answers. 'As you wish.'

The picture's finished. Pierre steps back. He makes a minor readjustment to a patch of colour.

'Can I see now?' Renée skips across the room and slips her arms around his waist. The painting shows her standing with her back to him, the weight on one leg, her arms crossed over her chest, her head thrown back so that her blonde hair seems to be dissolving in the light. She recognises objects in the room – the worktop with its jars of oil next to the easel, crumpled drapes and cushions on the chaise longue and the cane chair with her wrap thrown over it. But everything has been transformed. Paint crackles on the surface. It's a glittering kaleidoscope of colour into which she blends so seamlessly that Renée wonders how she ever managed to exist outside it.

'Pierre, it's beautiful!'

'I simply put down what was there.' He kisses her. She reaches for the wrap. 'I can't wait to see what it looks like in the exhibition. Will there be a lot of people there?'

'The opening is an opportunity for an invited audience to see the work and meet the artists. I'm not sure that anybody looks much at the paintings. They're too busy eyeing one another.'

Renée goes behind the curtain and pulls on her clothes. For weeks the only thing that anybody's talked about, apart from Caro's disappearance, is the Salon exhibition. 'What day is the opening?'

'The eleventh of September.'

'Does it last all evening?'

'Normally it lasts until the champagne runs out.'

'Are you putting any other pictures in?'

'Two.'

'What are they of?'

Pierre doesn't answer. It occurs to her that from this moment she no longer has a role. What will she do now? She pulls back the curtain. Pierre is sitting by the easel.

'Dearest, you do know that I can't take you to the opening, don't you?'

She stands looking at him. Pierre leans back. He sighs. 'I'm sorry if that's what you thought. You see, it's not the sort of thing the painters take their models to. It simply isn't done. We'll go together later and have tea somewhere. We'll make a day of it. How's that?'

She nods. Of course, she thinks. He couldn't take her to a thing like that. He would be telling everyone she was his mistress. 'What about the other pictures? Where are they?'

'They're in the studio at Saint-Germain.'

'Are they of Marthe?'

'Well they're of the garden and the living room and Marthe's in there somewhere with the dog and both the cats.' He smiles but Renée feels a chill inside her at the thought of the domestic life she is excluded from.

'What does it feel like to be married?'

There's a pause before he answers. 'I don't know.'

'You must know. You and Marthe ...'

'We're not married,' he says. 'Did I say we were?'

She can't believe she's hearing this. She searches backwards in her head. 'The way you talk about her ...'

'Why would I talk any other way about her?' Pierre tips up the bottle of white spirit, waiting for the liquid to soak through the sponge. 'Are you upset? You thought that I was married when I wasn't.'

She picks at a loose thread in the wrap. 'It doesn't matter.'

'It would seem it does.'

'It's only that if you're not married ...'

'What?'

She shrugs. 'You're free.'

'I'm not sure what that means.'

'You're not obliged to stay with her. That's what I mean.'

He's shocked. 'You don't just stay with somebody because you're married to them, Renée. Marthe's been with me for nearly thirty years. To leave her would be cruel, ungrateful. It would be unthinkable.'

'It's not because you love her, then?'

'Love doesn't mean the same thing when you're old.'

'I wouldn't stay with someone if I didn't love them.'

'But I do love Marthe. I'm just saying it's a different kind of love.'

'Why didn't you get married?'

'I suppose because it seemed unnecessary. We were all right as we were.'

'Did you ask Marthe what she wanted?'

'I think Marthe would have told me if she wasn't happy.' Renée's tracing with her index finger in the dust. 'And so would you, I hope.' He wipes the cloth over his fingernails. 'Are you unhappy, Renée?'

'No, of course not. I'm just wondering where I'll be in ten years' time. I'm worried I'll end up like Caro.'

'We don't know how Caro's ended up.'

'Most people seem to think she's dead.'

He sits down next to her. 'You won't end up like Caro, Renée. Caro only had Roussel. You have me.'

'What's the difference?'

Pierre looks at her reprovingly.

'No, I don't mean that!' Renée presses both hands to her temples. 'You're the only man, the only person who's been nice to me. It's just . . . oh, I don't know.' She bangs her fists against her knees. 'Since Caro disappeared, it all feels different. It feels wrong.'

'In what way, wrong?'

'I never even knew her name.'

What is preoccupying Renée is the thought that in a

month or so she'll have forgotten Caro, just like everybody else here. She'd thought they were friends, but they weren't really friends, thinks Renée. She feels as she did when she was little and a doll she hadn't cared for much until then had been given to her sister. It had left behind a space out of proportion to the space it occupied when it was there.

'Nobody here knew anything about her. I suppose she told us what she wanted us to know.' He throws the cloth into the box of rags under the workbench. 'You'd be wise to stay away from Roussel, Renée. If the police arrest him . . .'

Renée glances quickly at him. 'Why would they do that?'

'The girl has disappeared. It's his responsibility. He's her protector.'

'Would you feel the same about me if I disappeared?'

'Of course I would.'

'It took you long enough to come and find me when I did.' The words are out before she has a chance to stop them.

'That's not fair. I didn't want to harass you if you'd decided not to see me any more.'

'Perhaps that's how Roussel feels.' She is using Roussel to provoke him, but it's the equivalent of stroking someone's bare arm with a nettle. It's impossible to have an argument with Pierre. 'She had a friend, a man called Gallagher. She said he was her cousin.'

Pierre smiles. 'He couldn't . . .'

'No, I said that. Caro said his name was Charlie. They just called him Gallagher.'

'I don't recall you mentioning it at the time.'

'I only met him once.'

Pierre nods. So why talk about it now? is what he is implying.

'Roussel's wife has left him. Did you know?'

Pierre lets out a little sigh. 'Where did you hear that?'

'Roussel told me, that day when he asked me if I'd sit for him.'

'You must have had a fairly lengthy conversation.'

'He looked terrible. I asked him what the matter was.'

'And he said Isabelle had left him.'

'And she's taken both their daughters. It's because of all the trouble over Caro. Maybe this man Gallagher . . .'

'It's rather late to mention something like that now. The police will wonder why you didn't tell them straight away.'

'You think I shouldn't mention it?' He doesn't answer. 'Don't you think we ought to help Roussel?'

'I don't think we should feel obliged to,' Pierre says calmly.

'Isabelle has separated from Roussel.' Pierre is sitting in the armchair with the paper open on his knees as if that's where he read about it.

'I'm surprised the marriage lasted this long.' I sound churlish, but I have no sympathy for either of them. Édouard's always said that Roussel married Isabelle for money and she married him because she thought he would be famous, so she's stupid and he's greedy. Even if they weren't, I wouldn't like them.

Pierre shakes out the pages. 'Still, you'd think that with the two girls to consider, they'd have come to some arrangement.' He puts down the paper. 'This is the arrangement, I suppose.'

The news appears to have depressed him.

'Did she leave him?'

Pierre nods. 'There's been gossip recently. His model disappeared. She was an addict, so she'll probably be on the streets by now. Or dead. While Isabelle put up with his philandering as long as Roussel was discreet, she wouldn't want the family name dragged through the mud.'

'So Roussel is a single man again?'

I see his mouth twitch. 'He's an alley cat,' Pierre says. 'He's been lucky not to have been taken into custody. I doubt the girl was more than fifteen.'

'Who told Isabelle?'

I can't believe what I see next. When Pierre is having trouble distancing himself from something that he wants to get away from, he creates a barrier by crossing one arm on his stomach. He then rests the elbow of the other arm against the wrist and hides behind the hand. And this is what he's doing now. When someone's face is permanently hidden by a beard, you soon learn to interpret gestures.

'Who knows? I'm surprised she's left him, that's all. I'd have thought she'd want to hold the family together.'

So he got it wrong. No wonder he's depressed.

'I know the past weeks have been difficult for you,' he says.

Have we moved on to something else now? Keep up, Marthe.

'You've been very patient,' Pierre says.

I don't bother pointing out that I had no choice in the matter. I sit staring doggedly in front of me. I may not be entirely following this conversation, but I'm not about to interrupt.

'I'm grateful to you,' he says. 'I'm not ignorant of what it's costing you.'

He looks away. Is that it, then? Is this the conversation I've been waiting for since they declared the peace? The fate of Germany was argued over and decided months ago. Ours we have yet to haggle over. Pierre folds the paper carefully and puts it on the table.

'What do you want me to do?' I say.

'Do?' He blinks. 'Nothing. There is nothing you need do, except . . .'

Except to go on putting up with it, I think. Well, after all, it's what I'm best at.

'It's the opening of the Salon next week, he says.

'Yes, I know.' The invitation has been on the mantelpiece for months.

'I don't want you to feel obliged to go. I know you don't like these events.'

He's right. I may not want to do the things I do, but Pierre knows I will do them anyway. 'I'll go,' I say.

He nods. 'Good', he says in a voice that isn't giving anything away.

The studio is not the sanctuary it was before. Outside, too, there is something in the air – a febrile energy that she finds disconcerting and unsettling, given that the city is officially at peace. At least when they were still at war, the threat was real and you knew which direction it was coming from.

The painting, now in its ornate frame, has been ticketed and propped against the door, awaiting its transferral to the Salon. She had thought she would spend hours looking at it. It was the equivalent of opening a magazine and seeing yourself reproduced there – beautiful, immaculate, cut off from everyday reality.

She wonders why the painting troubles her now that it is no longer on the easel. She is not a work in progress any longer; she is finished. In the painting, she will look like this for ever. In reality she is already older than she was when Pierre signed off on it. This is the Renée that will be immortal. It is what she thought she wanted. But the painting isn't her; it is instead of her. She turns it to the wall.

'Pierre. Your face!' There is a cut across his forehead. It slants upwards from the eyebrow to the hairline so his face looks as if he's just asked a question and is waiting for an answer. Underneath the eye there is a bruise. 'What's happened to you?'

'I was set upon outside the studio.' He jerks his head as if there's something stuck inside his skull that he is trying to dislodge. 'It's nothing. There's no need to make a fuss.'

She strokes the lesions on his knuckles. 'Did they steal from you?'

'I had my wallet in my inside pocket. The man ran away without it.'

Robbery was not the motive, then. In any case, thinks Renée, why would anybody pick on you? You look as if you haven't got two sous to rub together.

'Did you tell the gendarmes?'

'By the time I got to the gendarmerie the man could have been tucked up in his bed in Lille or Rennes.'

Or Bobigny, she thinks. 'I'm frightened, Pierre.'

He hangs his coat up on the peg behind the door. 'Dear, nobody can get in without buzzing first. Make sure the outer door shuts after you when you come in and that you know who's there before you open it.'

'But if somebody can't get in, they only have to wait for someone else to open it.'

Pierre goes over to the sink and fills a glass with water. 'I don't know what to suggest, except that it's not you he's targeting.'

'I don't want him to hurt you either.' He sits down and Renée kneels in front of him. She cups her palm over his hand.

'Could Marguerite have told your family you'd moved out of the rue des Peupliers?' he asks.

'She didn't have to,' Renée says. 'I wrote to Maman. I knew Marguerite would send back any mail. I didn't want her finding out like that.'

'What did they say?'

'They wrote back that I needn't bother coming home again.'

'Your mother said that?'

'It was Tonio, but Mother let herself be bullied by him.' Renée sighs.

'You should have told me, Renée.'

'You'd have worried.'

'Well, of course I would. You need your family. I hate to think that you can't see them any more because of me.'

'I knew what I was doing.'

'Have you had no contact with your mother since that day?'

'She writes to me. She sends the letters poste restante. I thought it better not to let them have the address of the studio.' But still they knew it, Renée thinks. She runs her finger lightly down the cut above his knuckle. 'They're not going to forgive me, Pierre.' She looks at him. He doesn't need to ask, 'For what?'

'I see.'

'In their eyes I've been damned. There's no way back. You know what Tonio is like.' She rests her head against him.

'But I thought your mother was more sensible.'

'She's torn. If she sees me, she'll upset Tonio and she thinks I'm a bad example to the girls. She's right.'

'You couldn't be a bad example. Alys loves you; both the girls do.'

'You can love someone and still believe they've sinned. They're not condemning me for loving you. What they're condemning is me giving in to it.'

'If anyone should be condemned, it's me.'

'Yes, well they disapprove of you as well.'

He takes her hand and turns it over in his lap. She feels the pressure of his fingernail along the lifeline of her palm. 'It's my fault this has happened. When I asked you to give up your rooms in Belleville to come here, I didn't think of it affecting anybody else. It was short-sighted of me. We can't carry on like this.'

Her eyes flick anxiously across his face. 'It's what I wanted; to be here with you.'

'Yes, but you're not with me, not in the way you want to be.'

'I'm happy when you're here.'

'And when I'm not? You need a proper home, a place that you can call your own, where you can spread your things out and not worry that they might be getting in my way. With Caro gone and now that this has happened, living in the studio is not an option.'

'But I've nowhere else to go,' she whispers.

He puts up a hand to stall her. 'I've been thinking we might rent a small apartment for you.'

She feels panicky. 'You mean I wouldn't come here any more!'

'Of course you would still come here; you're my model. But you wouldn't have to cram yourself into this small space. You'd be living somewhere else, just as you were when you shared rooms with Marguerite, except that you would have them to yourself. You'd like that, wouldn't you?'

'It's not because you don't want us to be together?'

He spreads out her hands and kisses them. 'You said that you were frightened you'd end up like Caro. I want you to feel secure. You need a home and living here was always going to be temporary.'

She looks around the room. The smallness of it is what Renée likes, but she knows Pierre is maddened by the lack of space and by her need to fill whatever space there is. 'But won't it cost a lot?'

'Dear, that's what money's for.'

She feels a vague sense of misgiving. Somehow, being kept in an apartment seems more reprehensible than simply being Pierre's lover. On the other hand, by giving her a place that's hers alone, he's giving her the one thing he has never given anybody else. Not even Marthe.

When he doesn't mention it again, she wonders whether he regrets his offer. In the run-up to the exhibition, there is no time for discussion. Pierre is rushing back and forth between the studio and Saint-Germain, negotiating with his dealers for the other paintings he's been working on and itemising pictures due for transfer in a small black notebook. When the couriers arrive to take 'her' painting to the Salon she feels as if she is saying goodbye to a friend she's spent a lot of time with, but has never really got to know. The next day when Pierre tells her that he has a picture to deliver to a client and invites her to accompany him, she is grateful for an opportunity to get out of the studio.

The cab heads north-west out of Montparnasse and soon the crowded streets give way to tree-lined vistas. They are in the 9th arrondissement. The cab turns right onto the Boulevard de Clichy. This is not the most expensive area of Paris, but the shops are still so smart she is amazed that anybody can afford to patronise them. She sees couples wandering arm in arm along the avenue. It's not like Montparnasse where everyone is in a hurry.

They walk from the Boulevard des Batignolles and turn

into rue Clapeyron where Pierre's client lives. She gazes at the white façades, the wrought iron balconies and windows that reach almost from the ceiling to the floor. There is a porter's lodge and Pierre speaks to the man inside it. He nods, and they start to climb the stairs.

There is a faint breeze blowing through the stairwell and the air is delicately scented like the gardens in the square below. They reach the third-floor landing and Pierre takes out a key.

'You've got a key.'

'The man's not there at present.' He stands back to let her in. The newness of it is what strikes her first. It smells of fresh paint. The apartment has been simply furnished, but it reeks of class.

'Your client must be very rich.'

'He's comfortably off.'

'He's not a painter, then?'

Pierre smiles: 'Actually, he is.' He holds the key out. 'The apartment's yours.'

The key hangs in the space between them. 'I don't understand. You said your client lived here.'

He laughs. 'You're the client.'

Renée gapes. 'You've taken this apartment just for me?'

'Well, naturally I hope you'll let me visit you, but yes, it's yours, dear.'

She looks round. 'It can't be ... something this size and in Clichy.'

'There's no point in doing things by halves. You won't be able to move in just yet, but you can plan on seeing in the new year in your own home.'

She's still staring at him. Pierre waves his hand in front of her. 'This lovely flat is all for me?' she whispers.

Pierre adjusts his glasses. 'All for you.'

She throws her arms around his neck. 'I'm dreaming,' she says. 'Tell me that I'm dreaming.'

Word gets around, of course. The next time Pierre and Renée go down to the café, all eyes are upon them. When Roussel comes in, he glances witheringly at Pierre and then at Renée. She looks boldly back at Roussel, but Pierre sees the flush begin to rise up from her neck. 'Would you prefer to leave?'

'No thank you. Why would I prefer to leave?'

'You seem uncomfortable.'

Roussel is staring at her. Since their conversation, Renée has avoided him. She tells herself she doesn't owe him anything. A part of her would like to boast that she's been set up in her own apartment, although something tells her Roussel wouldn't be impressed.

I choose to wear a full-length dress with leg of mutton sleeves and a constricting ruff around the neck, the evening of the Salon opening. It doesn't suit me, but I need the high neck and the sleeves to hide the rash. There is nothing I can do about the hands, however. They were beautiful – small, quick, efficient. They spoke for me. Now they're also covered in brown stains.

There are the usual nods of greeting as we cross the concourse. I see Édouard with the Hessels, Lucy clinging to his arm as if she was the wife and Hessel standing next to them as if he's no idea what's going on. Perhaps he isn't such a fool. Perhaps he's honoured to be cuckolded by somebody like Édouard.

Pierre loops my arm around his elbow and puts one hand over mine protectively. We do a slow tour of the room. Nobody recognises me in my disguise; they're looking for the woman in the bath. I'm told that I look smaller in reality. I have a grandeur in the paintings; I fit into that world. Here, I just feel dowdy. There is no one in the room I want to speak to. Pierre greets a Jewish banker and his wife, whose garish friends are crowding round a landscape that's as loud and vulgar as themselves. The war has done this, Pierre says. People want an art they can escape into.

We wander down the line of paintings till we come to Pierre's. I stop in front of it. So that's her. The air freezes round me. It's the first time we've met face to face. Pierre could have picked a better way to introduce us. It's not only thirty years that separates us.

Pierre glances at me, but my face is empty. Next to her is hung the picture of the sitting room in Saint-Germain-en-Laye. The paint on it is not yet dry. Still, I suppose I should be grateful to be there at all. I shall be leaning on the windowsill for ever now, the garden with its rhododendrons and its riot of lobelia behind me, Poucette on the table, Blanco with her tail curled round a chair leg.

'Shall we move on?' Pierre says, but I go on looking at it. I feel clammy underneath my arms and there's a film of moisture on my top lip that I can't do anything about. Pierre is hovering beside me. Someone calls his name.

'There is a man I need to speak to,' he says. 'Can I leave you for a moment?' And he moves off, leaving us together, me and this girl.

'Marthe?' It's Roussel. I turn. He is about to kiss me on the cheek. I tilt my head away. He gives a sly smile. 'You don't often come to these events. Now that the war is over, maybe we'll see more of you.'

I doubt that very much. I'm standing with my back towards the picture and I see his eyes slide past me. There are red veins in his cheeks and shadows underneath his eyes.

This isn't a well man. He drinks too much and eats too little and he looks as if he never gets a good night's sleep. He bites his nails too. If I didn't bite my own nails I might not have noticed. He looks like a single man who needs a woman to look after him, but if the rumours are correct, he has an army of them. Surely one can sort him out.

He nods towards the pictures. 'Do you like the paintings Pierre has put into the exhibition?'

'It's not up to me to say.'

'You have as much right as the rest of us to an opinion.' He is looking at the one of Renée. 'How he's caught the light is brilliant, don't you think?'

It's not the light I'm interested in. 'Who is she?'

He looks baffled for a moment, as if he'd not noticed that there is a naked woman in the middle of the canvas who is nothing like me. 'Ah, you mean the girl. That's Renée Montchaty.' He tries to make it sound as if she's nothing special, but his voice tells me she is, and not just to Pierre.

'He found her working on a perfume counter. Once the Salon's over, I expect he'll let her go. The only thing a girl like that has going for her is her beauty and that doesn't last long.'

Long enough to do for me, I think. 'What interests you about her, then?'

He looks as if he's going to deny it, but then he seems suddenly relieved that I've seen through him. 'I was hoping she might sit for me, but Pierre isn't keen to share her.' He takes out a cigarette. 'My model took off just before the exhibition opened. It's the reason why the painting I've exhibited is ... well, the way it is. It's better not to say 'unfinished'. Hoffstadt's trying to explain it as a change of style. From now on, I shall have to leave them all in that state.' He laughs grimly. 'Isabelle has left me, I expect you heard. I lost my wife and model within two weeks of each other.'

'Sounds like you were careless,' I say and then wish I hadn't. There is something in Roussel that reaches out to women even when he isn't trying to ingratiate himself. He's looking for a chance to move away. We've probably said more over the last five minutes than we have in all the time I've known him.

I look round for Pierre. He's left the Jewish banker and is standing at the far end of the room with Édouard. I push through the crowd towards them, nodding as I go in case somebody recognises me. As I get closer, Édouard blurts out, 'For the love of God, man, have you gone completely mad?'

I stop. I don't catch Pierre's answer, if there is one, but because he is half-turned towards me, I hear Édouard mutter.

'She's got class; no doubt about it. But you see, old fellow, that's the danger.'

This is not a conversation that I want to interrupt, but it appears it's over anyway. Pierre says something else and Édouard prods him with his rolled-up catalogue. 'All right, you didn't ask for my advice, but that's it. Let it run its course. But don't make any rash moves. Leave yourself with an escape route.'

'It's too late,' Pierre says. 'It's already done.'

She's standing at the entrance looking round the walls as if she's searching for a friend. And then she sees it. She lets out a little squeal.

'Please, Renée, try and calm down.' He sees people turning round to look at them.

'It's not a library, is it? You're allowed to talk.'

'To talk, yes.'

'Can we have a proper look?' She takes his arm and drags him over to the painting. Then her eyes move to the painting next to it, of Saint-Germain-en-Laye. She puts her fingers up to touch it. 'What did Marthe think of me?'

'She didn't say.'

She taps her toe against the floorboards. 'Didn't she say anything at all?'

'She never comments on the paintings. She accepts that there are things about my work that she's not qualified to talk about.'

'She didn't even ask you who I was?'

'No.'

'That seems odd.'

'The fact that she's not curious? She recognises that what happens in a painting isn't necessarily related to what's happening outside it.'

'Does she like the way you paint her?'

'It's not something we've discussed.'

She snaps back, 'Is there anything you talk about?'

'When you've been with somebody for a long time, there are certain things that you no longer need to talk about.'

'Like me?'

'If Marthe has a question, I expect she'll ask it.'

'There are questions I would like to ask her.'

'What? What would you like to ask her?'

'Well for instance how she feels about us hanging side by side without our clothes on in a public place.'

'How do you feel about it?'

'Cheap.'

'Why would it make you feel cheap?' He looks round. 'There must be fifty paintings here with nudes in them.'

'You didn't have to put us side by side; that's all I'm saying. It looks . . .'

'Well?'

'It looks as if we're just the same to you. It could be either of us in the painting.'

'That's not how it is. I could have gone on using Marthe and not bothered bringing you in, if that was the case.'

'Why did you bother bringing me in?'

He is trying to be patient. 'When I saw you in the street that day it was as if you were already posing for the pictures that I had in mind. From then on you were indispensable; they couldn't work without you. Everything that happens in a painting has to be the way it is; it can't be otherwise.'

'I don't see.'

'You don't have to see. Just take my word for it.' He's trying tactfully to move her on. She was determined to come here today and having brought her, now he's keen for them to leave.

She hangs back. 'I thought we'd be looking at the other pictures, too.'

'He waves his arm. 'By all means have a look round.'

'Don't you want to come as well?'

'I've seen it once.'

He watches as she stands in front of each work for a regulation fifteen seconds before moving on. She stops in front of one of Édouard's paintings – a concoction of blues, greys and yellows that appear to have been thrown onto the canvas like a handful of pebbles at a window.

'Do you like it?'

'For a moment I thought it was one of yours.'

'Some critics say they can't tell us apart.'

She bends to read the caption. 'It's called *Madame Vuillard in the Breakfast Room*.'

'Yes.'

'So where is she?'

'Madame Vuillard? I expect she's in there somewhere.'

'I can't see her.'

'She's not really what the picture is about, you see. And even if she was there, even if it looked just like her, it would still not be her. Paintings are just dabs of colour on a flat plane. You can call the picture what you like but that's still what it is.'

'Why call it *Madame Vuillard*, then?'

'The organisers like to have a title for the catalogue.'

She scans the picture. 'Did she pose for it?'

'Yes, I expect so.'

'I'd feel quite put out if I'd done that and then I couldn't see myself in there when it was finished.'

'Édouard's mother is an understanding woman. Anyone who lives with Édouard has to be.'

'Édouard? That friend of yours we met outside the Louvre? He lives with his mother?' She turns back towards the painting. 'Was he part of that group you belonged to?'

'Édouard was a Nabi, yes.'

'Why would he paint his mother?'

'Maybe for the reason that I go on painting Marthe. We feel freer to express ourselves in situations we know intimately.'

Renée goes to speak and then thinks better of it. She looks round and catches sight of Roussel's painting. It's as if she's looking at it through a mist. The figure's ghostly presence pulses through the picture. Caro seems more spookily alive there than she had when she was sitting in the café with her ice creams. 'Roussel put the painting in the exhibition after all, then?'

'It caused quite a stir. His dealer seems to think it's an improvement.' Pierre clears his throat.

'I think so too,' says Renée.

She moves on. When she comes to a painting by Roussel of Isabelle at Pont Aven, however, she stands staring at it. Renée can't help but compare herself to every other woman she encounters. 'Is that Isabelle?'

'Yes.'

'She's quite beautiful.'

'It's one thing Roussel's women have in common. Sadly, by the time he's finished with them, most of them have lost it.'

On the 8th of January, Renée moves to the apartment in rue Clapeyron. Place Clichy is five minutes' walk away with Parc Monceau a quarter of an hour in the opposite direction. In the past she'd sometimes taken tram rides though the more exclusive areas of Paris, but she'd never dreamt that she might live in one.

The day she moves out of the studio, she entertains Pierre 'at home.' They've spent the afternoon together in the 'English' gardens of Napoleon III, a famous landmark of the area. She's fed the black swans on the lake and posed before the waterfall for Pierre to sketch her. From the grotto there's a view across the whole of Paris with the Eiffel Tower on the horizon.

It's now seven in the evening. Renée is preparing their first 'proper' meal together. She has bought a dinner set from 'Lafayette'. The serviettes are made from Irish linen and the place mats feature pictures of rare fruits with a metallic sheen on them. Light from the candles in their silver holders flickers back and forth theatrically across their faces, pausing intermittently as if debating whether to go out and plunge them into darkness. Renée feels as if she's on a stage, but this time it is she who is directing the production.

Pierre sits back and lets her serve him, complimenting

her on everything she puts in front of him. She pictures him in Saint-Germain and for the first time she appreciates how normal people live, with homes that somebody comes back to in the evening. She has even bought pyjamas and a toothbrush, so that Pierre won't have to bring his own.

He laughs. 'You've thought of everything.' He kisses her. 'Do you think you'll be happy here?'

'Of course. How could I not be?'

They clink glasses: 'To the future,' he says.

The first task she faces when she moves into the flat is how to cover up the walls. She isn't used to white walls. In the war they covered them with news-sheet. You could read the headlines of the news from 1914 four years later. It was as if there were other people in the room with you. The trouble with white walls is that they make the whole apartment feel as if it's someone else's.

'Well, dear, you've been busy,' Pierre says when he comes the next time.

Renee loops her arm through his and leads him on a guided tour from one room to the next. He takes in the improvements she has made. The knick-knacks that were previously in the studio have now been ranged along the windowsill. The walls are hung with scenes of fresh-faced children wandering in the Alps and photographs of famous film stars.

He makes little grunting noises of approval that she senses aren't entirely genuine. She loved the pictures when she saw them in the store but now she wonders if perhaps she should have taken Pierre's advice on what to buy. She's cluttering up the apartment in the way she cluttered up the studio. But she can't help herself. She needs these things to fill the gaps that seem to constantly be opening up inside her.

Pierre stands looking at the painting she has hung above the mantelpiece, the one he brought with him when they first came to the apartment – a self-portrait 'so that you'll have me for company if ever you feel lonely,' he had said.

But just as what she's done inside the flat does not entirely satisfy her need, nor does the portrait.

She has been there less than three months when her isolation starts to chafe on her. Although the rooms above her and below are occupied, sound never seems to percolate between the floors. She leaves the windows open to let in the sounds from down below, but this is one of those quiet residential areas that are considered so desirable. It's almost as if the apartment's sound-proofed. Nothing penetrates it. In the studio, she'd felt a kinship with the objects that surrounded her. They were like children – loved and cherished, even by the light that fell across them. She remembers how the shadows used to creep around the studio like footpads, pocketing the things they came across and leaving something different in their place. A white box might look grey or even black along one edge depending on the angle of the light. If you looked hard at any colour and then looked away, you'd see its opposite. The light in the apartment is too sharp and brittle. It illuminates the objects in its path, but it does not engage with them.

She had thought, when she moved to Clichy, that she would be going to the studio as usual, but since she's been in the apartment Pierre has hardly painted her at all. One week when she's been on her own for three days, she decides to take the tram to Bobigny. She knows that Tonio will be at work and Maman will be by herself. She isn't there, though. The back-door key is still underneath the mat, where anyone can find it. On the table, there are school books and a smock thrown carelessly across a chair back.

Renée sees her mother coming up the path. She's laden down with shopping. 'It's you!' she says, putting down the bags and hugging her. She's pleased, but Renée sees her eyes already moving nervously around the room. Will Tonio know that she's been here when he comes home?

'Let's have tea,' she says. 'I'll fill the kettle.' Renée hasn't brought a suitcase, so she knows she won't be staying. 'You look pale, dear. Are you all right?'

'Fine. I've got my own apartment now, you know.'

'I'd heard,' she says. She'd normally be desperate to hear about it – what the area was like, what sort of outlook there was from the window, did she have nice neighbours?

'It's in Clichy. It's a lovely flat. I wondered if you'd like to come one afternoon and have a look at it. We could have tea and walk down to the square.'

Her mother strains the tea into her cup and puts the cosy on the teapot, absently.

'You haven't poured yourself one, Maman.'

'So I haven't,' she says. 'What a goose I am.'

'I'll do it.' Renée reaches for the teapot. 'What about it, Maman? Will you come?'

Her mother keeps her eyes fixed on the table. 'I don't think so, dear. It's such a long way.'

'It's not far. I'd meet you off the bus.'

'I need to be here when the girls get back from school. And then there's Tonio.'

'He needn't know.'

'I didn't mean that. I meant he expects his dinner to be on the table when he comes home.'

'I do miss you, Maman.'

'Yes, I miss you too. We all do.' She is scratching with her index finger at the pattern on the tablecloth. It makes a shushing sound against the rough weave of the hessian. She always did that when she had her mind on something.

'Pierre is not a bad man, Maman. You would like him if you knew him better.'

'I thought he was very nice,' she says. 'He struck me as a gentleman.'

'What is it then?'

'I think you know that, dear. The way you're living isn't right. It's not what God intended.'

'It's more complicated than you think. Things aren't that simple.'

'No, I dare say. We shall have to hope that God appreciates that.'

What's it got to do with God? she wants to shout. Why should God bother if I'm living in a flat in Clichy with my lover? And in any case, I'm not. I'm living there alone.

'I can't persuade you then? You won't come?'

'I don't think so. It would only cause an upset.'

'What about me coming here? Is that all right?'

'Of course. We'd love to see you ... every now and then. The morning is the best time. Then you can get back to Paris while it's still light.'

When she goes, she tries to give her mother twenty francs. 'You can buy something for the girls.'

'You're very kind, dear, but no thank you. Keep your money, I expect there's lots you need.'

'There isn't. I've got everything I need. Why won't you take it?'

She holds out the twenty francs. Her mother cups her hand round Renée's, gently pushing it away from her.

'You're sure about that, are you, dear?'

She's walking down the rue de Ménilmontant when she catches sight of Marguerite. She's walking in the opposite direction with her head down. Renée, when she walks, sees everything. She likes the sense of life unravelling before her eyes. But Marguerite sees only what is in her head already.

Renée turns and follows her. The shoes she has just bought are bouncing up and down against her thigh, as if they too are going for a walk. These days she can buy anything she wants. Before, when she was shopping she could only stare in at the windows, coveting the things she saw. She wonders why it doesn't cheer her up to buy things when she used to think it would make all the difference to her happiness if she could only have that hat, that shirt, that pair of stockings.

Marguerite is elbowing her way through the arcade, her drab blue gabardine occasionally swallowed up, then re-appearing further down. She goes into a café. It's not far from the apartment that they used to share. These days whenever Renée's wandering the streets, she always seems to end up in the same arrondissement. When she was living here, she couldn't wait to get away. The area seemed drab, the population pale and starved of light. It throbs with life now. People say hello to her. In Clichy no one speaks to anyone.

A young girl sitting at a corner table gets up. Marguerite is threading her way down the room. They kiss each other on the cheek. The waiter brings a pot of coffee to the table.

Renée crosses over so the girl is in her line of sight. She's in her early twenties and she wears a shabby-looking dress under her coat. She has a moon-like face and an expression that is vacant but expectant. Suddenly she laughs, a brittle little laugh like breaking glass.

It's Marguerite who pays the bill. They leave the café arm in arm and walk along the pavement. There's a light rain in the air. They cross the road and turn into a side street. Renée wishes fleetingly that she were on her way back to the flat, the night ahead filled with the promise of companionship;

what sort seems immaterial. The only thing that counts is not to be alone.

The streets are suddenly deserted. They are in the residential quarter. Renée falls back. Marguerite and her companion disappear under the archway leading to the courtyard. Minutes later, Renée sees a light go on in the apartment.

She returns to Belleville three days later at a time when she knows Marguerite will be at work. The door is on the latch, but Renée rings the bell before she lets herself in. Opening the door, she feels the difference straightaway. There is a strange coat hanging on the hall stand, with a felt hat looped over the peg. She jumps – it looks like someone standing there.

The drapes she bought to cover the settee have been replaced by flowered chintzes. In the bedroom, blankets have been roughly pulled into position on the bed. A shirt that doesn't look like Marguerite's is slung over a chair and she can see a sandal poking out from underneath it.

There's a sound behind her. Renée turns. The girl is standing in the doorway with her arms crossed.

'I suppose you're Renée,' she says. She seems unsurprised. 'I'd gone to take the rubbish down. That's why the door was left unlocked.' Her sleeves are rolled up. Renée glances at her arms to see if there are any bruises there.

'Has Margo mentioned me?'

'She said you lived here for a bit, but you kept going off, so in the end she threw you out.'

'That isn't how it happened.'

The girl shrugs.

'I came to get some things I left behind . . . drapes, cushion covers.'

'Were those yours? I don't know what she did with them.'

'It doesn't matter.' Renée tilts her head back. 'I can buy some more. I've got a place in Clichy now.'

'Nice.' She looks unimpressed.

'At least I've got my own bed.'

Colour floods the girl's cheeks. So they're lovers, Renée thinks, and any sympathy she might have had for her evaporates.

'You're sharing the apartment, then?'

The girl looks straight at her and gives a brief nod. 'I stay over two or three nights every week.'

'Where did she find you?'

'We've been friends for ages.'

You're not friends, thinks Renée, even if you think you are. It's hot inside the room. She wishes she could take her coat off.

'You can't just walk in like this, you know. It's not as if you live here any more.' The girl is bolder now. She's asking for the keys, thinks Renée. She has taken the precaution of removing Marguerite's ring and although it would have reinforced her status, she's reluctant to relinquish the one proof she has that Marguerite might once have loved her. She feels less proprietorial about the keys. Now that she's been here, Marguerite will have the locks changed anyway.

'I only came to get the drapes. It doesn't matter if you haven't got them.' Renée tosses her the keys. 'You can tell Marguerite I shan't be coming back.'

Pierre is looking at the latest acquisition which she hasn't yet got around to hanging. It's an etching of the Colosseum that she picked up in the Marché aux Puces. He takes his glasses out and turns it over in his hands. 'The Colosseum.'

'It's in Rome.'

He smiles. 'Yes.'

'I expect you knew that.' Renée wishes he would be less deferential. He has taken off his shoes so that he doesn't leave mud on the carpet. Even though he has a key, he always rings the bell. It's so she'll feel that the apartment's hers, not simply one that she's allowed to live in, but it distances her further from him.

'I was there once. Many years ago, of course.'

'I know. You went there with Roussel.'

There is an awkward silence. 'Did he tell you that?'

'He said you went as friends, but you stopped being friends while you were there.'

'Did he say why?'

'He said he stole a girl from you.'

'Ridiculous!' He puts the etching down abruptly and goes over to the window.

'Don't be angry, please.'

'I'm not. I'm irritated by the way Roussel manipulates events.'

'You're saying that you were friends afterwards?'

'We weren't friends to begin with. We were never friends.'

Her eyes are on his face. 'There wasn't any girl, then? Roussel made it up.'

'The two of us were drawing in the Vatican. A girl asked whether she could see the drawing I had done. She liked it. I'd have given it to her, but Roussel whisked her off before I had a chance. That's all it was.'

She takes his hand and eases him into an armchair, perching on the carpet by his knees.

'What did she look like, this girl?'

'It was thirty years ago; I've no idea.'

'Did she have yellow hair?'

'Perhaps, yes, I believe she did.'

'Did she look anything like me?'

'I don't know. She was blonde and there aren't many girls in Rome with blonde hair. That's all I remember.'

He is tapping with his fingers on his knees. She knows he does remember, that he's not forgotten his humiliation or the girl who witnessed it, but that if she pursues it she will lose him. The engraving of the Colosseum lies on the low table next to them. 'It must be wonderful to live with all those ruins round you,' Renée murmurs.

'You need only ride round Paris on a trolleybus if all you want to see are ruins.'

'But it's different. Other countries are so . . .'

'What?'

'Exotic, I suppose.'

'What other countries have you seen?'

She bunches up her shoulders. 'I went to Marseilles once on the train.'

He bends his head towards her. 'Marseilles doesn't count,' he whispers. 'It's in France.'

'It's still exotic. When you're seven, anything outside your own home is exotic.'

Pierre reaches for a stray strand of her hair and curls it round his fingers. Now he's smiling. He will be regretting his ill-humour. She could ask for anything she wants now. Pierre gives the curl a playful little tug. 'You're right. Rome is exotic. It's like walking through a dream. The past is all around you; everywhere you look.'

'The Colosseum's been there for a long time, then?'

'The Colosseum is a Roman amphitheatre. It was built two thousand years ago.'

'And is it like the picture?'

'Yes, but what you don't get in the picture is a sense of scale. It's vast. You feel diminished. No, diminished is the wrong word. You feel overwhelmed.'

'You never wanted to go back?' She gazes up at him.

'I would have done but Marthe doesn't like to travel. I suppose I could have gone alone.'

She rests her chin against his knee. He goes on curling her hair absently around his finger – curling and uncurling.

'I would love to travel,' Renée whispers.

'Well, perhaps we'll go together one day.' Pierre strokes her cheek. '"See Rome and die," they say, but then they say that about most Italian cities.'

'Why?'

'They're saying nothing can live up to the experience.'

She draws her fingernail along the rough grain of his trousers, delicately picking off a dog hair clinging to the fabric just above the knee. She smells the porridgy aroma of the cat he has had sitting on his lap. His body is an archive of the life he lives away from her.

'I'll never go to Rome with you.'

'Why not?'

'It wouldn't happen, that's all.'

He stops stroking her. His hand rests on her head, the thumb still pulsing. She looks up at him. He draws his top lip in under the beard as if he's suddenly aware that they have strayed a long way from the path that they were on and he's not certain of the way back.

'There's no reason why it shouldn't.'

Her head drops onto his knee. 'There are a hundred reasons. For a start, what would you say to Marthe?'

'I don't know. I'd have to think about that.'

'Would you tell her it was me who you were going with?'

'I wouldn't want to lie to her. I don't tell Marthe everything and there are things she keeps from me, but we don't often lie.' He clears his throat. She hears that little click behind it. 'It might take a while to organise, of course.'

She nods. Of course. She gazes round her at the décor of the room. It looked much better, she sees now, when it was empty. Nothing in it seems to fit. She doubts that anything of hers will ever fit in anywhere.

Pierre sighs. 'Darling, please don't look so disappointed. We will go, I promise.'

Renée looks into his face. She isn't certain whether this is just a way of getting through an awkward moment. 'Even if she doesn't want you to?'

'I've said we'll go; we'll go.'

She goes on staring at him. 'Will we stay in a hotel?'

'That's normally what happens.' Renée's frowning. 'Have you ever stayed in a hotel?'

She shakes her head. 'I knew a girl once on the perfume counter. She'd been to a hotel with a man.'

'That's different. That girl . . .'

'What?'

'She wasn't in the same kind of relationship.'

'I wouldn't like to be mistaken for a prostitute,' says Renée, softly.

'Oh my dear girl,' Pierre takes her chin between his hands and raises it. 'You'll never be mistaken for a prostitute, I promise you.' He hesitates. He nods towards her hand. 'I've noticed that you still wear Marguerite's ring sometimes.'

Renée curls her thumb over the ring self-consciously. 'It's not because I miss her.'

'And you seem to wear it on the same hand all the time now.' Renée colours. Pierre leans forward, putting his hand over hers. 'I understand. It was insensitive of me not to have thought of it. Of course, you'd want some sign for other people that you're more than just a mistress.'

'But I'm not,' says Renée, hopelessly. 'That's all I am. My

brother, Marguerite, the man downstairs ... they all know what I am.'

Pierre sits back. He stares up at the ceiling. 'I had no idea that I had made your life so difficult. I thought that having the apartment might be a solution; somewhere of your own where you could feel secure and where you'd have your own possessions.'

Renée curls her fist against his knee. 'It's not that I don't like it here. I know I'm lucky.'

'I ought to have given you a ring myself, not let you make do with a second-hand one, certainly not one that Marguerite had given you. Before we go to Rome, we'll go and buy a proper one. How's that? Then nobody we meet will be in any doubt about us. I'll be able to look after you the way I should.'

'And after we come back from Rome, we'll be together?'

'Yes, we'll be together.'

Renée's eyes flick back and forth across his face. 'You promise you won't ever leave me?'

Pierre dabs his fingers on her cheek. 'I'll never leave you. You're my ...' He looks past her. Renée waits. 'My own dear girl.'

That night after he's gone, she wants to rush into the street. She has to tell somebody – Maman, Tonio, the elderly Algerian who runs the all-night café on the corner of the square, the blind accordionist in the rue des Batignolles who knows exactly how much someone throws into his hat by listening to the sound the coin makes as it lands. She wants to hug his dog – that lice-ridden old mongrel with the ribbon round its neck that raises one paw every time a passer-by slows down. She wants to bang on Marguerite's door and say, 'See, he loves me.'

But when Pierre doesn't come the next day, Renée feels a tremor of anxiety. The sun is shining. It's a lovely day; she could be sitting in the gardens. But she is afraid to go outside in case she misses him. She thinks of the scenario that at this very moment might be playing out in Saint-Germain-en-Laye. Not only will all Marthe's worst fears be confirmed, but she will know that Renée isn't just a ship that's passing in the night. She'll be reminding him how long they've been together; she'll point out that Saint-Germain-en-Laye is where he's comfortable. It isn't just where Marthe is; the dachshund and the cats are there, the sun-drenched parlour and the garden overflowing with lobelia, the comforting routine of wholesome meals, a warm bed and the undemanding presence of another human being. And if that is not enough to sway him, Marthe can remind him that she is his muse, and nothing can take that away from her.

The next day, Renée hears the postman. She goes out onto the landing. He is knocking on the door below. The man who lives there only comes back at the weekends, so she offers to take in the package. When the postman hands the parcel over, his eyes catch hers for a second. He knows from the letters that arrive for Pierre about the lease and from the name that's on the bell, that she's not married. Maybe he's assuming that she doesn't just have one protector but a number of them. Renée takes the parcel and turns back into the room. He won't be treating her like this when they come back from Rome, she thinks.

The postmark on the envelope is Avignon. The viaduct is pictured on the stamps. The package gives her an excuse to go downstairs on Friday night and have a conversation with the man who lives there. He might ask her in to look at his apartment. She props up the envelope against a vase and looks at it. Today is Wednesday. Friday is two days away. And then she thinks, how sad is that? She's waiting for a man she doesn't know, who's never shown the slightest interest in her; somebody she might not like much even if he did. She's desperate for company because the only man she cares about is not here.

Death. Why are we never ready for it when it has been waiting for us all our lives? I'm thankful that we're in the kitchen when the news comes. I sit Pierre down in the chair next to the stove. We don't speak; there's no need. When Pierre's in shock, his body closes down. The first bits to stop working are his eyes and hands, the only things that do work on a normal day. I sit him in the armchair and take off my shawl to drape around his shoulders, tucking it behind his neck the way the barber tucks the towel in at the corners. He once told me that it smelt of me – a combination of soap, earth and something else that comes from having animals around you day in, day out. It's as if I've wrapped my body round him.

I begin to stroke his hands as if they're creatures that are poorly and need coaxing back to life. His wrists are narrow even though his hands are large. There is a huge vein on the right hand running from the inside of the wrist across the back towards the index finger. I think of the work involved in carrying the messages that travel from his eyes into his brain and out again along the arteries until they reach his fingers.

I'm the one who calls the family to ask about arrangements. It's not something I like doing. My experience of human beings tells me we are better off without them. If I had to choose between Poucette and Madame Hébert, Madame Hébert wouldn't stand a dog's chance.

For the next two days I treat Pierre as if he were an invalid.

I bring him beef tea and the newspaper to read. I leave the sketchbook next to him because it's only when he picks it up that I shall know we're past the first stage. In his head he will be summoning the necessary energy for what's to come. In his class you don't simply dump the body in the ground and shovel earth on top of it; there is a ritual to go through. Once, when he'd been asked to speak at someone else's wake, I asked him why he felt obliged. 'You can't stand by and let your friends go down into the darkness without saying anything,' he said.

There are some consolations for religion, I thought, even if it only gets you through the funeral, but Pierre wouldn't lie. Accepting that there was an afterlife in order to make this one bearable would not occur to him. The morning of the funeral, he gets up early and puts on a suit. I brush the shoulders for him. Arnulf's coming to collect him in the cart and take him to the station. I did offer to go with him, but he said no, he would rather go alone. There's one thing; for the next three days at least I shall know where he is.

The man in the apartment down below seems less reserved. If anything, he's slightly more familiar than is comfortable.

He has a small dog, something in between a Corgi and a Pekinese. She wonders what he does with it when he goes off on trips. Perhaps he takes the dog and smuggles it into his hotel, brings it scraps of food secreted from the dining room and walks it after dark around the block. If they had known each other better, Renée might have offered to look after it. An animal would have been company.

It's been a week now since she spoke to Pierre. She can't eat; she can't sleep; she can't bear being by herself in the apartment, yet she dare not leave it. She begins to wonder whether any of it's real. She is afraid that if she doesn't talk to someone, she'll go mad.

Eventually she takes her coat and goes down to the street. She walks until she reaches the glass-fronted cafés and the bustling restaurants of rue de Furstemberg. She glances in the windows of Les Deux Magots. Inside, the tables are all occupied. Now that the war is over and the lights are back on, Paris never sleeps. There is a mad, sad gaiety about it. She stands for a moment staring in. She could afford to go in and sit down herself and order one of the expensive pastries from the trolley, rather than stand outside on the pavement looking in, but if she went inside she would be sitting at a table on her own.

She is about to move on when her eye is drawn towards a couple seated in the corner. Renée thinks at first that it's a father and his daughter, but the way they're dressed immediately tells her this is not the case. The man is smart but in a slightly coarse way. He's the kind who boasts about his suits and tilts his hat back on his head – a Jack-the-lad. He isn't old enough to be the father of the girl he's with. She's very thin and has a wasted look about her, but there is a dish with three huge boules of ice cream on the table by her elbow and she's tucking into them with so much dedication that the man, who has a cup of coffee and a cigarette in front of him, lets out a guffaw.

It's not possible, thinks Renée, and yet it could not be anybody else but Caro. Caro is alive, and she has found another man to buy her ice cream. She looks up and Renée thinks she's seen her, but it's dark out on the pavement. Caro won't be able to see anything but darkness outside. Inside, all is bright and warm. As long as she is inside, she will be all right. Why would she look beyond it?

Renée feels the rain against her face like tiny shards of

glass. She pulls her collar up and walks on. She goes past the Louxor cinema in Barbès and is tempted to go in. It's one way to get through the evening, but a woman sitting in a cinema alone is just as likely to attract attention as she is out on the streets in darkness. She goes past an alleyway that stinks of beer and urine and is jostled by a prostitute and someone she is trying to coax money from. She turns towards the river and then doubles back into the narrower but less intimidating streets of Montparnasse. She isn't ready to go back to the apartment. She will walk all night if necessary. She is in an area she knows now and occasionally somebody acknowledges her.

This world, with its shifting population, is the only one still open to her. There is nowhere else that she can go for company and even here there's only one of all the people that she knew who might still welcome her. She walks along the pavement, past the café where the painters congregate, and sees a crowd of them inside, but there is no one there she recognises. She walks on. She is impervious to everything around her – the incessant noise, the music, the ripe scent of bodies pushing past her. She wants to be sucked into the vortex that is Paris.

She's been walking back along the Boulevard du Montparnasse and has come out on rue Delambre, metres from where Roussel has his studio. She hasn't seen him since she moved to Clichy. It would have been easy, once upon a time, to knock on Roussel's door with the pretence of asking after Caro. She had done it once. But she can't do it now. She is an exile here, too.

Then she sees him, talking to another man outside a bar across the road from her. He doesn't look as run down as he did the last time Renée saw him, though he's not as dapper as he was when she first met him. She's walked on another fifty yards when he calls out to her. She stops and waits for him to catch her up.

'It is you!' He stands back to look at her. 'I was afraid we'd seen the last of you. It's months since anybody saw you in the café.'

'I don't often go there these days. It's too far to walk.'

'I haven't been in there myself much, lately.' He draws Renée in under the awning of a shop where they're less likely to be jostled. 'It changed after Caro went. I learnt a lot about my so-called friends after she disappeared.' He offers her a cigarette. His eyes take in the modish coat she's wearing and the leather bag over her shoulder.

Renée wonders why she doesn't tell him that she's just seen Caro sitting in the window of a café. Any other time she would be bursting with the news, but somehow what this tells her is that nothing's changed, whereas a week ago it seemed that everything had been about to alter. Caro vanishing without trace had a certain grandeur to it. Caro simply moving from one minder to the next did not.

Roussel has that familiar smell of oil and turpentine about him. She's been missing that. 'Have you been working?'

'Like a black. My dealer Hoffstadt sold two pictures this week – both of them in what they call my "new style".' He grins.

'Caro brought you luck, then?'

'You're the one who brought me luck.'

'Me? What did I do?'

'It was you who told me to stop working on that picture.'

'Without Caro, there was nothing else you could have done with it.'

'Let's say it was a happy accident.'

'I'm glad it's all worked out for you.' She goes to move on.

'What about you, Renée? Has it all worked out for you, too?'

'I'm all right.'

'A lot seems to have happened since we last met.'

'You've got famous, for a start.'

'As I said, I got lucky. It won't last. The critics will find someone else to write about. It helped me through that business over Caro and it helped to compensate for the divorce. I'll never get over the loss of Lisel and Annette but that's another story.' Roussel throws the cigarette away. 'Why don't you come and have a look at what I'm doing?'

'Oh no, I don't think so. It's too late.'

'How long have you been walking?'

'I lost track of time.'

'Lose track of it again. Another half an hour isn't going to make any difference.' Roussel takes her arm. 'It's not the first time you've been up there, after all.'

'Did Caro tell you that?'

He laughs, and she knows suddenly that everything she ever said to Caro has been passed on. Caro has betrayed her not once but continually, all the time they've known each other.

In the studio there is a range of pictures stacked against the walls, all painted in the rather hazy style that marked the Caro painting, though without its ghostly presence.

'Rumour has it that Pierre has set you up in an apartment.' Roussel puts out glasses. 'Clichy, isn't it?' He gives a snide laugh. 'Quite the little princess. Are you happy?'

'It's a lovely flat.'

'That wasn't what I asked.'

'Of course I'm happy. What girl wouldn't be?'

'A girl who wanted more from life than sitting in a gilded cage and waiting for her lover to stop by two afternoons a week. It's not what I would have expected of you.'

'Why can't you accept that Pierre and I just want to be together?'

Roussel pours a measure into each glass. 'But you aren't together, and you never will be. He's not going to leave Marthe. He could never reconcile it with his conscience.'

'If you must know, Pierre is buying me a ring.' She knows she should have kept it to herself. To blurt it out like this is madness. It will be all round the café by tomorrow night. 'He's making plans for us to go to Rome together and when we get back we're going to be married.' She says it defiantly, but in her head she's feeling shaky. She's been wondering if she misunderstood him.

'Renée.' Roussel sits beside her on the chaise longue. He takes Renée's hands in his and brings his face up close to hers. 'You really think Pierre will marry you?'

'I told you, he's already said he's buying me a ring.'

'That isn't quite the same thing, is it?' Roussel moves his face so that he has her in his line of sight. 'Believe me, I'm not saying it to hurt you. I'd just hate you to be disappointed.'

'Why would you care? You just want to spoil it for me.' Renée tries to tug her hands free.

'If Pierre leaves Marthe he will hate himself and in the end he'll hate you too. You know that what I'm saying is the truth.' She feels tears rising in her. 'Is this really how you want to live?' He waves an arm towards her that encompasses the coat she has on and the handbag she's just looped over the chair back. 'All these "trappings",' he throws back his head, 'that's what they are. They give you the illusion of security, but they entrap you.'

'I've got everything I want. I'm all right.'

'Everything? What have you got? A box to live in. I imagine it's a very nice box, but it's still a box and when the lid comes down, you will be in it on your own. Pierre has taken you away from everything you know and what he's given you is nothing.'

'What would you know?' Renée wrenches her hands free. She stands up, pulling her coat round her. 'I don't want a drink. I'm going.'

'Can I ask what you were doing here in Montparnasse this evening? If Pierre's in Clichy, why are you here?' Renée doesn't answer. 'But he isn't, is he? He's in Saint-Germain-en-Laye.'

'He's going to come back. I know he is.'

'He wasn't there to start with, Renée. I know Pierre better than he knows himself. Whatever passion he possesses goes into his work. There isn't anything left over.'

'You must be a bit like that, too. You're both painters.'

'I could never be that single-minded. I'm a man and women matter to me. Human beings matter to me.'

'No one matters to you. You're the same. You're all the same. You take what you can get and afterwards you couldn't give a damn. No wonder Caro left you.' Renée needs her exit from the studio to be dramatic. She can't bear to creep away humiliated for the second time. Roussel is sitting on the chaise longue with his legs apart and his hands draped between his knees. Now that it's just the two of them, she might have talked to him. But she remembers how he treated her that day when she was in the café and how Caro has betrayed her. She gets up and flounces out.

He doesn't follow her. She pauses on the landing to do up her coat and rearrange her hair. Inside the studio, she hears the clink of glass as Roussel pours himself another drink. She grips the bannister and feels her way downstairs. There's no light in the stairwell. She steps out onto the pavement.

She has no idea what time it is. The rain has stopped but there's a chill wind. She had kept her coat on in the studio and now she feels the difference. She pulls up the collar and heads for the Boulevard du Montparnasse where she can take the tram or find a cab.

The key to her apartment is inside the pocket of her coat, but as she nears the tram stop Renée realises she's left her bag inside the studio and in it is her purse. She has no choice now but to walk the six kilometres from Montparnasse to Clichy. She takes refuge in the doorway of a shop. Her anger has used up whatever energy she had.

She whimpers with frustration. It's not just the prospect of the walk. She wonders if Roussel will look inside the bag. Of course he will. She would if it were her. There's nothing in there of importance: lipstick, rouge, a metro ticket, maybe, and of course, the purse. Then she remembers something else. There is an inside pocket, with a zip, in which she keeps her *carte d'identité* and which contains the letter she received while she was living in the rue des Peupliers with Marguerite, the one that told the whole world what she was.

She'd told Pierre she had destroyed it. Now she wonders why she didn't. Did she keep the letter to remind her what could happen to a girl like her unless she took care to secure her future? She occasionally took it out and read it. It was like a hair shirt that she wore in private under the expensive blouses and the camisoles. But once Roussel has found it, it will not be private any longer. In her mind's eye, Renée sees the painters in the café passing round the note and laughing. Caro had betrayed her. Was there any reason to suppose that Roussel wouldn't, too?

She has been standing in the doorway for the past ten minutes and twice men have slowed down as they walked past. She can't stay like this. She turns and looks back down the street in the direction she's just come from.

It is less than a quarter of an hour since she left the studio. Roussel is sitting on the sofa with his back to her. She waits until she's sure he hasn't heard her coming up the staircase. He remains hunched over with his head bent. Renée sees her bag still looped over the chair back.

She creeps over to the chaise longue. She has never looked at Roussel from behind. His hair is flecked with grey and while the shirt he's wearing is expensive, Renée sees that it is threadbare at the neck. Since leaving Isabelle he clearly hasn't bothered keeping up appearances, but he seems more at home in his run-down atelier than Renée is in her apartment in rue Clapeyron. 'A box' is how Roussel described it and this is exactly what it's come to feel like.

Rather than risk going round in front of Roussel, she leans over him. She has secured her fingers round the strap and is about to ease it off the chair back when his hand darts out and closes round her wrist.

'Well, if it's not the little princess. Changed your mind?'

'I left my bag behind. That's all I've come for.' Renée struggles but he holds on.

'There's no need to rush back to your gilded cage. The door won't close until the bird's inside.'

'Why would I spend time in a dump like this when I've got four rooms to myself in Clichy?'

'You know you could cut yourself to ribbons on that tongue of yours.' He lets her go.

She slots the bag across her shoulder 'Let me leave, then. You won't have to listen to it.'

'I like listening to it. It reminds me what it was like living with a woman. Are they programmed to complain from birth?'

'Yours probably had plenty to complain about.'

'Ah yes, I had forgotten all those little tête-à-têtes you had with Caro.'

'What about the ones she had with you?'

'She took a childish pleasure in revealing secrets. I suppose it gave her some control over her life.' Roussel goes over to the workbench and begins to squeeze paint out onto the palette. Renée watches as he riffles through the brushes till he finds the one he wants.

'What are you doing?'

'Since I haven't got a home to go to, I sleep in the daytime now and work at night. I'd just come back from having breakfast when I saw you.'

'If you're going to ignore me, there's not much point in me staying.'

'I thought you weren't staying anyway.'

'I'm not.' She takes a step towards the door.

'So Pierre is taking you to Rome,' says Roussel without looking up. 'I wonder why.'

'Why shouldn't he?'

'I'm just surprised that he'd choose Rome.'

'He didn't. We were looking at a drawing of the Colosseum. I said I would like to see it.'

Roussel nods. He squeezes out a worm of cadmium and adds a touch of yellow and a scoop of lead white, mashing them into an oyster pink. He starts to hum.

She lowers herself down onto the sofa. 'It's not what you think.'

'What isn't?'

'That girl. When I asked him, he said he'd forgotten all about her.'

'Did he?' Roussel turns back to the easel. 'You're afraid that's what all this has been about; that it's not really you we're fighting over?'

'Why should I care? It was years ago.'

'You do, though, don't you?' he says, quietly.

Renée doesn't answer. Roussel reaches underneath the workbench for a rag.

'Be careful, Renée.'

'What's that meant to mean?'

'You're not like Caro, but there's one respect in which you are like her. You let things happen to you.'

'What did she let happen to her?' Inside the expensive shoes, the blisters on her toes feel raw. She wishes she could kick the shoes off, but she'd never get them on again. Has Roussel found out Caro's whereabouts himself? she wonders.

'My guess is that Caro will have found herself another minder.'

'She's all right, then.'

'She's all right. But you're not.'

'I don't need another minder.'

'You need someone to look after you.'

'I told you . . .'

'You might fool the others, Renée, but you don't fool me. We were both tempted by the promise of a more fulfilling life and cast adrift. Believe me, I know what that feels like. You yearn to be better than you are; you look for somebody who's better educated, more refined, a person who can teach you something. Then you find out they can't teach you anything. You move on. But each time you leave someone, you leave something behind, you see, until at last there's nothing left to leave. You're travelling with an empty suitcase. It's the only thing you have to barter with.'

Is this what Marguerite meant? She feels almost paralysed with weariness. 'I must go.'

Roussel shrugs. He turns back to the easel and starts

dabbing paint onto the canvas. Renée goes on sitting there. It's stuffy in the room; the heavy scent of paint and linseed oil seems to have drained the oxygen out of the air.

A door slams somewhere in the building. Renée jumps. She makes a pawing gesture with her hands but there is nothing to cling on to. She sinks back. A floorboard creaks, as if the room is settling down around her. Somewhere in the distance, Roussel is still humming. It's a tune she's heard somewhere before. It's from that opera Pierre is always singing snatches from. The sound is not as far away now. Suddenly it feels as if it's all around her. There's an urgency about it that reminds her of a swarm of insects looking for a place to settle. Then it stops.

From the balcony in Saint-Germain you have a clear view of the road. I see her long before she sees me. It's apparent from the way she's walking – hesitantly, looking round her all the time – that she's not just out for a stroll. The clip-clop of her heels goes through my head like tin tacks. As she snips the shadows of the trees beside the road, the yellow flowers on her dress turn black. The hat she's wearing shades her face, but I can see how young she is.

I step back from the balcony. I could pretend there's nobody at home. Perhaps she'll walk on by. But I don't want her coming up the path. I'm rushing now to reach the gate before she can unlatch it.

'This is not the house you're looking for,' I want to shout. 'And anyway, he's not here.'

'Marthe. Is it all right if I call you that?' She gives a little smile that wavers at the edges when she sees the look on my face. I may not be married to him – she will be aware of that – but I will not have her referring to me as if we were equals.

'No,' I say. 'I would prefer it if you didn't.' In the space behind her eyes, a door shuts. 'I shall call you Mademoiselle. My title is Madame.'

The little bit of confidence she had has fallen at the first fence. She looks round. The door behind her is still open. If I were to say 'Shoo', she'd turn round and bolt. I'm trying not to look at her, but most of all I don't want her to look at me. She's probably already seen me in the pictures. Half of Paris has me on their walls. They know exactly what I looked like a quarter of a century ago. Pierre might not have noticed that I don't look like that any more, but she can't fail to.

'Do you know who I am?'

'Pierre's floozy,' I am on the point of saying, but I leave it up to her to introduce herself. I'd hoped that she would have the kind of used look models have in Paris, but I can see straightaway that Renée isn't one of these, not yet. She's beautiful; no doubt about it. She has dainty feet in shoes that must have cost a fortune and her stockings are expensive. I stare blandly at her. I'm not giving anything away. 'Why have you come here?'

She's begun to wonder that herself. 'I hadn't heard from him for several days. I was afraid he might be ill.'

'A relative of his has died.'

'Oh.' Sympathy is battling with relief. 'I didn't know.'

'There isn't any reason why you should.'

She looks round. 'So he isn't here?'

I would have thought that much was obvious. The idea that she is here alone with me is not that comforting, perhaps. 'He's gone back to the family home in Fontenay.'

'I see.'

'He hasn't talked to you about his family?'

'No, only you. He talks a lot about you.'

Now she's started, it's all coming out at once. Her cheeks are flushed; she's nervous and the words are tumbling over one another. She's afraid that if she leaves gaps in the conversation they might open up and swallow her. Pierre won't thank her when he finds she's been here. He might jumble things together when he's painting, but he doesn't like his life to be a muddle. He would never have allowed her to walk into our home like this – stray cats, maybe, mice, yes, anything on four legs, but not Renée Montchaty. He will have wanted to keep her at bay.

'This must be quite a shock,' she says. 'I know you've been together for a long time.'

'Yes, we have.'

'Although of course he isn't married to you,' she says, in a sideways swipe.

'Nor you, either,' I say, brutally.

'No, but he's asked me.'

Is she lying? I keep my voice flat. 'You'd be a fool to pin your hopes on that,' I say. 'Pierre is married to his work. He's fond of animals and he prefers his women when they are as much like animals as possible. The objects in his living room are next in line. I've seen him passionate about the butter dish, for instance. He's head over heels in love with that old radiator. Oh yes, you would probably be in there somewhere, as a blob of yellow maybe or a stripe of purple – not much more than that. Are you sure it's enough for you?'

'It's more than anybody else has offered me.'

I wonder why. She has the sort of looks most men in Paris would go crazy over.

'Will you let him go?' This is the question she's come here to ask.

'It isn't up to me.'

'You want him to be happy, don't you?'

'You think you can make him happy? You're a child.' This upstart of a girl is starting to annoy me. 'You have no idea what you'd be taking on.'

'I'd learn. I'd learn from him. We'd both learn. Fifty isn't old.'

'Too old to start again, you'll find.'

She goes to speak and stops. She knows I'm right. 'You're not a bit as I imagined,' she says, stubbornly.

I stick my chin out. 'What did you imagine?'

'Once when we had been comparing animals to people, Pierre said you were like a mole inside the body of a wren.'

'What sort of animal were you, then?'

She's begun to wish she hadn't started on this tack. 'A whippet.'

'What about Pierre? He must have been an ostrich.'

I imagine all their post-coital conversations, giggling like children as they tore apart the world we had inhabited for quarter of a century.

'I thought you'd be a bit more ...'

'Like a mole?' Now she's embarrassed. Meeting me must be a challenge, if a mole was what she was expecting. Think of Jane Eyre meeting Mrs Rochester. I never read the book, but Pierre read bits of it to me in bed.

'I'd hoped we could be friends.'

'A whippet and a mole? That isn't very likely. Did Pierre suggest you came?'

'No. I just happened to be passing.' Now she's blushing. She's aware of what she's just said. This is not the sort of place you happen to be passing. 'Would you rather not to have met me?'

If she'd asked me in advance, I would have said no. I'd have been afraid by the comparison between us – her eyes, my eyes, her skin, my skin, her age, my age. All I have on my side is the fact that I have been here longer. She is like an orchid in a cabbage patch. Her eyes are hungrily devouring the objects in the room – the vase of flowers on the window-sill, the rug, the cat curled up on the settee, the pipe next to the fruit bowl and the spent match on the plate. She wants to understand the world he lives in when he's not with her, so she can recreate it somewhere else.

'Don't look!' I want to scream. 'How can you cast your eyes around our home? As if you haven't plundered it enough already!'

'Pierre, I'm sorry! Don't be angry.'

'You went to the house in Saint-Germain! But why?'

'I wanted to see where you lived when you were not with me. I thought if I could picture you there, I would feel less lonely.'

'But you knew that I'd gone back to speak to Marthe. Couldn't you have waited?'

'I did wait. I waited eight days! I thought I would go mad waiting.' Should she tell him that she did go mad, that after eight days she could not endure another minute on her own?

'It was more difficult than I'd imagined. I had no choice but to put it off. There was a crisis in the family.'

'Marthe told me. You'd gone to a funeral. I'm sorry.'

'What did Marthe say to you?'

'It was as if she had been waiting for me.'

Pierre puts one hand to his forehead, drawing in the skin towards the centre with his thumb and forefinger.

'She wasn't what I had expected. I thought she would be more homely, somehow. You know, like my mother.'

'Like your mother!'

Renée reaches for his hand. She needs Pierre to reassure

her that what's happened won't make any difference to the two of them, but she knows it already has.

'I wish you hadn't done this,' he says.

I sit with my hands clasped in my lap. I haven't even looked at him yet.

'Dear one, tell me what's the matter?' He takes off his overcoat and kneels down next to me. He reaches for my hand, but I withdraw it, like a child refusing to be comforted.

'You let that woman come into our home and then you ask me what the matter is!'

'I didn't know that she was coming.' Pierre pulls up a chair. Perhaps he's feeling at a disadvantage down there on his knees.

'You haven't been like this with any of the others,' I say. Now's the moment to point out that every time he strayed, I knew about it. He is looking at me now as if I haven't just confronted him with something that he thought I didn't know. Like all the other things we've never told each other, it's as if it simply slipped our minds.

'The others weren't important,' he says.

What he's saying is that this one is. I wish I hadn't asked. 'How did you meet her?'

'She was on her way to work at Printemps. You remember?'

'Like me. I was on my way to work, the first time you set eyes on me. You're lucky you don't get arrested, going up to women in the street like that.' He gives a joyless laugh. 'How long before you slept with her?'

'Don't torture yourself like this, Marthe.'

'How long?' I insist.

'A long time; that's all.'

So it could have started years ago. Perhaps the last time I

thought he had been unfaithful, it was her he was unfaithful
with.

'It's just something that happened, Marthe. Neither of
us wanted it.'

He makes it sound so reasonable and in a way it is. What
right have I got to deny him someone who has captivated
his attention in the way that I did quarter of a century ago.
But it is this that breaks my heart and makes me wilful – I
have no choice.

Yesterday, he pointed to three overlapping apples in a still
life and said, 'That's us.'

'There are three of them,' I said.

'Yes,' said Pierre.

This evening when he comes downstairs, I'm chopping
onions in the kitchen. Usually I wait until he's in the room
before I start preparing dinner so that he can watch me
doing it. I may be only standing at the stove but what I'm
doing is important if he's watching me. It's like we're doing
it together. When I turn round this time, he's still watching
me but there's a glazed look on his face and I know that it
isn't me he's seeing. It's her. Then I slam the knife down and
he jumps.

'Don't bother sitting down to dinner with me if the only
person you can think about is that whore!' I shout. I can't
bear the noise my voice makes. I sound like a fishwife. I told
Pierre my surname was 'de Méligny', but if I really were 'de
Méligny', I wouldn't be reacting like this.

'Renée's not a whore,' Pierre says. And he gets up quietly
and leaves the room.

I'm wondering if I should bring the chopper down across
my wrist. It's hard to know what Pierre's thinking at the best
of times, but when I shouted at him something happened to

his face. It was as if he had been looking at the same thing for a long time and had just seen something different in it. It was not so much discovery as disappointment. If he didn't know before, he knows now which class I belong to.

I should go up after him. I did get halfway up the stairs once. I was going to say, 'All right, if it means so much to you, you'd better go to her.' But not to know what they were doing, now that I know she exists, imagining the worst ... I'd rather he was here, unhappy, cursing me.

'I'm going to get out of Paris for a while.'

'If you want me to leave, you only have to say so.'

'Don't be silly, Marthe,' he says. 'This is your home. Where else would you go?' He doesn't say he doesn't want me to; he only says I couldn't. 'Stupid Marthe,' he might just as easily have said. 'You surely don't think after all this time that you can get by on your own?' He's right. I need the fruit bowl and the butter dish, the rugs and curtains just as much as he does. It's as if the whole house and its contents have been grafted onto me.

I've seen Pierre weep when the cat knocked something off the mantelpiece. At the beginning, I'd say, 'Don't fret. I can get another one. It didn't cost much.' Then I realised that what he was suffering was grief. And yet he's talking about leaving me. Am I the only object in the house he can get by without?

'I want to visit Rome. I'm going there with Renée,' he says.

No, I think. I can't be hearing this. It doesn't make sense, any of it. Pierre, who likes the things around him to be ordinary and familiar, faced with all that grand art, those vast buildings.

'Are you going to be coming back?' I have to ask this.

How can I get through the days unless I know there is an end to them?

'I won't be coming back to this house,' he says. 'Renée...' For a man who doesn't trust words, this is hard for him to say. 'We shall be getting married,' he says, finally, and gives a little sigh as if to marry Renée is the saddest thing imaginable. And for me it is.

'You'll miss the animals,' I say.

His mouth curls. 'Yes,' he says. 'I shall. And I shall miss you too.'

'Then why go?' is what I would like to shout out. But I don't. In the silence, I can hear the clock tick. It's the one that stopped at five o'clock in every picture. I feel angry that it goes on ticking now. 'Life goes on,' it says, cheerily. 'Tick, tock.'

I stand there dumbly and eventually he takes my arms and kisses me.

'Is this your daughter's first experience of Italy?'

Pierre replies without the slightest hesitation. 'It's the first time she's been out of France.'

The woman looks at her with wide eyes. 'What a marvellous adventure for you. Rome is wonderful!'

'I've told her that,' says Pierre. 'She's looking forward to it, aren't you, darling?'

He smiles down at her. She leans her head against his shoulder and pretends to doze. The woman whispers to him, 'What a beautiful young girl; you must be very proud of her.'

'Yes,' says Pierre. 'I am.'

Her little boy is playing with a toy car, running it along the ledge beside the window. Next to him, his sister's playing with a doll. She's talking to it and she looks up coyly every now and then to see if Pierre is looking at her. The performance is for him. His smile is distant but it is enough. If she were ten years older she would be behaving in the same way, shyly giving him the 'come on'.

Renée feels a wave of jealousy. She'd thought the ring Pierre had bought her would transform her magically in other people's eyes, but no one bothers looking at her hands; they have already come to a decision about who and what she is. She's either this man's daughter or she is his whore. The silver band is too discreet. She'd hoped for something more substantial, but presumably that's why he chose it. If it was a wedding ring it would be gold, so even if she does succeed in bringing it to people's notice it will only reinforce what they already know – that she is not what she pretends to be.

The woman leaves the train at Lazio. 'I hope you have a lovely trip,' she says.

Pierre helps them with their baggage, summoning a porter. When he comes back, he finds Renée staring from the window.

'Anyone would think you did this all the time, the way you answered her.'

'Believe me, it's not something I would do from choice.'

Does he mean being here at all, or posing as her father? 'Are you going to pretend that's what you are when we arrive at the hotel?'

'I can't. They'll want to see our passports.'

'Won't you be embarrassed?'

'I'll try not to be. They charge enough. I'm paying them to turn a blind eye.'

'What if they say no?'

'Then we'll go somewhere else.' His nerves are on edge. When he signs the register in the hotel, the man behind the counter in reception glances at her. When the porter brings their bags up, Pierre tips him. Once the man has gone, he leans against the door a moment with his eyes closed.

There's a choice when they go down to breakfast of meat, cheese, papaya, cereal and croissants. Renée orders everything. Pierre makes do with coffee and a slice of brioche. 'Aren't you hungry?'

'Not as hungry as you seem to be.'

'It's so delicious. Did you ever see so much food all at once?'

'You'd better save some space for lunch.'

'We're having lunch too? Aren't there any shortages in Italy?'

'There may be now.' He smiles. 'You ought to have some lire on you so that if you get lost you can take a cab or buy yourself an ice. And you should memorise the name of the hotel.'

'To listen to you, anyone would think you were my father.' Now that they've got over the misunderstanding on the train, she can start teasing him about it. After all, if anybody was to feel insulted it would be Pierre. In restaurants, he lets her choose things from the menu that she likes the sound of and then tells her what they are. She is his lover and his little girl. Now that her family is lost to her, Pierre is standing in for all of them.

Occasionally, she thinks of Caro. She has not told anyone that she's seen Caro. At the start she was preoccupied with what was happening in her own life. Later, Caro seemed irrelevant. No one had mentioned her for months. Somewhere inside her head she's thinking that she might have shared the same fate. She is thankful to have left that life behind her. It's strange how irrevocably 'past' all that seems now – the café, Caro, Roussel, even Margo. It's as if a door has shut on it.

There's been no word from Pierre since they left. Perhaps that woman is already Madame Bonnard. Once he's married her, she'll be respectable and I shall be the harlot. Our roles will have been reversed. He's marrying her, I suppose, to show me there's no going back. If there's a message, it's for me, not her. I wander through the house imagining them in a carriage on the train, the country slipping by outside the window, Renée chattering, Pierre not saying anything, just looking, noticing the way the powder on her cheeks is pink with greenish shadows in the hollows, how the lilac of her eyes affects the colour of the scarf around her neck. She'll ask him what he's thinking and he'll smile. He isn't thinking anything, he'll say, he's looking. She needs nobody to tell her that she's beautiful. She'll know it every time she looks into a mirror. She could have had anyone. So why destroy me?

There's a moment when I wake up in the morning and I feel quite normal and then I remember what it is that's lurking in the shadows. Even if there isn't such a thing in pictures as an empty space, in life there is. The rash is getting worse. I lie for hours in the bath, but even in the water it's as if there are ants crawling over me. Because the water dulls the pain, the tramlines I make with my nails across the skin are deeper. Sometimes I draw blood. I watch it seep into the water and make swirling, cloud-like patterns and I think, 'Pierre would find that beautiful. He would be captivated by the swirls of red dissolving. He would turn my suffering into art.'

The first week, all they do is eat and sleep and see the sights. They follow lunch with a siesta. Sleep comes easily and when they wake up they make love and lie there with the windows open and the roar and bustle of the city down below. The curiosity that greeted them when they arrived has faded, or perhaps they're simply getting used to people in the hotel staring at them. Sometimes, when she wakes up, she sees Pierre is sketching on the balcony. He comes in once he knows that she's awake.

She's never been as happy as she is now, Renée tells herself. For once there isn't anything she longs for, nothing that she wishes hadn't happened, or had happened differently, except perhaps the night she had been lured by loneliness to Roussel's studio. But like so many other things that she associates with that time, it's been docketed and filed away. Her whole life up till now has been a preparation for this moment. Renée wishes she could stop it moving on. She tries to slow the seconds down by concentrating hard on each thing individually – a grey hair in Pierre's beard, the small patch above his pocket where the weave has parted and been darned by Marthe with a thread that's one shade lighter than the jacket, the small scar on Pierre's knuckle that he got when he was dragged along a gravel pathway by the family dog when he was four years old. She tries to stash the images away inside her head, so that they're there for later.

When she puts her hand into the *Bocca della Verità*, she says she loves him and it doesn't bite her hand off, so it must be true. It is their destiny to be together. They will make each other happy and then no one else will matter.

They are in the square outside the Vatican. He hasn't taken out his sketchbook, but she sees him pat his pocket to make sure it's there. He turns to her. 'What would you like to see, dear?'

'Can I see what you were drawing last time you were here?'

'The *Laocoön*? Yes, if you like.' He guides her to the entrance of the Vatican Museums. They walk endlessly down corridors that open into larger spaces and then there, in front of her, is an enormous sculpture of three figures struggling to escape from serpents coiled around their bodies. She is shocked that there are life-sized statues of nude figures in the Vatican. They represent the suffering of humanity, Pierre says. She knows from the way he's looking at it that it's not the statue that's preoccupying him.

'You brought your sketchbook. Did you want to draw it?'

'Oh no, that's not what I had in mind.'

What did he have in mind? she wonders. He is gazing at the statue with a fixed expression.

'She'd be old now,' Renée says.

He turns his eyes on her. 'Who?'

'That girl.'

Pierre looks at her a moment and she wonders whether he's comparing them. He takes her arm. 'Let's go and see the Sistine ceiling,' he says.

Pierre has locked the workroom. What is in there that I'm not supposed to see? I check the row of keys on hooks next to the back door. That one's missing. In the end, I find a chisel in the scullery and force the lock. There is a sharp crack as the spring goes.

He has left a roll of canvas stacked against the far wall with the string still holding it together. Normally I wouldn't dream of touching anything in there, but it's like finding someone's diary in a drawer. You have to look inside it, even though you know that what you find might hurt you.

Pierre likes to paint the picture first, then cut it down.

There have been times when I've been in it one day and the next there's just a hand or half a head. There are four paintings altogether, on a single canvas. She's in every one of them and here she isn't simply posing. She is sitting at the table with me. Sometimes she's there helping me to lay it. She stands in the doorway watching while I feed the cats. She stands beside the window gazing out onto the garden or steals quietly up the stairs when I'm not looking. We don't speak. Pierre won't lie to that extent.

There is a book about Italian cities open on the workbench. I had never been abroad before I met Pierre. I turn the pages till I come to Rome. It's big. It's only when I see a photograph of the piazza with Saint Peter's in the background and the crowds like swarms of ants in front of it, that Paris suddenly seems small. I can imagine Pierre and Renée walking arm in arm through the museums, Pierre explaining patiently, as he once did to me, why one work or another is regarded as a masterpiece.

'You like it then?' I asked once when we stood in front of a Uccello in the Louvre. How was I to know if I should like it, when I didn't know if he did?

'I respect it,' he said. That seemed odd until I learnt that it's impossible to love something you don't respect. Respect without love, that was possible. But not the other way around.

'I thought I might go out alone this morning,' he says one day over breakfast. 'I would like to do some drawing.'

'Can't I come?'

'Of course, but won't you find it boring? Wouldn't you prefer to find a café where you can sit for an hour with a cake, or spend the morning in the gardens?'

He suggests the Villa Ada. There are butterflies so huge

they look like kites. 'If you sit still, they come and settle on your arms,' he tells her. They are not the only things, unfortunately. Men look back over their shoulders when they've passed her. One begins to talk to her. He sits down. Renée shifts up, but he moves up with her, till she's wedged into a corner. He keeps pointing to the butterflies. 'Farfalla', he says, and then grins at her and nods. He wants her to repeat the word. She gets up. He calls after her.

'Va-t-en!'

He laughs. He doesn't think she means it. They would never dream of pestering their own girls, but then you don't often see them walking by themselves. No girl would do what she's done – go off with a man who has a wife already, or as good as, try to make out that she's married to him, let him book them into hotels as a couple and then leave their passports on the counter so that anyone who cares to look inside can see immediately what they're up to. If she felt bad when she was in Paris, she feels worse here.

She can't shake this man off. 'Non!' she shouts. 'Non, non, non!' Even somebody like him must get the gist of that. He stops and stares at her. And then he throws his head back, waggling it from side to side. 'Si!' he says. 'Si, si, si!'

Why doesn't someone help her? She keeps walking till she reaches the hotel. He's still there, needling her now that he senses he's not getting anywhere. When she begins to climb the steps, he stops. He spits the last few words, then melts into the crowd.

She's shaking when she gets up to their room. She wants Pierre to put his arms around her, but he isn't there. She waits an hour and a half.

'You're back already, darling,' he says, taking off his jacket. 'Did you have a nice time?' He sits down beside her. When

Pierre's been working, he gives off a special scent. It's full and rounded. When he isn't working, or it isn't going well, there is a non-scent, but it has a whiff of something sour. If she hadn't spent so much time on that bloody perfume counter, she would be less sensitive. If he was less preoccupied, he might have noticed that the scent she's giving off is not one you would pay good money for.

She has two choices. She can cry so that he feels obliged to comfort her, or she can whinge because he's left her on her own and she feels vulnerable. She can't decide and so she does both. First of all she cries and then she snaps at him. Eventually, when she's got it all out of her system, she lies quietly in his arms and goes to sleep. She wakes up half an hour later and he's sitting in the window. Her first thought is that he's drawing, and she feels a rush of anger. Then she sees he isn't doing anything. He's staring out over the square.

He turns. 'How are you?' This time he does not say 'darling.'

'I'm all right.'

'What happened when you went into the gardens? Do you want to tell me?'

'An Italian started pestering me. I was frightened.' She tries not to sound pathetic. Where she lived in rue des Peupliers she ran the risk of being pestered every time she put her foot outside the door. 'He didn't seem to understand the French for "Go away".'

Pierre nods. 'It's because you're fair. Italian women all have dark hair. You're a novelty.'

'I think it's more because he saw that I was on my own.'

'A combination of the two, perhaps.' He moves the chair back from the window and puts on his jacket. 'It's as well you woke up. Any minute now, the gong will go for dinner.'

She untangles herself from the counterpane. 'I'm sorry you were frightened. We'll go out together from now on.'

It's what she wanted him to say but it sounds grudging, as if he suspects she made the story up in order to achieve this. Normally they chatter over dinner about what they've seen that day. After they'd visited Saint Peter's, Pierre told her about the argument between the Pope and Michelangelo over the Sistine ceiling. On it, you can see God disappearing off into the clouds after he's finished the creation and he's got no clothes on.

'It's the only painting of God's bottom anywhere in Christendom,' Pierre said.

Then there's Donatello's *David* with this silly hat. Pierre said Donatello was a homosexual – that's why his *David* was so lean and sinewy and wore a hat with flowers on it. Michelangelo was homosexual as well, but there's no doubt his *David* is a man. There seem to be a lot of artists like that. Pierre says it's because they needed to be sensitive as well as strong. 'You manage,' she said and he smiled, which made her wonder whether there was something she had missed.

'Where did you go to draw?' she asks him, finally.

'The Church of Santa Croce. Later on, I did some drawings in the ruins. You can see them later if you like.'

She nods. She ought to have been more enthusiastic, but it's as if he is justifying having left her on her own by showing her the work he's done. 'What do you want to do tomorrow, then?'

'Why don't you choose?' he answers, carefully.

'I don't know what there is to choose from.'

'We could hire a car and go into the countryside.'

'Not look at art, you mean?'

'The best things in museums tend to be the windows. And a day off wouldn't go amiss, in any case.'

'For me?'
'For both of us.'

It's no use. I have tried but I can't bear it any more. The whole house has become a mausoleum. I still fill the bath mechanically each morning and it gives me some relief, but once I'm in I feel I might as well just sink under the surface and allow my head to go the same way as my body. What would Pierre do then? Perhaps he'd simply sit down on the footstool in the bathroom and do what he's done each morning since we came here – look at me.

I say that, but the truth is that he hasn't looked at me for years. What other woman looks the same at fifty as she did when she was eighteen? Twenty-four, that is. He got it right then. He'd immortalised me once. What more could any woman ask? And would I rather he'd kept up with me as I got older? Pierre was always honest in his portraits of himself. If he had painted someone else like that, it would have seemed unkind. He wasn't merciless, except when it came down to looking at himself.

Mind you, who'd want a picture of an old crone hanging on their walls? The bathroom pictures never sold well. There must be a hundred of them upstairs in the studio. I will say one thing for Pierre; he never cared much whether people bought the work or not. He did it for himself.

I'm filling up the bath and thinking how nice it would be to feel the water all around me. *All* around me. I get in and sink up to my neck. It feels good. If I raise my knees and stretch them out again, it makes waves and the water sweeps across my breasts.

How long would I be lying here before they found me? They were going for a month and it's been less than three weeks. I imagine Pierre walking through the downstairs rooms and calling. He will look in all the other rooms first, knowing that if I am in the bath I shan't be getting out of it again.

What happens to the skin when it has been in water for a week? Will it have cured the rash? Perhaps my skin will finally be like it was when Pierre first painted it. Of course it might be night when he comes back. He'll have to bring the lamp upstairs and stand there in the doorway, straining to see whether that dark shadow in the bath is me. Was me.

There is a scratching at the door. Poucette jumps up onto the stool beside the bath. What will I do about the animals? I had forgotten them. I've not left any food out. What will happen when tomorrow they discover there is no milk in the saucer, that the herring I get every weekend from the market isn't in the bowl, that there is no lap to curl up on in the evening? I ought to have given this more thought.

The water's getting cold. When you first get into the bath it's as if arms are wrapping you in an embrace, but then you feel the temperature dropping by the second. It's too late to put my head under the water. You would think that once you'd made your mind up, you could do it any time; an hour more or less is neither here nor there. But other things get in the way – the animals, the laundry, getting to the market, hunger. I stand up and wrap the towel around me. Poucette jumps down from the stool.

Deciding not to kill myself – at least not yet – has given me an unexpected lift. I give the cats an extra helping of the herring and decide that I'll prepare myself a proper meal this evening. I imagine Pierre sitting in the corner, watching me. I move as if I'm only there for him to draw. I turn the peppers slowly in the pan. I think about how this will look once it's been drawn and wonder if I'll ever be there in another painting. Poucette smells the herring on my fingers. I hold out my hand and feel the rough tongue graze my knuckles.

Will I go mad, locked up in this house where every object interlocks with every other, where you can't take anything away without the rest collapsing? Maybe other people live like this. How would I know? If I had really been eighteen when we began to live together, I suppose I would have thought of it as normal. If I hadn't seen my father hurling crockery across the kitchen and my mother tearing off the tablecloth before the contents of whatever had been toppled seeped into the fabric, where the only routine was the constant threat of violence, how could I have borne the luxury of so much constancy?

It's cooler once they reach the outskirts of the city. They go up into the hills and drive on to Frascati. Pierre says that the wooded slopes here were created by volcanic action. Pine needles are spread over the ground like matting. She knows from the way he's looking at the landscape that he'd like to get his sketchbook out, but he has left it in the hotel. Normally he takes it everywhere, so she knows it's deliberate. He's brought a picnic with a folding table, two chairs and a cold box with a bottle of Prosecco.

Renée goes out of her way to tempt him with the food. She takes small bites of things and puts them in his mouth. She tells him he should take his hat off, so he doesn't have that line of white between his hairline and his eyes that makes his face look like Venetian blinds. She's chattering and if she goes on too long he'll stop listening, so once lunch is over she spreads out the rug. Pierre takes his jacket off and folds it carefully. He puts his hat on top of it and then he stretches out beside her and she wraps her arms around him.

It's the sharpness of the air that wakes her up. She's shivering. Pierre is lying with his eyes half-closed.

'What time is it?'

He takes his pocket watch out. 'Half past six.'

'We'll be too late for supper at the hotel,' she says, desperately, and he laughs.

'It doesn't matter. If you're hungry we'll have dinner somewhere else.'

'I think I've caught the sun. My skin feels hot, but underneath it's cold.'

Pierre wraps his jacket round her. By the time they reach the hotel, she feels feverish. That night she dreams she's woken on the picnic and found Pierre with the paring knife they've used to peel the fruit protruding from that little hollow underneath his Adam's apple. There's a single spot of blood, but it's on her. She tries to pull the knife out, but it's stuck and when it finally comes loose it brings his beard and chin away with it. There's just his mouth, then nothing.

'Renée'. Pierre is shaking her. 'Wake up. You're dreaming. What on earth's the matter?' She begins to sob. He's worried that the people in the rooms on either side of them might hear.

'I dreamt that you were dead.'

'Well, as you see, I'm not.'

'And I dreamt it was me who'd killed you.'

'Ah.' He says 'Ah' as if now he understands. But what is there to understand? He presses one hand on her forehead. 'Here.' He pours a glass of water. 'You must drink as much as possible. You're feverish.'

She spends the night alternately cocooned under an extra eiderdown and throwing off the blankets. By the morning, she's exhausted. Pierre arranges to have breakfast brought up on a tray. 'You'd better stay in bed this morning.'

'What will you do?' she asks, trying not to make it sound as though she thinks he's engineered this for his own advantage.

'I shall stay here with you.'

Now she's feeling guilty. 'No, I'll be all right,' she says, reluctantly. 'You go and draw.'

'I'll draw here. I can sit out on the balcony.'

From where she's lying, she can prop her head up on the bolster so he's in her line of sight. Once he has settled down, he starts to hum under his breath. He's soon oblivious to everything. She wonders whether Marthe feels this kind of loneliness. His head is turned away from her, but she can see the outline of his face. He bunches up his shoulders when he draws, as if his drawing needs protection. He protects her in the same way, but she knows she'll never mean as much to him as this.

The sun moves round until it's in his eyes. The heat is building up inside the room. They ought to close the shutters now or by the middle of the afternoon there will be nowhere they can go to get away from it. In Paris you don't see the sun from one month to the next. In Rome there is too much of everything – sun, food, religion, art, but shade is what you long for in the end.

She's better by the next day and Pierre suggests they spend the morning at the Villa Medici. The Medici were like a Mafia; they ran the city as if it belonged to them. If anybody crossed them, they would have them murdered – even children, if the wrong one was in line to take the throne. The one good thing they did, Pierre says, was to patronise the arts. They paid for everything in Rome between the 15th and the 16th centuries – banks, churches, palaces, the paintings inside and the sculptures outside.

She would rather they had been a bit less generous. She

follows Pierre through the rooms, which all look just the same. The sight of so much grandeur is exciting when you see it for the first time, but it palls. She hangs on Pierre's arm. She wants everyone who passes them to know that they're together. He detaches himself sometimes, so that he can go up to a painting and look closely at it. That's the way he makes it look, but what he's telling her is that he'd rather be here on his own. He isn't showing her his sketches any more. He sometimes takes the sketchbook out and makes a few marks. 'Records', he says. Then he puts it back into his pocket and they go on walking. It would be more sensible for him to go off on his own; she knows that, but she's frightened that if she begins to let him go, he won't come back. She thinks of Caro. Caro's shadowy existence has become a metaphor for all that could still happen in her own life. He is all she has now.

'Please allow me, Signorina.' It's a man she's noticed sitting with his wife and daughter in the hotel restaurant. She's seen them looking round and whispering to one another when she takes her seat at table next to Pierre.

There's no one in the hotel under fifty, other than the daughter. Pierre does not encourage anyone's familiarity. He is polite, but distant. They would have done better staying in a *pension* where no one bothered who they were or where they came from. Here the atmosphere is so respectable, it's stultifying.

Renée has twice passed the man outside her room. She'd sensed an interest in the way he looked at her and as he takes the fob from her and fits the key into the lock, she knows that this will be the prelude to a series of ingratiating overtures that will eventually finish with him pressing her against the wall in one or other of the hotel corridors and fumbling underneath her dress.

He pushes the door open and holds up the key. She has to reach for it and, when she does, he moves it fractionally away.

'The doors in the hotel are very stiff,' he says. 'I often have to struggle with the key to get mine open.'

'I find this one opens fairly easily,' says Renée. He must have seen Pierre walk out of the hotel that morning after breakfast. She reclaims her key and turns to go into the room, but he is in the way. 'Excuse me.'

'You and your ... er ...' he looks innocently at her with his eyebrows raised, 'are finding your stay here in Rome enjoyable?'

'Yes, thank you.'

'I was here before the war. I know the city well. I would be happy to advise on places of interest, even possibly to act as guide.'

'That's kind but we've already planned our stay.'

'But you have different interests possibly. My wife and daughter are content to spend the whole day shopping. I find shopping a horrendous bore. And I'm the one who has to pay for it.' He looks at her in mock despair. 'There is a charming little cinema on Via Reggio that shows the latest films. I know how young girls love the cinema.'

It is the kind of banter she was used to on the perfume counter. Every day she would be fending off attention from men just like this one. She'd felt threatened in the gardens of the Villa Ada but here she was well within her depth.

'Shall I come inside for a moment? You may care to take my card.'

'No, thank you. In a few days we'll be moving on to Florence.'

'Florence? I know Florence very well. Before the war ...'

'Goodbye, Monsieur. I hope you have a pleasant stay.'

He still has one hand flat against the door. As Renée shuts it after her, his wrist cracks. He lets out an 'Ouf'. She leans against the door and listens, conscious that the man is listening from the other side. Eventually she hears his footsteps going back along the corridor.

This time she doesn't tell Pierre what's happened. They are sitting on the terrace of the hotel later on that day. He is describing an encounter he's had with an artist painting in the square, when he breaks off and stares at her.

'You've taken off your ring.'

'It's on the other hand.' She brings her right hand up to show him.

'But I thought the whole point of the ring was to tell people you were spoken for.'

'It didn't seem to make much difference last week in the gardens.' She sits back so that the waiter can refill her glass. 'It's better if we stop pretending. People here are gossiping about us anyway. It makes it more humiliating if they think we're trying to convince them we're respectable.'

He reaches for her hand. 'I'm sorry if it's spoilt your stay here.'

'Who cares what they think?' She gives a bright smile.

'Maybe we should have let people go on thinking that I was your father.'

'You said you had never wanted children.'

'I said artists made neglectful parents.'

'There you are, then.'

'Are you saying I'm neglecting you?'

'I'm saying I don't always want to be your daughter.'

Pierre is looking at her curiously. 'I'm afraid I might have been a touch insensitive when you came back to the hotel and told me you'd been pestered that day at the Villa Ada.'

He sits back. 'You'll tell me, won't you, if you run into that sort of thing again?'

'Of course.' She smiles.

Pierre takes out his pocket watch. It's half past six. The gong for dinner goes at seven thirty. Renée takes an olive from the saucer. 'Did you want to have a walk down to the river before dinner?'

'I feel rather tired. I thought we might go back up to the room and have a nap, unless you're keen to have a walk.'

'No, I'll be happy with a nap too,' Renée says. She takes another bite out of the olive. She had never tasted one before she came to Italy. She'd found the first one bland and bitter. Pierre is right; it's an acquired taste. She quite likes the combination now.

Pierre suggests they take a train out to Assisi. Renée's face falls. 'Are we looking at more paintings?'

'I think these are pictures you'll like looking at. They're all about Saint Francis and his miracles. They're set out like a story book along the walls of the basilica.'

He's been there once, she thinks. Why should they need to go and look at them again? But she enjoys the train ride through the gently rolling hills of Umbria after the stifling atmosphere of Rome. They walk through dusty medieval streets and climb the hill to the basilica. Inside, she finds the same hill she has just climbed, with the same basilica on top. She sees Saint Francis in his friar's cassock, feeding birds and exorcising demons with the raddled faces of Italian peasants and the scaly legs and wings of dragons. This is art that she can understand.

There is a painting showing kitchen porters scraping food into a bowl for an emaciated dog, while Jesus and the twelve apostles sit in an adjoining room and argue about which of them is going to betray him. Renée thinks the dog's a mongrel, but Pierre insists that it's a terrier. She likes it that they're both more interested in what is happening off-stage. For an instant, she is totally absorbed, the line between them open because all their energy is flowing in the same direction. Sometimes, as they're looking at the pictures, he assumes the role of *professore* talking to a pupil. Often they discover they've attracted a small audience. When Renée sees what's happening, she giggles. He pretends he hasn't noticed.

'Do you think that in a hundred years' time somebody will stand in front of your work and explain it?'

'My work doesn't need explaining.'

'It makes me feel shuddery to think that I'll be dead and so will you, but people will be looking at me in your pictures. It's like being dead and not dead.'

'Only half-dead, do you mean?'

'But in a way we shall be more alive than ever.'

'Only if they tell the truth about us.'

'Better if they don't,' says Renée.

'Is the truth so terrible?'

She sighs. 'They wouldn't understand.'

'Perhaps the world will be more liberated in a hundred years' time. They won't blame you, anyway, my darling.'

'Yes, they will.'

'What matters, Renée, is how well you fit into the picture, not how well you fit into the world.'

'You think so?'

On the homeward journey, she is tired. He puts his arm around her and she dozes. When she wakes up, Pierre is leaning on her shoulder with his free hand resting in her lap. She sees the way his fingers jerk involuntarily when he's asleep. His hands are never really still. Like sentries they remain on duty even when the rest of him is sleeping. She looks at the hand and wonders whether it can sense her looking at it. While they've been in Rome, the skin has coarsened and the knuckles have turned brown. It doesn't look like his hand any more. She feels a frisson of excitement at the thought that this hand could belong to anyone. Or even that it's not a hand at all, it's a gigantic stag beetle nestling in her lap. She feels a stirring in her loins. The insect rises on its six legs and sinks down into her lap again.

At the far end of the carriage is an old man with a crate of guinea fowl perched on the seat beside him. Renée takes her shawl out of the basket next to her and drapes it casually across her knees. She feels the bony segments of the creature's body underneath the silk and presses lightly on it. There is no response.

She makes an effort to distract herself by concentrating on the rhythm of the wheels over the tracks. She looks out at the landscape rushing past them, children playing in a field, a peasant herding cows along a dirt road. This is what she's seeing, but what she is feeling is the throbbing pulse between her thighs that's turned the flesh to liquid.

She spreads out her hand and presses harder, clawing at the shawl. The creature underneath, alert now to its situation, gives a series of small jerks. It scrunches up her skirt and slides in underneath it. Renée feels its tentacles brush lazily across her skin. She's thinking of the night she lay with Margo's hand across her thigh. The creature carries on with its exploratory sorties, pressing gently down on her, refusing to be hurried, moving at its own pace. Renée bunches up her fists. She doesn't care now if the old man at the far end of the carriage knows what's going on. She hears the squawking of the guinea fowl, the flutter of their feathers on the cage bars. She lets out a little sob.

At Tiburtina station they walk out into the sunshine arm in arm, the artist and his muse, the fallen woman and her lover.

'You should not be going through my pockets, Renée.'

'It fell out when I was hanging up your jacket.'

He comes over to her, takes the sketchbook, slots the card inside the cover and replaces it inside his pocket. On the back, there is a sketch of the Borghese Gardens. Underneath, he's scrawled, 'A wilderness. Love Pierre.'

She can remember when he bought it. They were in the square outside the Vatican. He'd asked if there was anyone she'd like to send a card to and chose half a dozen for himself. 'They serve me as an aide-memoire,' he'd told her.

'It's the postcard that's upset you, I suppose?''

'I'm not upset. I wasn't looking for it. How could I know it was there?'

'That's why it's better not to look in places where you might find things you'd rather not see.'

'Better to be in the dark, you mean?'

'I tell you what you need to know. I'm trying to protect you, Renée.'

'I wish you'd stop treating me as if I were a child.' She wishes that she didn't always feel the need to answer back.

He reaches for his jacket. 'Let's go down to dinner?'

'I'm not hungry.'

He regards her patiently. 'Why don't you come down with me? Who knows, once you're there you might be tempted.' He goes over to the door and stands there holding out his arm.

As they go through the dining room, they pass the table with the man who she'd encountered in the corridor outside her room. He nods to her. The woman glances their way and then lifts her eyebrows to her husband. 'It's the painter and his whore.' That's what they're thinking.

'Will you send it?'

'I expect so.' Pierre dips his spoon into the soup. At least they have stopped playing games. He knows what she's referring to.

'Have you said when we're coming back?'

'I don't think even we know that.'

It was supposed to be a month and it's been less than three weeks so far. She feels panic. 'Will you go to Saint-Germain-en-Laye when we return?'

'I think I'll have to. There are things I need to sort out.' He puts down the spoon and wipes the serviette across his mouth. There is a flake of parsley clinging to his beard. Once she would have leant over, scooping it onto her tongue and offering it back to him. He would have laughed.

'You've got a bit of parsley in your beard.'

He wipes it off.

Once they're in bed, she cuddles up to him and they make love in a desultory way. A minute later, he's asleep. She lies there wondering if Marthe – plain, old, shabby Marthe – nonetheless has something she lacks. She puts up with things. She doesn't make a fuss. She would not search his pockets and then challenge him because she found a card in there addressed to someone else.

He's up before her in the morning, leaning out over the balcony. When he comes back into the room, he stands beside the bed and she pretends she's still asleep. She doesn't have to look to know there's something merciless about the glance he's giving her.

It seems as if the energy that's channelled into everyday things has been blocked and now it's ready to explode.

That evening in the restaurant, she's picking at a sliver of prosciutto on her plate, not eating it but shifting it from one side to the other. When the waiter takes Pierre's plate and then leans across to pick up hers, she makes a grab for it. 'I haven't finished.'

'Oh, for heaven's sake,' Pierre exclaims. 'You've spent the last half hour toying with the food.'

The waiter hovers. She puts down the fork.

Pierre draws breath. 'I'm sorry. That was rude. I didn't mean to rush you. Obviously, you take whatever time you like to eat your meal.'

She wants to leave the table and go out into the street, but they are stuck here until both of them have finished or at least done justice to the meal. She feels obliged to eat now, rather than provoke another scene. While they wait for the next course to arrive, she traces round the pattern on the side-plate with her index finger.

'More wine?' Pierre tilts the bottle and she shakes her head. She looks towards the window. Outside it's still light. 'Shall we miss out on the dessert and take a walk?'

'Yes, please.'

Outside the hotel is a gypsy selling sprigs of lavender. 'Good luck,' she says. It's bad luck not to buy one, is what she's implying. Pierre buys a sprig for Renée and attaches it to her lapel. She sniffs her fingers and then holds them out to him.

'That smell reminds me of the house in Dauphiné where I grew up,' he says.

She sniffs at it again. 'You've never told me anything about your childhood.'

'There's not much to tell. I have an older brother and I had a sister.'

'Don't you still have one?'

'She died.' He takes her arm and they walk on. 'She wasn't very old. She had a daughter who is only fourteen.'

'Not the mother of your niece ... the one who has my name?'

'That's right.'

She stops. 'You never told me.'

'I said I'd been at a funeral.'

'Not hers.'

'You'd never met her. I suppose I didn't want to make you sad.'

She stares at him. She's thinking of the woman she saw step out of the cab that afternoon on rue de Rennes, the tender way that Pierre took her in his arms and kissed her on the cheek; his sister.

'Don't you miss her?'

'Yes, of course I do. She was the only person in my family I felt close to.'

'Aren't there other people you feel close to?'

'Not in that way.'

They walk on. There is a moment in the south where once the sun goes down, the city seems to hold its breath. The heat of day has not yet given way to the first chill of evening, but you feel the promise of it in the air. She stumbles suddenly and grabs his arm. The heel has broken on her shoe. She bought them last week on the Via Borgognona. Pierre takes the shoe and turns it over in his hand.

'Can it be mended?'

'I don't think so, but at least it's not the same foot as it was the last time. You can make a pair with the survivor of the other two.' He smiles. Has he discovered that she kept the broken sandal as a keepsake to remind her of the day they met?

In the hotel he puts them side by side against the wall,

his own shoes, scuffed and battered, next to them. He hates new clothes. He says he has to wear them in and it distracts him from the things he needs to concentrate on. It's true, when he does wear something new it always looks as if it's meant for someone else. She's staring at the shoes. The left one, with the broken heel, looks cowed beside its partner. The toe faces outwards as if it intends to creep away as soon as they're not looking.

'They were so expensive,' Renée whispers. 'How can they be broken?'

'Money doesn't guarantee a long life, I'm afraid.'

'They were the nicest shoes I ever had.'

'We'll buy another pair just like it.' Is she really going to get so upset over a pair of shoes when there is so much else to grieve about? 'I've bought two tickets for the opera tomorrow. Have you ever seen an opera?'

'No.'

'Italians are huge opera lovers.' Carefully he hangs his suit up on the rail. 'I'm taking you to one of Verdi's operas, *Rigoletto*. It's the story of a father who is treated like a clown but loves his only daughter to distraction. Everything he does, he does for her.'

'What happens?'

'Love destroys them both.'

'So it's a tragedy?'

'No, dearest, it's a comedy, Italian style.'

'It was amazing, wonderful.' Pierre has given her the programme as a souvenir. She wishes Gilda hadn't died. She hoped it would end happily, but Pierre says there's no such thing in opera as a happy ending. Someone always dies. 'At least they do it beautifully,' he says.

Pierre begins to get undressed, but Renée wants to stay

out on the balcony and watch the stars. 'You'd better come to bed,' he says.

'Can't I stay here a little longer?'

'We've a busy day tomorrow.'

'Have we?'

'I've told the *patron* we shall be leaving after breakfast.'

She's not certain that she's heard him properly. She stands there looking out over the street. It's quiet again. Somewhere a dog barks, someone calls, a man laughs. When she turns into the room, he's lying propped up on the pillows, one arm folded on his chest, the other lying by his side, palm up, the way that beggars wait for alms. She shuts the doors onto the balcony. It isn't only the mosquitoes; moths come in, attracted by the light, and throw themselves against the lamp until their wings are shredded.

'Why do you suppose they do that when they know they'll die?' she'd asked Pierre.

'Because their love of light is greater than their fear of death.'

He bunches up his hand in case the open palm is misinterpreted. 'Did you hear what I said?' He doesn't turn his head towards her, but his eyes have shifted. She nods meekly. 'I don't think this place is doing either of us any good.'

It's not the place, she thinks. It's us. 'But we've had such a lovely evening.'

'Yes. I'm pleased that you enjoyed it. I did too. It would have been a pity to have ended on a bad note.'

'When did you decide?'

'I've been considering it since you told me you'd been pestered at the Villa Ada. Rome is wonderful but I'm afraid Italian men are volatile. A woman on her own – young, beautiful, fair-haired, is something they find irresistible.'

'It only happened once.'

'You only went out on your own once.'

'Are you saying that's the reason why we're leaving?'

'I'm frustrated, and you're bored. There's no point in our staying.'

'Why are you frustrated?'

'I suppose because I want to work and I'm unable to.'

'Is that because of me?'

He looks away. 'No, I'm not blaming you. I thought that Rome would be the same as it was thirty years ago. Of course it's changed and so have I.'

'We could go somewhere else.'

'Where else?'

'I don't know. We were happy in Assisi.'

'Yes, let's not forget that.'

She is standing on the carpet with her hands clasped and her head bent. 'I did want to please you.'

'Dear girl, yes, I know you did. I've said it's not your fault. You need someone who's younger and less self-obsessed, a man who'll give you the attention you deserve.'

'You're saying that it's over?'

'We can't make each other happy, Renée. We've discovered that much while we've been here.'

'You want me to be in Clichy on my own?'

'Until a reasonable alternative presents itself.' He looks away.

She wonders what a 'reasonable alternative' would be.

She's sitting at the dressing table, staring at her own reflection. She lifts up the towel he's draped across her shoulders. There's a dark bruise on her right breast and another on her upper arm, but it's her face that frightens her. There's a distracted air about it. It's the face of somebody emerging from a nightmare to discover that the dream is real.

She can remember lying next to him the night before, the pillow pressed against her mouth, and crying silently until it felt like she was drowning on the inside. She had heard the clock down in the square strike three, then four. She had got out of bed to fetch a handkerchief and stubbed her toe against the chair leg. Suddenly it was as if the pain in her had found an outlet and was pouring through the gap. Rage, misery, humiliation, all of it came tumbling out. She gave a wail and heard the bed creak as Pierre threw back the covers and rushed over to her.

'Don't scream!' he begged. 'If somebody hears, we'll have the *patron* up here.'

'You said you would never leave me!' she shrieked, throwing herself at him, bunching up her fists and pounding them against his chest. 'You promised!' She was clawing at his face and as he tilted back his head to save his eyes, she heard the skin tear on his cheek, like linen when you put a knife through it.

'For God's sake, Renée, stop this!' He was scrabbling to secure her wrists. She stumbled, giving him the opportunity to twist her round and push her down onto the floor. He sat astride her, pinning her arms by the wrists above her head. The only bit of her that she could still move was her mouth.

'I wish that Tonio had killed you. I wish I had! You've destroyed me. Bastard!'

He let go of one wrist, clamping his free hand across her mouth. Her teeth closed round the hand and she bit into it. He shrieked. She'd bitten him down to the bone. She tasted blood inside her mouth.

Pierre leant forward. 'Renée,' he said, menacingly. 'I shall take my hand away now, but if you cry out, I'll put it back and keep it there and if you choke, so be it.' She heard noises coming from her throat. His hand was covered in a sticky blend of blood and mucus. As she breathed, a pink froth bubbled on her teeth. Her body shuddered with a last involuntary spasm.

She watched Pierre get up and stagger over to the sink. He took a hand towel from the rail and ran it underneath the tap. He bathed her face, attempting to remove the dirt and blood still sticking to her cheeks. His hand was bleeding and he rinsed the towel again and wrapped it round his fist.

She lay there without moving while he brought a blanket from the bed and put a pillow underneath her head. She heard him stumbling round the bedroom, picking up the fallen chair and straightening the carpet, rescuing the opera programme that had fallen on the floor and gathering the stray shards of a broken tumbler before tipping them in the waste-paper basket. In the dull light of approaching dawn, the room seemed drained of colour. He'd sunk down into the armchair. Outside in the square the clock struck half-past five.

She'd drifted off into a troubled sleep and when she woke the next time he was leaning over her. His face looked odd. There was a red line down his cheek and where it cut into the beard the hairs were missing.

'You look funny. Something's happened to your face.'

She put her finger out to touch it. He stepped back. 'You'd better have a wash. We have to leave soon.' He picked up the eiderdown and put it back onto the bed.

Her throat felt dry. It was as if her body had been drained of liquid. 'Could I have a glass of water, please?'

He filled up the decanter. 'There's no glass; it's broken. I'm afraid you'll have to tip the jug.' As it came level with her mouth, she felt the bruises on her lips. 'There was a struggle; you remember?' He returned it to the shelf above the wash-hand basin.

∞

Renée stares at her reflection in the glass. She looks round at the rumpled carpet and the pillow and then slowly takes in the waste-paper basket with its bloodied towels.

He lifts the nightdress up over her head. She gives a little shudder. For the first time since they met, she feels ashamed of being naked. Pierre soaks the flannel and begins to wash her, starting with her face and neck, then holding out each arm in turn and wiping it. The flannel passes underneath her breasts, across her stomach. As it dips between her legs, she closes them instinctively. 'It's all right,' Pierre says. Once she's dry, he wraps the towel around her shoulders. Reaching for the hairbrush, he makes an attempt to tidy up her hair. She leans her head against him. 'Can you put your clothes on now, or shall I help you?'

'I can do it,' she says in a small voice.

He bends down to kiss her forehead. 'While you get dressed I'll go down and settle up the bill. I think it's better that we don't go in to breakfast. I'll bring back some coffee if I can.' He puts his jacket on. 'You ought to start. The train leaves in an hour.'

Is this what it's like when you go mad? She is afraid of being shut away. She knows what homes for the insane are like – dark corridors that echo, rooms with lights directly overhead so that you can't go anywhere to get away from them, cold water poured onto your head until the thoughts inside it are so jumbled up you don't know what's real any more. She must sit quietly so that when Pierre comes back, he'll know the person who did those things isn't her. She'll be his little girl again, obedient and biddable, not wilful and destructive. She gets dressed. She hears him coming up the stairs and down the corridor. He's brought up coffee on a tray and there's a plate of madeleines.

She lifts the cup obediently to her lips and winces. Pierre pours himself a coffee. While she's sipping hers, he takes the last of her belongings from the closet, adding them to the valise.

'I've made sure all your things are in a separate case so that you'll have them with you when we drop you off at the apartment.' He's pretending that he's doing this for her, but Renée knows he's doing it so that there'll be no need to go back later to return belongings that have got mixed up with his.

He drains his cup and puts it back onto the tray. She's hardly touched hers, but he says they can't wait any longer. They'll be sending up a porter any minute.

'We must go.'

She puts her cup down on the tray and Pierre takes her arm.

He lowers his valise onto the mat and stands there staring at me. 'Could I sit down?' he says, finally.

He sits down opposite me at the table. Now the light is shining on him, I see just how tired he is. His hair is matted and his beard's unkempt. He has the scent of someone who's been travelling for nights on end; the rancid smell of railway carriages and dining cars.

He puts his hand up to his eyes. His hands have aged, too, in the last month. I look at the finger of his left hand where the wedding ring would be. There isn't one. They didn't marry after all then; I suppose that's something. He would not deliberately lie; he's not like me.

'Pierre?'

He makes a little gesture with his hand to wave away the question. I can't think I've ever seen a human being looking so defeated. Even when the lines of soldiers passed through

Paris after being routed in the north they still had some life left in them, some hope. I feel indignant, as if someone's borrowed something from me and then broken it.

'I'm sorry, Marthe.'

'You had better go to bed.' His jacket's wet with mist; he's shivering inside it. I get up and take his arm to help him up the stairs. I peel the jacket off him and undo his tie. I kneel in front of him and carefully release the buckle round his waist. He goes on staring into space. I feel rage start to bubble up inside me. Rage because what Renée has sent back to me is no more than a husk. I wrench the buckle and he gives a little start.

'Get into bed.' I lift the covers up and he falls sideways. He's asleep before his head lands on the pillow.

I lie with my body folded round him, wedging my knees in behind his so that he's protected all the way down. His hands fumble blindly in the dark for mine. I put my own hands over his. We're locked together now so tightly that there isn't room for anything to come between us.

'Marthe,' he says in his sleep.

At least he's got my name right.

When he comes down in the morning, I have coffee ready on the hob. He's shaved his beard off. There's a moment, as he stands there in the doorway, when I want to laugh. His face is pink and raw around his chin, brown where the sun has weathered it over the past month and white underneath the glasses, like an owl's. I notice there's a scar across his cheek.

I wonder what the bathroom looks like. Madame Hébert's due this morning. I don't want to give her any ammunition that she hasn't got already. Earlier, when I came downstairs, I looked in the right-hand pocket of his jacket for the sketchbook. It was in the left-hand pocket.

Somehow, more than anything, this tells me that Pierre has lost his way. There was a drawing of a cat among the ruins, several views through open shutters and a stray dog on a dusty road – no more than half a dozen drawings. He would have done more than that here in a morning. At the end, loose, was a pencil drawing of a square. There were two women in the foreground and another in between them holding up a set of scales. He took us both to Rome, then, after all.

He looks around the kitchen, takes in Juno lying on the carpet underneath the chair and Poucette riffling through her fur for fleas. When he came back, he wasn't certain I would be there. What he'd hoped for was exactly what he got – me sitting at the table where he'd left me. Did he think I'd been there waiting for him all this time? I curse my own stupidity. I could at least have picked a different place at table.

'I'm glad nothing's changed,' he says. The silence after that is longer, as if both of us are struggling to get over what he's just said. He sits down. 'Of course, I don't mean ...'

I look dumbly at the coffee pot. He thinks that everything's the way it was before. It's not, of course. You can't break someone's heart and then expect to glue the bits together. Like a milk jug, it might look the same, but you won't dare put milk in it again.

Suppose he had come back last night and found my body decomposing in the bathtub with the skeletons of Juno, Blanco and Poucette splayed out across the tiles? Nobody to take off his jacket, tuck him up in bed, no sleep for him to sink down into. Just a nightmare that had no end.

'It was terrible,' he whispers.

'It can't all have been like that,' I say, although a part of me is hoping that it was, that he at least was suffering a bit of what I felt that morning as I ran a bath and wondered what would take more courage – getting out of it again or letting myself slide under the water.

'I'm so sorry, Marthe, I don't know what happened.'

I do. 'You're a middle-aged man in his fifties,' I could say. 'You fell in love with someone young enough to be your daughter. It's a common tale. It happens all the time. Don't bother giving it another thought.' But knowing that it happens all the time is not much consolation to the woman who's been left.

'I was afraid you might have gone,' he says.

'Gone?' I say with a little laugh. 'As you once pointed out, where would I go?'

He holds his hand out. I would like to reach across to him and take it, but there's more than two cups and a coffee pot between us.

I call Dr Dolbecq in to look at him. The doctor comes from Isigny, so he's a man of few words and I know that he will not waste any of them gossiping.

'Home cooking and a warm bed,' he says. He prescribes some chloral for Pierre to take at nights. Most people take a passing interest in the pictures when they come into the house, especially those in which I'm standing naked in the bathtub. Dr Dolbecq walks straight past them. He is not a man who sees much.

'Dr Dolbecq says you'll live,' I say. 'He's given you a sleeping draught.'

I pour some water for him from the jug and leave it on the windowsill. The sun is catching on the glass. I brought a bunch of the mimosa in, this morning, so that Pierre could see it from the bed. A bud drops down into the glass and floats across the surface. I bend down to scoop it out.

'Don't move,' Pierre says. 'Stay like that.'

It's over, I think. He's come back.

'You have to help me. Please.' She has both hands around my arm. The basket tilts and plums roll out across the cobbles. People turn and stare. They might not know her in the market, but they know me. 'Talk to me!' she says. 'I have to talk to someone.'

'Talk to someone else,' I tell her. 'I can't help you.' Tears are running down her face. Her eyes are red and swollen. She's been wandering up and down between the stalls.

'I'm going mad,' she whispers, putting her face up to mine.

She's clawing at my arm. Her face is streaked with dirt and tears. Dear God, to think I envied her. I back into the alleyway that runs down one side of the market square. I've been through this once with Pierre and I don't want to go through it again with her. But looking at the wreck in front of me, I can't help feeling sadness. This could be Suzanne come back for comfort with a broken heart, her dreams in ruins, all her hopes dashed. 'Pull yourself together, girl. You think he wants to see you in this state?'

'He won't see me at all,' she sobs. 'He doesn't want to see me any more.'

So he left her. In spite of everything, I dared not think that he could willingly have given up on so much beauty. 'You're not doing yourself any favours,' I say. 'Dry your eyes. You'll be arrested if you carry on like this.'

'I can't bear to be on my own,' she wails. 'I'll kill myself.'

'Tch. You'll do nothing of the sort,' I say. 'That's just the sort of talk that scares men off. Have you no pride, girl?'

'Do you think I'd be here if I had?'

There is a café nearby and I bundle her inside. The coat

she's wearing isn't thick enough to keep the cold out and she's shivering. I order her a bowl of soup. She says she isn't hungry. 'Warm your hands around it then,' I say. She follows my instructions, grateful to have somebody to tell her what to do.

'How did it come to this?' I ask, when she's stopped shivering.

'I don't know. It was lovely to begin with. Rome was wonderful. I didn't mind him working, but I felt shut out from it. It wasn't like it had been in the studio. The more I clung to him, the more remote he seemed. I felt I'd lost him. I was jealous, I suppose.' She looks at me. 'You wouldn't understand.'

Oh yes, I think. I understand. The people at the other tables have begun to listen to the conversation. They'll be wondering who this woman is and in the end they'll find out. I can see why Pierre was frightened of her. It's as if she's got a spring wound up inside her. It's so tight that once it starts unwinding, she can't stop it. 'He said he was sorry if he'd hurt me; he had never wanted to. "I've only loved two women in my whole life," he said, "and I've ruined both of them."'

'You don't think I can change his mind for him? You think I would have let him leave me if I'd had a choice?'

She's weeping, but more quietly now. 'I feel as if I have no value,' she says, sniffing in her handkerchief.

'Of course you have a value. What sort of a woman lets a man decide her value? You're young. On a good day, you'd be beautiful. You'd have men falling over one another for a chance to woo you.'

'Pierre's the only man I want.'

'Why? Why do you want him? You're sure it isn't just because he's someone else's?'

'It's not my fault that I fell in love with him.'

'This isn't Rudolf Valentino, Renée. It's a middle-aged man with a weak chin and a body that's begun to let him down. There's only one thing that he's really passionate about and it's not us. He wants a quiet life so he can get on with his work.'

'I wouldn't interfere with that.'

'You have, though. He had half a dozen sketches with him when he came back, so he can't have done much while he was away. Pierre can't live without his work.'

'I understand that!' she insists. 'I only wanted him to reassure me that he loved me.'

'That's a lot to ask a man like Pierre. He hasn't said it once to me. You have to take what you can get.'

'Please. Please just tell him that I'm sorry. If we were together all the time, I wouldn't be like that. I'd be the sort of wife he wanted me to be. Please.'

'You say you can't bear to be alone, but have you thought that if you married him you would be on your own again in twenty years' time?'

'I can't look that far ahead.'

'You should. I'm telling you it's hard to have to start again then. Find somebody of your own age, Renée, some young man who'll love you properly. Put this behind you.'

'I can't. Don't you see, I can't.'

'I spoke to Renée Montchaty this morning,' I say as I'm dishing up the evening meal. 'I met her in the market.' His eyes rest on me a moment, then he lowers them. I feel this conversation ought to be with both of us, so I hold out as long as possible before I give up waiting for him to respond. 'She's in a bad way.'

He looks like a rat trapped in a corner by a crowd of men with bricks.

'You ought to see her, Pierre.' He shakes his head. 'She says she's sorry,' I say. After all, I did agree to pass the message on. 'She understands why things went wrong between you out in Rome.'

'It wasn't her fault.'

'No, I don't suppose it was.' If I'd met Pierre now and was her age, I might well have ended up by battering him with my fists as well. 'She's no more than a child and you're a grown man. You have some responsibility towards her.'

'Don't you think I know that?'

'You can't run away from it. You have to talk to her.'

'Please, Marthe,' he says. 'Please don't do this to me. God, I wish that it had never happened.'

'I think all of us would say "Amen" to that, but still it has.' I'd like to bang their heads together and I sense that this might come as a relief for both of them. 'Imagine if you had a daughter her age and she'd gone off with a man of fifty. Think how you'd react.' Perhaps it's not a good idea to hammer home his guilt. It's guilt that's paralysing him. That's why he doesn't want to see her. He's afraid that it'll break his heart. 'Dear God,' I mutter, losing patience suddenly. 'What made you do it?'

'I was flattered, I suppose. I never thought she would be interested in me.'

'She came after you, then?' I need something to restore the balance in his favour. At the moment Renée's winning hands down.

'No,' he sighs, 'it wasn't like that. Neither of us really thought about it.'

'More fool you.'

'She seemed so innocent. She made me feel . . .' He stops. Perhaps he's seen me clenching my fists underneath the table.

'But you surely didn't have to say you'd marry her.'

'I don't know what came over me. It was the one way I could make her happy. I thought it would reassure her and that our relationship would settle down to something more like yours and mine.'

I catch his eye and hold it for a moment.

'Unforgivable,' he says. 'I did it out of cowardice.'

No wonder she's in such a state, I think.

'I don't know how to put it right. There's nothing we can do for one another. Can't you say that to her, Marthe?'

'If you think I'm running to and fro with messages between the two of you ...'

'I don't mean that. Of course not. But if you could see her once more ... make her understand it's hopeless.'

'Why would she believe me? After all we're rivals. It's not likely I would hand you to her on a plate.'

'But you're the one she came to.'

'Out of desperation, yes. Because she couldn't get at you.'

'I'm not sure I could answer for myself if we met up again. It might end with me marrying her after all and think what a disaster that would be.'

'You would get used to it, I dare say.'

'No, I wouldn't. Nor would you.'

There's no one in her street when I turn into it, but I can see that it's a genteel area, the sort of place men favour when it comes to setting up their mistresses. It's so much grander than the first apartment Pierre and I shared. Ours was two rooms with a wash-hand basin and a stove. There is a pleasant view onto the gardens at the back and inside there are three rooms and a kitchen. Through an open door, I see the bathroom. What I'd give for one like that. The rooms are in a starfish pattern and she goes into the first one. There are throws and cushions on the sofa and a vase of lilies on the table. Renée might have let herself go, but she's kept the flat nice, hoping no doubt that Pierre will come back into it. Her shoulders sag as she sits down. She must have hoped he would be with me, or perhaps that he would come without me.

'Would you like some tea?'

I would, but from the way she says it I can tell she isn't anxious to get up and get me some, so I refuse. 'Pierre asked me to speak to you,' I say. 'He thought it would be easier.'

She gives a tight smile. 'Easier for him.'

'I dare say.'

'Men are such cowards,' she says, tossing back her head and in the gesture I see what she must have looked like when he saw her first. If she can keep her anger, she may yet survive. 'All right, then,' she says. 'Tell me.'

I know how humiliating this must be for her, so I try not to overdo it. She might have a bathroom to herself that's twice the size of mine, but all I feel for her is pity.

'Pierre is sorry for the pain he caused. He knows it's his fault. There was nothing different that you could have done.' She is about to interrupt me, but I raise a hand to silence her. 'All I can do is tell you what he said.' Her mouth sinks back into a pout. 'He knows a man of his age had no right to take up with a girl as young as you. You don't know what it's like yet to be middle-aged, but when you are you'll realise how unusual it is to have somebody notice you. It came as a surprise that anyone would want him for himself.'

'You did,' she says.

'He's taken that for granted.'

'Don't you mind?'

'I've taken him for granted too. You do that when you've lived with someone for as long as we have.'

'That's not how it would have been with us.'

'You don't know. You're not old enough to know what happens when you live with somebody a long time.'

'You keep telling me how young I am, as if the young don't feel things just as much.'

'The young feel things a lot more. That's the trouble. In the end you were too energetic for him ... that's the way it looks to me, at any rate.'

She is about to tell me it's not any of my business until she remembers I'm her only link with him. 'It wasn't just sex. We did love each other.'

'That's not what I meant by energetic.' Surely I don't have to keep on labouring the point. 'Pierre is not strong. He can't give his energy to lots of things. He'd have neglected you the same way he's neglected me. You saw that in him and it frightened you. You realised you would have to share him, not with me but with his work, the one thing he would not have given up for you.'

'I didn't want...'

'Don't. Let me finish. What you want is not important any more. I'm telling you the way things are. They can't be otherwise. No matter who you were, no matter how hard you tried not to mind, the end would still have been the same.'

She's started weeping, but it's not the shrill, demented kind now. It's the sort you heard at funerals throughout the war. When you've lost two or three sons, or a shell has landed on your house and wiped out half your family, you're too tired to curse fate or shake your fist at God. However much I want to comfort her, I'm still the enemy. There's no point in me saying everyone has felt the way she's feeling now, that in a year's time she will have recovered, while Pierre and I are stuck for ever. It's too late for us.

'He's written you a letter,' I say. I don't hand it to her. I'm afraid of what might be communicated if our fingers touch across the envelope. I don't know what he's said; if he's agreed to let her go on living here. It's one way he can make himself feel better. Still, I can't help feeling that it would be best if she were to go somewhere else. I leave the letter on the sofa arm. 'Don't grieve too long,' I say. 'It isn't worth it.'

After leaving the apartment, I walk by the river. I feel shabby; there's no other word for it. I'm angry that Pierre could drag us into this. The more I see of Renée, the more anxious I become for her. I wonder if I shouldn't simply let her have him. I would grieve without him, but I'd manage. I shall never feel as vulnerable again.

He's pacing up and down when I get back. I put the kettle on.

'How is she?'

'What do you think? She's distraught. She looks as if she hasn't slept for weeks. She's skinny as a rake and she's been crying.'

Pierre sits at the table, burying his forehead in his hands.

'Oh, buck up, can't you?' I say. 'I can't stand the two of you behaving like a wet weekend. If you can't help each other, don't inflict your misery on me.'

'I didn't mean . . .'

'I'm tired of hearing that you didn't mean to hurt her. Be a man, face up to it; you have.'

'I've said that she can stay in the apartment if she wants to. She should have a roof over her head at least.'

'She should be with her family. I can't imagine what they're thinking of. She's not fit to be left alone. She must have friends.'

'She didn't keep in touch with them once she and I . . .'

'Perhaps she'll find another artist. There are plenty of them.' I resist the urge to wonder if he couldn't fix her up with one of them. I know that this is how it often works, though once a girl is known to have caused trouble, they tend to be wary. Even Roussel might think twice and he's not fussy normally.

Pierre puts both hands round his cup to drink it. He's relieved but he's ashamed of his relief. He looks at me and looks away again. 'We can't go on like this,' he says. 'Whatever happens now, we can't go back to things the way they were.'

That's true, I think, but there's a panic-stricken moment when I wonder if he's contemplating leaving both of us.

'Perhaps it's time we married.'

'Married!' My mouth sags.

'You'd like that, wouldn't you? You would feel more secure if we were married.'

What he means is that he would feel more secure. At least then he would not be tempted to propose to anybody else.

'We live together all this time and you make two proposals to two different women in the space of six months.' He looks sheepish. He may be in doubt about his motives, but he knows that I'm not. Up till now, I've been a background presence. One thing to come out of all this is that I shall never be ignored again. He might have taken me for granted in the past, but I'm the paste that's holding him together. If he'd only asked me earlier, before his life began to fall apart. If we'd been married, maybe it would not have happened, or perhaps it would have happened anyway. It hasn't stopped Roussel from running after women. I'm surprised that he had time to father Annette and her sister, having spent so many nights in other women's beds.

Pierre is looking at me anxiously. Perhaps he's thinking

I'll refuse out of perversity. If we get married, I shall have to sign the register. He'll know my name is not de Méligny and that I wasn't eighteen when he met me. He'll have something to forgive too, so perhaps that makes us equal.

'Yes,' I say. 'I'll marry you.'

Pierre and I are married three weeks later at the Mairie in the arrondissement where we had our first home. The only witnesses are Édouard and a lady borrowed from the wedding party next in line. Our families haven't been informed. I wear a light grey satin dress with imitation flowers round the neckline. Pierre tells me I look radiant and I believe him. It takes very little effort for a woman to be beautiful as long as someone tells her that she is.

Édouard provides a small reception for us at a neighbouring hotel where we drink champagne. There has been no word from Renée since I saw her. I suppose at some point we shall need to find out if she's still in the apartment. Without wanting to be harsh, Pierre cannot continue to afford a flat for someone who no longer models for him. I'm allowed to have a voice in these things now that I'm a married woman. After so long I thought being married would be neither here nor there, but I feel like a queen in waiting who's transformed the moment that the crown is put onto her head. I have authority. Of course I know that in the studio Pierre will carry on the way he always has, but even there I can at least determine who goes in and out.

'So, you're a married woman,' Édouard teases, twinkling at me from behind that massive beard. 'If you'd been anybody else's but Pierre's, I would have made a play for you myself. Too late now.'

It's the sort of joke he'd only make in company. I know the kind of women Édouard is attracted to and I've been grateful not to be one. Now I'm spoken for, of course, I might be more at risk. He wraps his arms around me in a bear hug and I feel his wet lips through the bristles of his beard.

A horse-drawn carriage comes to take us to the station. Pierre's friend, Manguin, is allowing us to use his house in Antibes for a fortnight. Once we're settled on the train, enveloped in the warmth and comfort of a first-class carriage, I feel pleasantly relaxed. I'm not sure how much notice Pierre took when I signed my name as 'Boursin', not 'de Méligny' and had to list my date of birth. He hesitated for a second before signing his name, but then he looked up at me and smiled.

I felt that Renée should be told about the marriage, but Pierre fears doing anything that brings her back into our lives. I dare say if she reads the papers she will see us listed under 'Marriages', or maybe one of Pierre's friends will tell her.

It will soon be dark. She never liked the twilight. It was like a slow goodbye, a gradual withdrawal – light, heat, colour. Is this what the body's like when it begins to die – it takes a while to notice? Lately, she's got used to sitting in the darkness. It stayed light in Rome till ten o'clock.

If it had not been Pierre's name in the paper, she would probably have missed it, though she always casts her eye along the lists of marriages and deaths. It's human nature. When you see a name you recognise, you're drawn to it. So Marthe lied about her name. It comforts her a bit to know that Marthe wasn't all she said she was; all that Pierre said she was. How can you know someone for quarter of a century and think they're someone else? It's possible; she sees that now. She and Pierre were closest in the first twelve months they were together. It was then that they began to drift apart. A decade on, they would have lost sight of each other altogether.

A young couple with a small child pass under the window. Suddenly the child looks up. She gives a little wave. There is a second when the child's eyes are locked into hers and Renée knows that forty, fifty years from now, she will remember looking up out of her stroller that day, straight into the face of a dark angel. With the light behind her, that is how she must look.

Sometimes, in the evenings, she sits with a cushion underneath her head and reads a magazine. She won't do that tonight. Tonight, she'll think about Pierre and Marthe on their wedding day. She shuts the windows. Inside, there is still a legacy of warmth. She needs to make sure everything is tidy. You should always leave things as you found them, Maman used to say. She wouldn't have included people in that. The whole point of other people is the marks they leave on you.

She's not the person she was when Pierre first met her. She will never laugh again. She'll never go to dances, cry her eyes out over sad films, make out that she knows who Tintoretto and Giotto are, insist she doesn't take her clothes off for just anybody, eat three mille-feuilles in a sitting, fall in love. These things are lost to her and what they've given her instead is this dull weight inside her chest that feels a bit like hunger. Eating won't get rid of it. There's only one thing she can do to make it better.

She lines up her shoes inside the closet and arranges the frocks tidily on separate hangers. She hopes Tonio allows the girls to choose what they would like. Last night she went to Saint-Pierre. She lit a candle for her father and went down onto her knees to say a prayer for him. She prayed for Maman and the girls and at the end she meant to say a prayer for herself. But by the time she got there, she was tired of praying, tired of saying sorry. She just said it like that. 'Sorry.' Then she got up off her knees and went out. It could have been anything that she was saying sorry for. Still, God's supposed to know; you shouldn't have to tell him. She thought she'd feel better afterwards, but she felt just the same. Perhaps that's what it means to be cast out; you don't have anybody to fall back on, even God.

She's not sure what to do about the magazines. They are the sort that Gabi would adore, the pages still smooth, no moustaches drawn onto the faces. She liked to come back to them when she'd forgotten how the stories ended or which actor recently divorced to marry someone else. It's odd that if you're rich and famous you can sin and no one bothers. Even God forgives you. No one in these pages has been cast out.

She turns out the lights in all the other rooms and goes into the bathroom. She enjoys the sound the boiler makes when she turns on the tap. The noise of water in the pipes has often been her only company. The bath looks like an altar with the candles at each end of it. She takes the portrait of Pierre and props it up against the mirror, tilted slightly so it looks as if he's gazing down at her. The bath is half full. Normally she'd turn the taps off now. Pierre said she could take baths twice a day if that was what she felt like, but you can't shake off the habits of your youth.

This evening she won't stint herself. She keeps the water running till it's nearly at the top before she lowers herself into it. She looks at Pierre's portrait. For the first time he seems to be looking back at her, or is that wishful thinking? Pictures can't look back at you; the traffic's all one way. She wouldn't want to be forgotten. Nor would she want someone looking at a picture of her in a hundred years' time, wondering what he saw in her. It matters not just that he should remember her as beautiful, but that the world should think she is.

The world. Now she sounds really like those women in the madhouse who insist they're Josephine. Five years ago, the perfume counter was her world. If Pierre hadn't come along, she'd probably have married someone Tonio approved of and had half a dozen children. Or she might still be with Marguerite. She was right in the end. She gave her good advice. But what use is advice when you're in love?

She might have gone on living here in the apartment, waiting for another lover to take over from Pierre. She's been 'kept' all this time; what difference would another year make? When you love someone, it doesn't matter which of you is making sacrifices. But it matters when you don't. The minute Pierre stopped loving her, he started paying for her. She was little better than a whore then. She was never that before, no matter what her brother said. What Pierre took from her wasn't just his love; it was the value that she put upon herself. So no, she can't continue living here, especially now he's married. Did he do that just to show her that he wasn't coming back, or was it Marthe who insisted? She'd have done the same in her place.

She turns on the hot tap and there is another gush of water. The steam rises round her in a cloud. She's thankful that she can't see anything too clearly. As the water closes over her, she hears the blunt sound of the street bell. So few people call on her now that she has forgotten what it sounds like. She hears voices on the ground floor and then, seconds afterwards, the sound of footsteps on the stairs. They come up to the next floor and the next, until they stop outside her own door.

For an instant it occurs to her that it might be Pierre. He has a key although he always rang the bell to let her know that he was on his way up. If it were him, he might save her, swooping down and gathering her up into his arms, his voice sad and distracted, murmuring 'Oh, Renée, Renée.'

Somebody is hammering on the door. There is a pause and then it comes again. It's odd what happens when sound has to pass through water. She remembers, in the park once, seeing two swans frozen to the surface of the lake and, as their bodies thawed the ice and it began to crack, it was as if the sound was all around her and the earth was breaking up under her feet. This time the sound is very far away, but she is very far away, too.

She's surprised that there is no last-minute struggle; that she doesn't rise up gasping to the surface and have to go through it all again until she wears herself out. If she'd known it was so easy, she might not have waited. I must tell someone, she thinks. I ought to tell Pierre that in the end, it wasn't hard at all. I ought to tell him, but I can't. Because I'm dead.

The days we spend in Antibes are among the happiest I've ever known. We go for long walks in the country and one day we take a picnic and a rowing boat out on the water and stay there until the evening. Pierre is sleeping better, tired out from the walks and wholesome food – rich soups and bouillabaisse, veal cutlets with wild mushrooms, salad laced with chervil.

Renée isn't far from either of our minds, but she's the one thing we don't talk about. It's like pretending that there's not a war on. I know dreadful things are happening out of sight, but whereas they would haunt me if I were in Saint-Germain-en-Laye, here they seem too far off to matter.

We don't see a lot of Manguin. He stays in his own part of the house. We sometimes ask him round for dinner and then he and Pierre stay up half the night discussing art or politics. Pierre thinks that the Allies are demanding too much in the way of reparations. Manguin thinks the Germans should be screwed for every penny. Both of them are Communists and all that either of them really cares about is painting.

When I asked him whether he was anxious to get back to Paris, Pierre said that it wouldn't bother him not to go back at all. He's even thinking we might buy a little house in Antibes as a summer residence. It will take years for Paris to get back to what it was before the war, but here you wouldn't know there'd been a war.

We've been there nearly two weeks when the telegram arrives from Édouard. I know when the boy delivers it that what is inside will destroy the peace Pierre and I have been enjoying here. He's gone across to Manguin's studio to help him choose the pictures for the Paris Salon next month.

It's Pierre's name on the telegram, but I could open it. We don't have secrets from each other any more. I don't, though. When I hear Pierre's steps on the gravel, I arrange my face so that it doesn't give away the terror I already feel. 'The boy came by this morning with a telegram,' I tell him.

He stands looking at it. He would rather that I opened it, but after all it is addressed to him. He slides his finger underneath the flap. There is a silence that seems to go on for ever, then he gives a sharp cry, like a rabbit when a weasel has it by the neck. He leans against the wall, his eyes closed. I uncurl his fingers from the telegram and smooth the creases out so I can read it. What is printed there, appalling as it is, is not entirely unexpected. Renée Montchaty has killed herself.

☞

The line is bad and Édouard's voice is rasping, so that every time he says a word with 's' in it, it's followed by a whistle. Pierre is leaning on the counter for support. The cashier's giving him odd looks. He's listening in to this side of the conversation and imagining the other side. He's also trying to add up the price of stamps and weigh the parcels handed to him.

'Do you know what happened?' Pierre says.

'I don't have the details, but the rumour is she drowned herself. '

'Oh God.'

'My dear chap, I appreciate that it's a shock. The girl must have been mentally unsound.' He knows this could have happened countless times in his life, but I don't suppose he ever thought that it would happen to Pierre. 'There'll have to be an inquest, I'm afraid. It's usual in cases where the cause of death is not established.'

'But you say she drowned?'

'She did, but they will want to know if it was accidental. Damn it, Pierre, you're a lawyer.'

'You said she had killed herself.'

He sighs. 'There's not much doubt about it. She had rigged the bathroom out as if it were a chapel – candles everywhere, your portrait propped up on the washstand ... It's not looking good, Pierre. I wanted to get hold of you before the police did.'

'Are they going to arrest me?'

'No, of course not. There's no evidence that you had anything to do with it. How could you have? You're at the other end of the country. But they'll be wondering if she had any reason to be suicidal. You need to prepare your story.'

'I shall have to tell the truth.'

'I wouldn't be in too much of a rush to do that, old chap. It's not your fault, what she's done.'

'Whose fault is it?'

'She got the wrong impression. She exaggerated the importance of the love affair. It's not unusual for women to convince themselves that they've been promised something when they haven't.'

'I said I would marry her.' He knows I can hear everything that's said between them, even if the cashier isn't able to. Of course he isn't saying anything I didn't know. It's strange that, hearing it again now is as painful as it was the first time Renée told me.

'That's just it, Pierre. By all means say you were her lover, but for God's sake don't imply that you agreed to marry Renée. Don't say anything unless you have to. Let them ask the questions, but don't volunteer the information. Marthe's sensible. I'm sure that she'll agree with me. You're in shock. Give yourself time to adjust. I'll let you know as soon as I have any information.'

The train journey back to Paris seems interminable. By the time we get to Roussillon the skies have clouded over. We stare mutely at the devastated landscape outside Paris, blighted trees and shell-scarred meadows, sodden ditches and a cold wind riffling the grass beside the tracks. The cab is waiting outside Montparnasse to take us on to Saint-Germain-en-Laye.

It seems that Renée had been found by police when water started dripping through a neighbour's ceiling. She had left the hot tap running to prevent the water going cold. My first thought is, how dare she kill herself like that? Now every painting of me in the bath will give rise to the same snide comments. Is the woman Pierre has painted me or Renée, or a combination of the two of us? Had he been hoping I might die like that and leave him free to marry Renée, or perhaps by taking up the same pose I was showing callous disrespect of someone else's suffering? I might have been the injured party at the start, but I can hardly claim the role of victim now.

The morning of the inquest, Édouard helps me bundle Pierre into the cab. He started smoking cigarettes when we got back to Saint-Germain, as if he didn't have the patience any more to light the pipe, and he starts fumbling in his pockets. Édouard lights a cigarette and gives it to him. We exchange a glance. I haven't always had a lot of time for Édouard in the past but in the last two weeks I have relied on him to help me bolster up Pierre. I don't think I can do it on my own. It's different from the situation we were in when Pierre came back from Italy. There was a problem to be solved then. It was action that was needed. Now we have to come to terms with the result of what we've done. I feel guilt just as keenly as Pierre. If I had had no dealings with the girl, I could have coped more easily with what is happening now, but I feel like a man with scarlet fever asked to nurse another man with measles.

I know, having contemplated suicide myself, that it's a thing you do without consideration for the people round you. There is no more selfish act than suicide. She must have known what she was doing. She was making sure she wouldn't be forgotten. Not a day would go by when Pierre would not wake up and think about her.

I see Roussel at the inquest, sitting hunched up in the public gallery. He's like those buildings you see everywhere in Paris now the war is over, their façades apparently untouched but without anything behind them. He's not being called, but it seems that the evening Renée died he'd gone to her apartment. He had seen the notice of our marriage in the paper and had been afraid for her, he told the police. Perhaps he thought he stood a chance with her himself with Pierre no longer in the running. Luckily for him, the man downstairs had heard him beating on her door. He said that Renée hadn't answered and ten minutes later he'd heard Roussel coming down the stairs again. Without his testimony, Roussel might have found himself in trouble – one girl missing and another dead. A man soon gets a reputation.

Monsieur Mauberger, from the apartment underneath, when asked if he'd had any contact with her, said she'd taken in a parcel for him some months earlier. When he collected it, she had invited him into the flat. He had declined. Why? 'I sensed she was lonely,' he said, as if loneliness were a disease.

The inquest brings a new shock. She was pregnant when she killed herself. How could she do that? Not just kill herself but kill her child. I think of Suzanne and how much I wanted her. It's fortunate that we're a good way into the proceedings before this is mentioned.

'The deceased was known to you in what capacity?' Pierre is asked.

'Professionally, to begin with. I employed her as my model. I'm an artist.'

'The apartment Renée Montchaty was living in was in your name, according to the leasehold documents.'

'That's right.'

'It wasn't merely a professional association, then?' It starts to look as if it's Pierre's own reputation that he is defending. This is the conclusion that the coroner has come to, anyway. 'Is it correct that this young woman was your mistress and you'd set her up in this apartment?' Pierre looks round for me. 'Please answer.'

'That's correct.'

'When did you last see Renée Montchaty?'

'It was the evening of 23rd April. We'd returned from Rome and took a cab to the apartment. We'd decided not to see each other any more.'

'And why was that?'

'We realised we weren't suited.'

'How long had you been together?'

Pierre frowns. 'Four years.' He turns one hand palm up as if reading from a script. 'No, on reflection it was nearer five years.'

'Your relationship was such that you had set her up in an apartment. After all that time you suddenly decide the two of you aren't suited. What took place in Rome to lead to that decision?'

'I suppose it was the first time we had been together constantly. We went in preparation for . . .' He stops, aware of the significance of what he's been about to say. Beside me, Édouard groans.

'In preparation for . . .' the coroner prompts, glancing at his watch.

'Our marriage.'

Suddenly the room falls silent. You can hear a fly up in the skylight, buzzing.

'So you planned to marry Renée Montchaty?'

'At that time, yes.'

'You had proposed to her? She was a party to these plans?'

'Of course. I couldn't marry her without her knowing.' Pierre is not deliberately being flippant, but his last remark does not go down well with the coroner.

'This is an inquest. We are trying to determine why a beautiful young woman in the prime of life was seemingly so desperate that she took her own life.'

Pierre grips the stand.

'I'm right in thinking you already had a common-law wife?' Pierre nods. 'Was she made aware of your relationship with Renée Montchaty?'

'She knew about it when we left for Italy.'

'And how did she respond?'

'She wasn't very pleased.' There is a titter in the court.

'One might think that if anyone was going to be desperate, it would be her.'

'My wife is an exceptionally strong person.'

I'm not certain if this is a tribute and in any case it isn't true.

'Your wife, yes. You were married shortly after your return from Italy, but not to Renée Montchaty?'

'No.'

'You decided after thirty years, to marry Mademoiselle Boursin, with whom you had been living prior to your love affair with Renée Montchaty ... indeed, throughout your love affair with Renée Montchaty.'

'Yes.'

'How do you imagine the deceased would have reacted on discovering the status you had offered her had been afforded to another?'

'I know she was terribly unhappy.'

'How would you describe her state of mind when you returned from Rome?'

'Excitable. She was erratic – laughing, crying.'

'Had she always been like that?'

'No, she was lively but much calmer, normally.'

'What brought about this sudden change of personality?'

'She thought I was withdrawing from her.'

'And presumably you were. You'd told her you no longer wished to marry her.'

'I hadn't said that, no.'

'She didn't know that you intended going back to Paris and proposing to your common-law wife?'

'That was not what I intended.'

'But you did go straight back, having left her by herself at the apartment. And that was the last time that you saw her?'

'Yes.'

'So you have no idea what happened to her in the interval between that evening and her death a few weeks later?'

'Only through my wife. She was approached by Renée Montchaty one morning in the market. Later, she went to the flat and took a letter from me.'

'Your wife acted as an intermediary?'

'She tried to reason with her. Renée was behaving in a way that made us all concerned for her.'

'You didn't try to reason with her personally?'

'I knew it wasn't any use.'

'One wonders if it wouldn't have been more upsetting for one mistress to be told her lover didn't want her any longer by another.'

'I don't know.'

'You will have been aware that Renée Montchaty was pregnant when she died?'

There is a murmur in the courtroom. Pierre sways. I think he is about to fall. So does the clerk, who hands him up a glass of water.

'No,' he whispers. 'No, I wasn't.'

I'm afraid the coroner might go on questioning him, but he doesn't. 'I think it's apparent that the reason Renée Montchaty committed suicide was that her expectations had been disappointed. She had been led to believe that she was to become your wife. The trip to Italy took place on that assumption. For whatever reason, you decided you no longer wished to marry her. Not only that, but shortly after your return you marry someone else. One doesn't have to look far for an answer to the question, "Why was this young woman driven to decide that life was not worth living?"'

Pierre leaves the court supported between me and Édouard. Outside, standing in a sullen group, is Renée's family. Her mother has her arms around the younger children. One of them is crying and the other twists the tassels of her mother's shawl around her finger silently. I catch the woman's eye and she looks back at me in anguish. As we pass, a young man turns and spits at Pierre. The gobbet of saliva lands on Pierre's lapel. I don't know if he's even noticed.

Édouard guides us into the first bar we come to, pushing Pierre down into a pew. I sit down opposite him. Édouard brings three shots of Calvados. 'Thank God that's over,' he says.

'I don't think so,' I say.

'In the end it doesn't matter who's responsible. They merely need to know she did it.'

'He said it was my fault,' Pierre mumbles.

Édouard looks at me and grunts. 'I'm glad I've not been brought to book for all the misery I've caused along the way,' he says. 'You were unlucky. In a sense, you were too principled. You wanted to do right by everybody. Better, probably, to be entirely selfish, like me.'

'What do we do now?' I say.

'Wait. It'll all blow over. People will find something else to talk about.'

'I don't think we can stay in Saint-Germain-en-Laye. The findings will be in the newspapers tomorrow. There were journalists in court.'

'Perhaps you ought to spend a few months out of town.'

'We've only just come back.'

'Still, if you stay, the hacks will root you out. You're welcome to come back with me until you've made your mind up.'

'Thank you, Édouard, but we must find somewhere we can settle. Pierre needs to work.'

'Keep him inside then.'

We've been talking as if Pierre wasn't sitting next to us and he has taken no part in the conversation. 'Drink your Calva,' Édouard orders him and Pierre lifts it to his lips. He chokes. 'Good stuff, eh? That's the spirit. Drink it down.'

We sit in silence, each of us preoccupied, but all of us in one way or another thinking of the girl whose body will already have begun to decompose, whose beauty will be turning into dust.

I'm not sure how I'll get through Monday when Madame Hébert is due, but she pre-empts me with a letter telling me that she will not be working for us any longer. I'd assumed that Madame Hébert's thirst for gossip would have over-ridden any qualms she might have about coming to a house as saturated with debauchery as ours, but it seems even Madame Hébert has her limits. All of France now knows officially that I was not Pierre's wife, that he had a mistress he supported independently in an apartment and that she committed suicide because he wouldn't marry her. It isn't an uncommon story in the circles that we move in. Even so-called upright men have mistresses, but it's unusual for them to cause so much upheaval.

Pierre spends all day upstairs in the studio, but there is no suggestion that he's doing anything. I find him staring at the wall once as he would have done if there had been a canvas pinned to it. 'What are you doing?' I ask.

'Thinking,' he says. But he doesn't tell me what about. I don't think it's a still life somehow.

Manguin writes that there's a house for sale up in the hills, a few kilometres from his. He thinks the owner might agree to lease it. He describes the house. There are enough rooms to convert one for a studio, a garden and, because it's something I can't do without, a bathroom. I am not expecting Pierre to take an interest in the house, but he seems desperate to get away from Saint-Germain-en-Laye.

'And this house is for sale?'

'Yes, but he thinks that we could lease it.'

'We could buy it, Marthe.'

Once, the thought of even owning one home was a distant dream, but we could do it now. If Pierre could afford to keep a mistress in a flat in Clichy, I think bitterly, he could afford a second home elsewhere.

'Why would we want to stay here?' he says. 'There is nothing here for either of us any more.'

Pierre insists that he wants nothing from the flat in Clichy but, as usual, it's not that simple. We've invited Renée's family to take whatever they would like of hers, but there's been no response. It will be up to us to clear it out, which means it will be up to me. I go there with a notebook and a bag of luggage labels. I feel heavy as I climb the stairs up to the top floor. Renée's spirit will be up there, lingering. I stopped off on the way here to say prayers for her and light a candle. It's a long time since I spoke to God. He didn't seem to be there in the war and if you can't depend on someone in a crisis, why would you be bothered with them once it's over? When Pierre left, I was lonelier than I had ever been before, but on the whole, I'd rather have the company of Juno and the cats. They may not be as powerful as the Almighty, but they're more companionable. Still, there's nothing I can do for Renée now, except to pray for her.

In the apartment it's so quiet that I can hear my own breath. I unlatch the windows to let in the street sounds from below and then begin the grim task of examining the contents of each room in turn. I start with the least intimate – the kitchen. Out of habit I fill up the kettle from the sink and make myself a pot of tea.

I sit down at the table with my notebook and write 'kitchen' on the first page. After that, it's easier. I lose myself in the routine of putting certain things aside and putting others in the pile for throwing out. I ought to be more ruthless, but I can't bear waste. I keep the caddy, for example, partly for the tea and partly for the tin, which has a picture of a tree in blossom on the front. I'm keeping too much back, so I make a reserve pile to consider later. I could do with Madame Hébert being there. She was a demon when it came to clear-outs. Secretly, I think she took the things away and kept them for herself. It's practically unknown for anybody born in Normandy to throw a match away unless they've used it twice.

I work my way round the apartment. All the time, I can feel Renée at my elbow, watching as I sift through towels and linen, docketing the tablecloths and crockery. She must have tidied up before she died. There is a sad finality about the rows of cups, the chairs pushed tidily into the table and the stopped clock on the mantelpiece that will have gone on ticking for the best part of a day after her heart had stopped.

There is a cache of photographs addressed to 'M' without an address, and a pile of magazines with 'Gabi' scrawled across the top one. I'm not sure if these are meant for someone or if 'Gabi' was the one who left them. Given all the other items that I need to sift through, I decide a heap of magazines and photographs are neither here nor there. I put them in the pile to be disposed of.

In an alcove off the bedroom there's a pile of sketches, some of Renée sitting at the table, one of her reclining on the bed and one in which she's washing at the sink. My impulse is to rip them into shreds. I keep on having to remind myself she's dead. But here she is alive and always will be. If I keep the drawings, I'm immortalising her. If I destroy them, I'll have killed her twice. I put them in a neat pile. Everything in here must be preserved. This is the only room that has a feeling of unfinished business in it. It's the only space that still has life.

I don't like going through the drawers, especially in the bedroom. Taking out the lingerie, I'm pricked with envy at the luxury of Renée's underwear – silk stockings, corsets where the whalebone is replaced by tunnels of material through which the straps run delicately and emerge with ribbons on the ends of them. I could afford to buy such things myself now, but what would a woman in her fifties look like wearing something that cries out for youth?

I shall give these to Pierre's niece. Poor thing, she hasn't had a lot to cheer her since her mother died. There are five pairs of shoes lined up inside the bottom of the wardrobe and a pair of sandals with a broken heel. I recognise the shoes that Renée wore the afternoon she came to Saint-Germain-en-Laye. She's left a jewel box on the bedside table. Inside, there are necklaces and bracelets, with her sisters' names attached to two of them with bits of cotton. There's a brooch here too, which she has labelled 'Maman'. Nothing for her brother.

I have left the bathroom to the end. The police will have been through the whole apartment thoroughly. There's just the dark stain on the floorboards underneath the bath where water gathered in a puddle before leaking through into the room below. I think she left the taps on so that she would not be left up there indefinitely. Apparently, the tenant downstairs was a single man whose business took him out of Paris every week. He only came back at the weekends. Is that why she chose a Saturday to kill herself? She couldn't do it on a Sunday. That would be unthinkable.

Each time I think of Renée dying in the bath, I feel as if it's my grave somebody has trodden on. Because the idea is uncharitable, I've tried to stop wondering if she chose to drown herself because the bathroom was the one place that was mine. The fact is, Pierre can never look at me reclining in the bath now without thinking of it as her tomb.

It's past four by the time I've finished itemising everything in the apartment. I shall never come back here again and so, before I leave, I go through every room and say goodbye to it and to whatever still remains of Renée. 'I forgive you,' I say, 'for the way you hurt me, for the careless damage you did with your youth and beauty, for the guilt and grief you've left us with. And I hope you'll forgive us.' If you don't, I think, we're damned.

Negotiations for the house we're purchasing are dealt with by the lawyer, Maître Bleicher, who we've also put in charge of selling on the leasehold of the flat. Of course, he knows the circumstances. Renée's suicide and Pierre's part in it have turned into a *cause célèbre*, not just here in Paris, but, if Manguin is to be believed, down in the south too. If Pierre behaves down there the way he has at Saint-Germain it could be weeks before the local population even catch a glimpse of him.

We haven't talked about the pregnancy. Pierre was so

distraught, I didn't feel that I could mention it. He will expect me to be angry, but the fact that it's his child as well as hers is probably the one thing in its favour. Oddly, it's the first time I've been on the point of telling him about Suzanne. 'She's not your only child,' I would have said. 'You had two.' But, since both of them are dead, he might have thought that didn't count for much. I get on better, generally, with ghosts.

When Madame Hébert hears we're going, she relents and asks me if I need help with the packing. This is something I'd prefer to do alone, but it'll take me twice as long and I need her no-nonsense attitude towards the things we don't require.

'They'll have butter shapers down south, I imagine,' she observes when she sees me attempting to find room inside an overflowing tea chest for an item you can buy here in the market for a few sous.

'Maybe you would like it, Madame Hébert,' I say, and she shrugs. She'll only take it if it looks as if she's giving in under duress. In this way we pare down the contents of the house to fifteen packing cases. We can auction off the furniture, although Pierre is clinging to things he insists he needs – like fruit bowls, carpets, plates. 'You wouldn't leave the cats or Juno,' he says. 'They have dogs and cats down in the south, presumably.'

It's not the same, but I don't argue. I'm relieved that he's not leaving everything to me.

'And how's the master?' Madame Hébert asks. When she's around, Pierre stays upstairs in the studio.

'Much better, thank you.' This is not the news she wants to hear. What right has he to go on living comfortably when that poor girl is lying in her grave? That's how they'll look at it in Saint-Germain-en-Laye. They've no truck with what happens in the mind. The idea that guilt is a cross on which you'll hang for the remainder of your life, is foreign to them. Someone throws a stone at you; you throw one back. That's their philosophy. They wouldn't spend time agonising over it.

I watch as Madame Hébert picks things up and puts them down again. She touches something and it's as if she has thrown a net across it. 'You won't want this,' she says, picking up a sugar bowl. 'It's got a hairline crack in it.' It would go nicely on her kitchen table; this is what she's thinking.

'Everything in this room has to go into the tea chests, Madame Hébert. Pierre needs them for his work.'

'You'd think that after all this time he'd welcome something new to paint,' she says. 'You could get ten for three francs in the market.'

'He's decided he wants this one,' I say, firmly. I've learnt one thing in the past months. Madame Hébert isn't here to do me any favours and unless it suits me, I shan't do her any either.

Yesterday I took a bunch of dahlias to put on Renée's grave. It was a bright day and her little corner of the cemetery looked almost gay. It's not exactly in the cemetery, of course. They wouldn't have her there, the bastards. Still, it's near enough. The wind has blown leaves from the line of elm trees bordering the graveyard, piling them against the raised earth. There's a bunch of lilies on the grave that must have been there since the funeral. We didn't go. The family asked us not to. I'm not sure we could have faced them, anyway, after the inquest.

When I touch the flowers, they're like paper. I can't bear dead flowers. I can hardly put them on the rubbish heap, but still their withered beauty is too much like Renée's and they make me feel uncomfortable. I don't like lilies at the best of times – they reek of bitterness. Of course, they might have been left by Roussel. It haunted me the way he'd looked, the morning of the inquest.

I explain to Renée that we shall be leaving Saint-Germain-en-Laye for good soon, so I won't be coming back. Perhaps somebody else will come by and take time to sit with her. Her mother, maybe, or her sisters. It's much easier to talk to her, now that she's dead. You'd think it would increase the barrier between us, but it doesn't. If I say the wrong thing now, she'll take it in her stride. We've passed the point of having to be diplomatic, which is why when I get around to telling her the reason for my visit, I don't mince my words.

'The thing is, Renée,' I say, 'and I hope you won't take this amiss. You weren't the first girl Pierre had fallen for, though you were probably the one who mattered most to him. He'll never think of me the way he thinks of you, but when it comes to which of us will be remembered for their contribution to his work, it's going to be me.' I let the words sink in. It's better that she comes to terms with it. 'You were the mistress, not the muse,' I tell her. 'That was always my role and I'm hanging on to it. I'm sorry if you hoped for more, but this is where it ends. There will be no more pictures of you and the ones that do exist will slowly disappear. You can't fight wear and tear. We muses are a wily bunch. We have to be. There's always someone waiting in the wings – more beautiful, more captivating to the eye and ready to take over at a moment's notice. That's not what it is about. A muse is like a tick that gets in underneath the skin. She is the thought the painter has before he knows he's thought it. She can make the journey from his eyes onto the canvas without going through his brain at all. He hardly knows she's there and yet without her he is nothing. She's the air he breathes. If you had listened to me when I tried to tell you, you might be alive now, though perhaps it's just as well you're not.'

Although the name suggests the house is grander than it is, the 'Villa Bosquet' seems to suit it. Houses have a personality and this one is accommodating from the start. It nestles in among the olive groves and trees in blossom. Sun streams through the open shutters when we wake up in the morning and the scent of jasmine and mimosa flood the room. Pierre drinks a glass of water when he gets up and then walks down to the footbridge over the canal with Juno, through the olive groves and up the hillside before coming back for breakfast and a morning in the studio. Our nearest neighbours are a couple of kilometres away. They're not the sort of people you make friends with – bankers, businessmen who've come here to retire and die more slowly and in greater luxury than they could do in Paris. We don't seek their company. If Pierre meets up with any of the locals on a walk, he says hello, but otherwise he keeps his eyes fixed on the ground until they've passed each other.

Though we're moving to an empty house, I know there's no such thing. A house contains the ghosts not only of the people you bring with you, but the ones already there. All one can hope is that the ghosts are friendly. Sometimes, when I'm in the kitchen kneading dough, or sitting at the sewing table, there's a flash of yellow in the corner of my eye or the faint rustle of a dress as someone brushes past me and I know it's Renée. I might wish that I could blot her out entirely, but I can't. She lives with us as surely as if she had moved into the house with her belongings. Having lived with ghosts, I know their habits. She and Suzanne keep each other company. Suzanne would have been twenty-three, the same age ... well, let's not go there again. I chat to them the way I talk to Juno and the cats. If you don't talk occasionally, you lose the habit.

There is only one place Renée's not allowed to go, and that's the studio. I take more interest in the paintings than I used to. Pierre knows what it's about. The studio is on a mezzanine, so I can wander in and out at will. I'm on the lookout for a shape reflected in a mirror, the suggestion of a profile in the pattern of a rug, a shawl that isn't mine, draped carelessly across a chair back. I become quite good at picking up the clues. Occasionally, we have words about it. Sometimes, if it's something insignificant – a hand that doesn't look like mine, or someone's shoe tucked underneath a sofa – I might let it go. I always make it clear I've seen it, though. My days of putting up with things are over.

Once a year, we take the train to Paris for the opening of the Salon. One year we run into Roussel. Like us, he had gone to ground after the inquest. You could not help feeling sorry for the man. His paintings were occasionally reproduced, but nothing that looked new. Whenever anyone referred to him, it was invariably in connection with that model who had disappeared – Chiara, was it? People liked to think he had exhibited that painting out of guilt. They say there's no such thing as bad publicity. The critics raved about it, other painters copied it. He copied it himself. But it turned out to be a one-off. Nothing he did afterwards lived up to it.

I see him turn and whisper to the woman he is with. Pierre is talking to a client. Roussel's pushing through the crowd towards me. He still cuts a figure in that lightweight linen suit of his and with a woman on his arm he looks more like his old self.

'Marthe,' he puts out his hand. 'It's been a long time.'

'Yes, it has.'

'Four, five years?'

'All of that.'

'How are the two of you? Do you like living in the south of France?'

'We get by.'

'Still the same old Marthe?' He laughs, but it's not the sort of laugh he'd once have given me. He turns towards the woman by his side. 'You won't remember this young lady,' he says. When I look at her, the face is certainly familiar, though I couldn't put a name to it. 'My daughter Lisel,' he says.

I remember Roussel telling me that neither of his daughters was remotely interested in the arts. They and their mother had reverted to the family name after the marriage broke up. He had had no contact with his daughters. But it seems that Lisel is a painter in her own right now. 'She was exhibiting while she was still a student at the Beaux-Arts,' he says, proudly. 'Lisel is a rising star.'

I smile politely. Now I think about it, I can see she has a lot of Roussel in her, although not quite in the same proportions. She's a handsome woman, but you couldn't call her beautiful. He thinks she is, of course, and for a moment I feel quite benign towards him. He has got his daughter back and I know what that means.

'What name do you paint under?' I say, and she glances at her father.

'Roussel,' she says.

We stand talking idly for a few more moments before she is whisked away by someone keen to introduce her to more influential people. Roussel gazes after her. He's utterly besotted with his gifted daughter. He turns finally and sees me looking at him. 'It meant such a lot, you know, her coming back to me.'

'I'm sure it did.'

'I didn't realise how important it was, having children, till I lost them.' It occurs to him that Pierre and I are not in a position whereby we are likely to have children coming back to us. 'Did you and Pierre never think of having children?'

'We had one. A daughter. Her name was Suzanne.' He looks surprised. 'She died.'

He makes a sound like a collapsed balloon. 'I'm sorry, I had no idea.'

I look at him implacably. He's groping for my hand and cups it in the two of his. Don't make a meal of it, I think. I can imagine Suzanne saying, as we leave, 'Whoever was that sentimental old ham?' and I would have told her, 'He was once accused of murdering his model. He was a philanderer. He had a wife he treated badly and two daughters who rejected him. He drank, he gambled, there were rumours that he slept with prostitutes.'

'How is Pierre?'

'He's managing.'

He hesitates. 'That business at the inquest about Renée being pregnant,' he says. 'I said nothing at the time. I didn't want to make things worse.'

I know what Roussel is about to say.

'There is a possibility the child might not have been Pierre's.'

I suddenly feel weary. Looking round, I search the crowd for Pierre. I'm finding these events increasingly a challenge.

Roussel's trying to be kind. 'It must have made it harder for you,' he says, 'thinking that it was.'

I need to get away from here. I can't think with this racket going on all round me. 'Thank you,' I say, in an effort to be gracious.

'Will you tell Pierre?' He's looking at me, keenly.

'I don't know.'

'It might be kinder if you didn't mention it.'

'To whom?'

'Why, to Pierre, of course.' He looks away. It strikes me that he wouldn't want Lisel to know about it either.

'I think you can count on me to do what's best,' I say.

I don't say anything to Pierre. It's partly that it's years since either of us mentioned Renée and I'd rather not exhume her memory and then have to bury it again. But also, I'm afraid that Pierre won't forgive me if I take away the last of his illusions. I'd been haunted by the thought that she might have a greater claim on him than I had, that I might eradicate her from the paintings, but I'd never manage to eradicate her from our lives. Pierre might still think that she has a claim on him, but I know that she hasn't. Once I have decided that she has no right to be here, I stop seeing her. Ghosts are like children. If they are ignored, they either clamour for attention or they fade away. There are occasions when I miss her company, but now at least I have Pierre completely to myself.

The years pass, and Pierre's reputation grows again. The Second World War sees off many of our close friends – Édouard fleeing from the Germans in the first year of the occupation, Maurice Denis whom Pierre had known since they were students, three years later, and Roussel, who by then was the only one left of the old crew, in the spring of 1944. The rumpus over Renée's suicide and the humiliation of the inquest has been long forgotten. Nobody these days has heard of Renée Montchaty. It's me that students of his work refer to now. They want to see the house that has inspired so many of his paintings and the woman who they say is always in there somewhere. They take photographs of Pierre and me together, flanked by pictures. Finally, I have the recognition I deserve.

And then I make a big mistake. I die. One day my heart stops beating; it has had enough. Well, after all, I'm over seventy. We never talked about my age, but I expect Pierre had worked it out. The next year, he attends the Salon opening on his own. That year will be his last. The painting he's exhibiting is called *The Women in the Garden*. It's a picture that he left unfinished after Renée's death. I thought he had destroyed it. If I'd known he hadn't, I'd have put the torch to it myself.

They say that if you want to influence the future you should be there, but in Renée's case the fact that she has not been there seems to be working in her favour. Looking at the painting, I remind myself that it is called *The Women*, rather than *The Woman in the Garden*, so there must be two of us, but at first glance you wouldn't know that I was there at all. It's Renée who is bathed in light; she positively shimmers. She is sitting at a wrought-iron table, her chin resting on her hand as if she's not aware of me. She isn't quite there, as indeed she wasn't.

Going back to it, he guilds the background yellow, so the light seems to be coming from within. It's beautiful. If I'd still been alive to see it, I would have been spitting bile. It isn't only that he's put me in the shadow and her in the light, that I'm dark and in profile whereas she's full-face and smiling, that I've been imprisoned in a corner of the picture by what looks like a wheel with cast-iron spokes but is in fact a garden chair. She's centre-stage. She is glowing. She's ALIVE.

She is the only thing the critics talk about, her and her tragic life. You'd think that dying was the worst thing that could happen to you. I have never thought that. After all, death comes to all of us; we're none of us let off. What matters is the timing. If you ask me, she chose well. I should have been the one who perished in the bath that day.

As if he still has one eye on a future in which he might have to answer to me, Pierre does one more painting. This time it's of me. I'm lying in the bath at Villa Bosquet, my flesh green, the water lapping all around me. I look like a corpse, but after all that's what I am and so, now, is Pierre.

I dare say we could go on bickering into eternity, but it won't change the course of history. I tried to wipe out Renée and I failed. The very fact that nobody knows anything about her, other than her name, will be enough to stimulate the curiosity of hacks and busybodies. In the future, they'll write books about her. What they don't know, they'll make up. She'll be his muse, his soulmate, his lost love.

And what will I be? There is only one place where my sovereignty is undisputed. Renée would have taken that from me as well, but no, when future generations talk about 'the woman in the bath', it will be me that they're referring to and maybe that's enough.

ACKNOWLEDGEMENTS

In writing *Painted Ladies*, I am indebted to the numerous biographies that have been written about Bonnard. I have used the facts, as far as they are known, as a basis for the story. Where there are gaps, events, characters and dialogue have been fictionalised.

I would like to pay tribute to my husband, Jeremy, for his unwavering support during the writing of this book and the books that preceded it. To my children, who suffered the usual neglect of a parent whose attention was all too often elsewhere and who responded by bringing themselves up rather wonderfully, this one is for you.

Thanks are due to Stuart Harling, a dear friend who offered invaluable criticism of the various MSS he's been asked to look at over the years; to David Llewelyn, Titania Krimpas and Alison Lang for their editorial advice and to Carol Smith and Christine Cohen-Park, fellow writers, for their friendship and encouragement.

I owe a special debt of gratitude to Tessa David at Peters Fraser and Dunlop for her enthusiasm and determination to find a publisher for the book and to Tim Binding, author and in-house editor at PFD for reading the MS and endorsing her decision to run with it.

Finally, I would like to extend a huge thank you to Moira Forsyth and the staff at Sandstone Press, without whom this book might never have been published.

Thank you all.